AQUILA AND THE SPHINX

AQUILA AND THE SPHINX

S.P. SOMTOW

Wildside Press
New Jersey • New York • California • Ohio

AQUILA AND THE SPHINX

First Wildside Press edition: January 2001

to
Art and Lydia, who
ground my coffee at a time
of direst need,

and to Ed Bryant,
who loves madmen

CONTENTS

PRIMA PARS:

THE PURLOINED PYRAMID

CHAPTER
I

LUCIUS VINICIUS

MY ARROGANT, SELF-AGGRANDIZING, SELF-righteous, self-centered half-breed of a half brother had the gall to compose the second volume of these memoirs, which you have undoubtedly read, else you would not be unscrolling this, the third papyrus of our outlandish adventures. Luckily for all of us, he is too occupied with other matters to continue to badger you, O reader, with his self-congratulatory prose.

It falls to me, the witty, handsome, aristocratic, and always self-deprecating Lucius Vinicius, nephew of the Emperor Trajan, to continue the tale. And it's about bloody time, if you ask me; my dear half brother is half-savage, you see, and though we Romans tried to instill in him the rudiments of a classical education, he's incapable of writing a decent Latin sentence, let alone a Greek one—he goes on for page after page without a single metaphor, litotes, zeugma, asyndeton, or any of the other figures of speech with which any decent writer must, by his very nature as a soul inspired by the Muse of Poesy, imbue those lines which fall not without grace from pen to papyrus.

In fact, I used several figures of speech in the above sentence, videlicet: alliteration, apostrophe, hysteron proteron, and litotes. But I shan't insult your intelligence by constantly alluding to my brilliant use of rhetorical devices; from now on we shall take that as read, unless, of course, I come up with a particularly striking turn of phrase.

On with the story!

As you will recall, we left the world in something of a shambles in the last volume. The entire universe, you will remember, had disappeared, and our Earth, along with its attendant sun and moon and a few other hunks of rock, had been shunted into what our friends the little green were-jaguars called a "holding universe," wherein our world, including this grand Roman Empire of ours at the dawn of the ninth century since the founding of Rome, was fated to remain until the Time Criminal, Viridiporcus Rex, a green pig from a distant galaxy, was apprehended. Because of the uncertainties of the laws of conservation of multiplex universes, however, it was uncertain as to whether our world had much longer to exist —there was a distinct possibility that it could vanish at any moment.

Also there was a certain urgency to our quest to find the Time Criminal. But you wouldn't have thought it. By and large, the citizens of Rome took the impending destruction of the universe in stride. Most of them didn't even notice the brief disorientation of our transfer to the holding universe; indeed, since the aliens had now put something they referred to as a "holographic simulacrum" around the Earth, even the stars and constellations looked the same as before, and most people simply went about their business as usual.

As Phoenix, the owner of the wineshop down on the Via Neronis, told me, "Destruction of the universe, my arse! My father got out of Pompeii in one piece—and I imagine we'll squirm out of this one somehow."

The empire had never been more prosperous. Our lands now stretched all the way to Armenia and Parthia on the east—and to the west, the province of Iracuavia had extended southward to reach the borders of the land of the Seminolii, and westward all the way to the Oceanus Pacificus (or Papinianus, as some call it). My uncle, Marcus Ulpius Trajanus, Caesar Augustus, the Living God, White and Greatest Father of the Western Peoples, and other titles too numerous to mention, was still emperor, and the Pax Romana reigned secure over every province. Grain poured in from Egypt—it was an abundant harvest—and the markets did not lack for exotic viands from the New World—giant chickens, aurochs livers, elk kidney sausage, hummingbirds' brains in aspic, and the intoxicating *aqua cocacola*, made from the leaves of the coca plant.

It was indeed the best of times, and only a handful of us—an incompetent old general, a wily old Lacotian chieftain, an Egyptian, a sasquatch, my aforementioned half brother, and myself—had the slightest inkling that it was also the worst of times...

Am I digressing? I fear that an inordinate fondness for the aqua cocacola occasionally dulls my wits.

Let me then bring you, O reader, up to date on what has transgressed since the last scroll—for I shall not attempt a summary of the chaotic events of the previous two—and then launch straight into our story.

We left Equus Insanus, my half brother, in the prairies west of Tachyopolis, riding off into the sunset, seeking his own solution to the fate of the universe. For the next three years we had no knowledge of his whereabouts.

Titus Papinianus, the bumbling Roman general, had been recalled to Rome after he had succeeded, against all odds, in building the ferrequus, or railway, from Omahopolis all the way to the Montes Saxosi. Aaye, the talkative Egyptian, and his friend Abraham bar-David, the learned Sasquatius, had decided to give up on adventuring; they were now in Egypt, cowriting an immensely edifying treatise on the sexual appetites of newly resurrected mummies. And Aquila had taken up residence in the slums of Rome, abandoning his senatorial toga praetexta to become a teacher of ancient Lacotian wisdom—

a homo medicinae—and joining the dozens of other purveyors of cults from the fringes of the empire who
haunted the marketplaces of Little Lacotia.

And I—I was no longer that reckless boy who had
flown across the Oceanus Atlanticus in a flying saucer. I
was a man—officially at least—having dropped the toga
praetexta of boyhood and adopted the pure white toga
candida. Back in Rome, I decided that worrying about
the end of the universe was a bit much, so I threw myself
into the study of poesy and rhetoric. My mother died,
and I became undisputed lord of the Vinicius fortune. It
seemed even more likely that I would succeed my uncle
as emperor, but I was not particularly interested in that
honor. I tried my hand at writing a few *scientifictiones*,
but my works were not well regarded, even when I distributed free scrolls to the poor. It was not surprising,
then, that I should have become thoroughly bored with
my existence and started to daydream more and more
about getting back together with my friends.

How our disparate group came to be together once
more, and how we subsequently embarked on an epic
odyssey that ended in our saving the universe for the
third time, will shortly be revealed.

But first I shall relate the manner in which news of my
long-lost friend and brother, Equus Insanus, first
reached me.

It was on the Saturnalia, more than three years since
our parting, on the occasion of a celebratory orgy at the
palace of my uncle the emperor.

Because it was being thrown by my uncle, it was naturally one of the dullest orgies in Rome that night. But
the emperor is the emperor, and so, after rising from my
bath, I donned the old party clothes—the purple tunic
with a fringe of gold thread, the cloak with its jeweled
brooch, the ostrich-skin moccasinae manufactured in
Africa by Lacotian émigrés, and—last but not least—a
laurel wreath, somewhat the worse for wear, I think, because I had accidentally rested upon it one evening.

It was the Saturnalia, so, in accordance with custom,
all the slaves had the day off, and I had to dress myself. I

could not find a thing—I stumbled about the house in the half dark, trying to find a pot to pee in. Eventually, I found myself in the atrium and managed to relieve myself in a little fountain that contained a statue of Jupiter ravishing the sea nymph Tridentina in the guise of a golden octopus. It was evening, and the moonlight was unnaturally bright. I looked up at the sky, and it was then that I had my first premonition of doom. There was a crack in the sky.

"By Jupiter Optimus Maximus!" I said to myself. "That aqua cocacola must have been jolly strong." I squinted. I peered skyward again. The crack was still there.

And through the crack I could see, or thought I saw, the leering visage of an enormous green pig! The brows were knitted together in an expression of wrath and puzzlement. And those beady eyes appeared to be staring right at me!

He was back. Adventures would soon follow. It all started to come back to me—the dinosaurs, the uranograph, the building of the railroad, the invention of the telegraph, the attack of the minotaur in the labyrinth of Tachyopolis, the journey to Mars, where enormous green elephants sat in judgment over the human race—and I knew that it would soon be time to save the universe again.

But at the moment it was time for one of my uncle's stultifying orgies.

I needed a gift—I did not wish to appear niggardly to my uncle—so after stumbling around the house some more, I pulled an amphora of the best aqua cocacola out of the wine cellar. Then I summoned a link boy to light my way to the palace and started trudging uphill toward the Palatine.

CHAPTER
II

A STUPEFYINGLY DULL ORGY

AT TIMES LIKE THIS I REALLY MISSED HAVING OLD Equus Insanus around. I mean, he was a Lacotian, and crazy by definition as well as by name, but you could always count on having a good time with him. I sighed as I prepared for an evening of enervating ennui.

I emerged from my little villa at the bottom of the hill and found the Saturnalia festivities going strong. Masked revelers were running about; large women with little clothing were prancing about in the middle of the street waving torches; Nubians bearing palanquins strutted up and down the street, their ostrich feathers flapping in the breeze.

Next to my house stood an enormous telegraph pole, in the Ionian style; the Gaulish slave who operated it lay chained to the platform on top, fast asleep, curled up around the smoke tripod. Despite the advancements of modern science, they still had not figured out how to send telegrams by night, for, no matter how close the intervals between the telegraph poles are, it is just too difficult to make out smoke signals in the dark.

It was an eyesore, this telegraph pole, for the wretch

who operated it could see right over my walls and into my atrium, and was addicted to drink besides. Put something of a damper on parties—one does not normally notice slaves, but to have one looking down from on high, like an Olympian, can be pretty unnerving when one is trying to get into the tunica of some senator's wife.

My link boy was waving his torch, prancing about in front of me, trying to elbow a pathway for me through the throng, crying "Make way, ho! Lucius Vinicius approaches!" to anyone who would care to listen. In the first hundred paces up the hill, I had already been accosted by two prostitutes, a soothsayer, three beggars, and a man peddling larks' tongues on skewers. It was a full hour before I made it to the palace, and then I had to go through several body searches, and park my link boy in an anteroom, before I was admitted into the presence of my uncle, the irrepressibly niggardly emperor.

It was every bit as dull as I thought it would be. There were seven or eight couches set around an almost laughable banquet—on a Terra Novan theme: six roasted giant chickens, an elk on a spit, a soup with alligators' eyeballs, a couple of roast armatilli stuffed with pumpkins, a paté of quoiotulus livers, and a purée of those exotic potatii that were all the rage when they were first brought back from Terra Nova. In short, the food was of the most boring variety, the sort of thing that might be eaten on any nonorgy evening even in a middle-class home—not that I've ever set foot in one, but one hears stories.

The emperor was being fanned by two young slaves, dressed for the occasion in little purple tunics and miniature war bonnets. About a dozen dancing girls moved languidly among the guests, swaying their hips, waving little wooden tomahauca, and ululating in an outlandish parody of a Lacotian scalp dance. All the guests seemed to be asleep, except for one little fellow who was staggering back from the vomitorium.

"Oh, goodness!" he said, seeing me. "Someone who hasn't passed out! An audience!"

I rolled my eyes. "Euphonius the bard," I said, recognizing the silly man from the time he had recited an epic poem at the Theater of Apollo and been roundly booed off the stage. What an unpleasant surprise! Not only had I come to the world's dullest party, but the only other person I could talk to was the world's dullest poet! I scratched my head as I sat down in the first available lectus, discovering to my horror that he was sidling up to the couch next to mine. "Jolly decent epic poem that was," I said. "*Leda and the Swan*, wasn't it?"

"*Leda and the Duck*, actually," he said, obviously bursting with pride that I even knew who he was.

"Duck? Whoever heard of Leda and the duck?"

I had obviously said the wrong thing, for he was no longer bursting with pride. "What a cultural ignoramus!" the little poet said huffily, wagging a finger at me as he drew an enormous lyre, almost as big as himself, out from behind the couch. He cleared his throat as though about to perform, but nobody woke up. "Haven't you heard anything about the new realism?"

I sighed and prepared myself for another lecture on the latest cultural fad to sweep our decadent city.

"My dear Lucius Vinicius," Euphonius said as he gnawed on the bone of a giant chicken, "this is the ninth century since Romulus and Remus founded Rome! We don't go by those silly old myths anymore. We've got to make them *relevant*, you see." He tossed the bone away, whereupon it was silently removed by a burly Scythian bearing a silver tray. "We've got to show the gods with warts—after all, the only gods we've ever had the privilege of seeing in the flesh, such as the divine Nero, the divine Caligula, and our own divine Marcus Ulpius Trajanus, have all had warts, or been paunchy, or suffered from satyriasis—and we wouldn't want these *living* gods, who are very much around to have us tossed into the arena or crucified, to suffer by comparison with the gods *upstairs*, would we, now?"

I thought I followed his logic as I distractedly sipped a goblet of second-class Falernian wine. At least, I thought, he's not singing!

"That's why," Euphonius said, "I cleverly *transformed* the myth of the coupling of the parents of Helen of Troy into the fornication of Leda and a duck—and I intend to publish my own version of the story of Helen of Troy, with a warts-and-all view of mythology, under the singularly *brilliant* title of *The Ugly Duckling*! A charming conceit, is it not?" He had demolished his second giant chicken leg and was working on the alligator eyeballs, sucking all the juice out of each with a perfectly horrid slurping sound and tossing the slimy husks onto the floor, where they were gobbled up by my uncle's tame cheetah cubs. "If you like, I'm prepared to offer you the supreme privilege of a prepublication performance—"

"No, it's all right, thanks," I began, but it was too late. Euphonius had already thrown his head back, opened his mouth wide like a goldfish out of water, and begun spewing forth the following hideous piece of doggerel:

Ugly as sin she was, and no one thought her
Remotely likely to be Zeus's daughter,
Though Leda kept insisting she had mated
With that great god whom she both loved and hated,
Who had assumed the shape and visage of a duck,
The better her chaste virgin form to—

At the sound of the bard's screeching falsetto, several of the guests actually woke up, and the fruit began flying.

"Philistines!" Euphonius shouted, and continued, his fingers flying across the lyre strings, his body assuming various classical poses reminiscent of some of the lesser-known vase paintings of the silver age:

Ah muse, ah muse, ah, muse, muse, muse, muse,
*   muse,*
How I importune thee me to amuse—

A piece of prime Terra Novan pumpkin grazed his left cheek and caught me square in the forehead. "I say, that's not fair!" I cried as a slave hastened to towel me off. I dodged potatii, tomatii, and various other exotic Terra Novan vegetables and was in imminent danger of being bashed on the head with a cudgellike zuccinum when my uncle woke up.

There was a dead silence; after all, my uncle, dullard though he was, did have the power of life and death over everyone and was, in any case, a god. I could see everyone slithering into his favorite toadying position; heads were bowing, knees were bending, eyes were darting shiftily from side to side. The slaves who had been fanning their master from time to time now did so with renewed vigor.

"Good heavens," the Emperor Trajan said. "Who are all these people?" He turned to the bard Euphonius, whose toadying position was one of the most convoluted I have ever seen—he had somehow managed to bow himself in two while still reclining on the couch. "Oh, you," he said. "How did *you* get invited?"

"If it please your Divinity," Euphonius said, "would you like to hear an ode or two?"

"Perhaps you would care to sing to the lions, you silly little man. We've an orgy planned for them, ah, next week." He winked at me as I plucked the remains of the exotic fruits from my party clothes.

"Ah, your Magnitude is pleased to joke with me," Euphonius said, swallowing nervously.

Then he launched himself into another interminable song, this one about the adventures of Jason and the Argonauts, except, in the interests of the new realism, Jason was now a sausage vendor from the wrong side of the ferrequus tracks, Medea a two-obol prostitute who worked the back door of the Flavian Amphitheater, and the Golden Fleece a particularly succulent sort of sausage made from the entrails of the Terra Novan armatillus. This was an excruciating performance, made even more painful by Euphonius's insistence on acting out all the parts himself.

The bard was being pelted with food again—at last I knew there was a purpose for all those inferior victuals

—and I, too, was receiving not infrequent (litotes here) tomatii in the face. As Euphonius reached the climactic scene, in which Jason and Medea were playing "hide the sausage" down in the subterranean passageways of the Circus Maximus, being hounded by a hungry lion that had somehow gone down the wrong off-ramp on its way to dine on a few criminals, the pelting gained in both frequency and accuracy, and I knew I was going to have to kiss my expensive new tunic good-bye. The slaves were not even toweling me off anymore, and even the dancing girls had started throwing vegetables, much to the emperor's delight. Euphonius was capering about wildly, waving his harp and yodeling ferociously over the hooting of the audience.

I did not think I would be able to stand it for another minute. But at that moment, I felt a tap on my shoulder.

I looked around. It was my link boy.

"What are *you* doing here?" I asked.

The boy pointed behind him, to where another child stood, even more diminutive than himself.

It was a Lacotian boy, dressed in a buckskin uniform, with a smart little silken headband in which reposed a single eagle feather. I knew at once what manner of child he was, but could not believe that his kind would be operating so late. "What is it?" I asked, avoiding a particularly large pumpkin.

The two boys dodged deftly at the same time, and it smashed into a bust of Homer by the wall.

"So much for Homer," I said as Euphonius began a stomach-churning rendition of Medea's curse:

> *Was't for this sausage that my sons I slew,*
> *Sautéed my siblings into stringy stew?*
> *Ah, wicked fates! I pray, give me surcease—*
> *I do not die for Athens, but for grease!*

Even the little slave boy winced, though he probably did not speak much Latin, let alone the Greek of cultured conversations. "Well, child! Speak, if you can," I commanded.

"Telegram for Lucius Vinicius," the telegraph boy said.

CHAPTER
III

VOMITORIUM ENCOUNTERS

I WAS GLAD OF ANY EXCUSE TO GET OUT OF THE PARTY, though I wondered how anyone could possibly have sent me a telegram at this time of night.

"If you'll come this way, Lord Vinicius," the lad said, tugging at my sleeve.

I took my leave of my uncle. "Off to the vomitorium, then, eh, Lucius?" he said, and waved at me. As soon as I stepped out of the triclinium, I felt much better, for the singing of Euphonius, the twanging of his lyre, and the thud of exotic fruits against the marble walls all blended together into a generalized murmuring as the sounds echoed through the labyrinth of corridors.

The vomitorium was to the right; I turned left, and the corridor soon led to an enormous parapet, one from which the emperor was wont to inspect the Praetorian guard. Beneath me was a breathtaking panorama of Rome: the magnificent dwelling places on the Palatine, the Tiber, the temples, the distant slums, the Capitoline and Vatican, the streets full of Saturnalia celebrants, the music wafting up to me on breezes scented with lemon and olive and wine and, alas, uncollected sewage. Now I

15

understood why the telegraph was still operating this late at night. For the sky was rent in several places, and a cold light leaked out of those jagged tears in the fabric of heaven, and everything was touched by the glow. And I was one of the few who knew what it meant—that the universe had not much longer to go before it would simply vanish—unless we could capture the Green Pig, the Time Criminal, who was still at large, roaming the multiplex universes, somewhere, somewhen...am I losing my readers? If so, I suggest that they return to their local libraria and have their scribes copy out the first two volumina in these chronicles...

The subject at hand, though. Yes, it was light enough to read smoke signals, and I could also see the operators who manned the telegraph poles, which stretched all the way across the city and along the major highways all the way to Egypt as well as northward to Gaul and even Caledonia. The poles were puffing away merrily into the distance as the slaves labored to relay messages. "It's coming now, sir," said the telegraph boy, who spoke Greek atrociously and was forced to fill in the gaps with words in Latin, the vulgar tongue.

A thin line of smoke stood at the horizon—I could barely make it out—and then, closer to the Palatine, another column of smoke, echoing the first. I realized that it must be the Gaulish slave chained to the pole beside my house and wondered whether the man was drunk or sober.

"Quick! What does it say?" I asked, for smoke signals are sent in a bizarre code that can be understood only by the Terra Novans of the Great Plains of the New World. That was why telegraph boys were generally Lacotians; they had a knack for deciphering the signals, and besides, the Lacota tongue had become a kind of telegraphic lingua franca; lacking declensions and conjugations, it was easier to codify into smoke form.

"Can't quite make it out," he said, squinting, and then, after a few seconds, recoiled in shock. "I think it's about Equus Insanus!"

I realized with a start that I had always known this

moment would come. My young friend had ridden off into the sunset three years before, and now the fabric of the world was so torn that fragments of other universes were shining down on us. There was bound to come a time when the son of Aquila learned something on his odyssey. Perhaps, I mused, he had already captured the Green Pig, and the rest of us need do nothing more. I hoped so. Saving the universe is all very well, but after two or three times it can get pretty tedious.

I was rudely awakened from my reverie, however, as the boy pieced together more of the message. "'Ha . . . so you thought you could elude me forever, you silly little creatures of the remote past! Little do you know that I've already . . . captured young Equus Insanus'—demoniacal laughter—'and intend to destroy him utterly'—demoniacal laughter."

"What do you mean, demoniacal laughter?" I asked.

"Oh, it's a special symbol," the telegraph boy replied. "You see those three quick spurts of smoke, followed by a long one? That's what that means."

"I see."

"Not to be confused with three quick spurts and two longs—that's the sign for 'large buffalo herd approaching,'" he added. "And *two* quick spurts followed by one long is 'enemy braves within range—balding—not worth scalping.'"

Bloody Lacotians. Give them an inch of civilization and they'll take a mile. "Just get on with the message." Even as I stood there I was overcome with fond memories of my half brother. Of the time he and I urinated from the eye of the giant statue of Jupiter Vacantanca down onto the heads of the senate—the time we battled the Green Pig on his flying throne—even our school days. My arse positively tingled at the remembrance of the flagellum of Androcles the schoolmaster, the almost daily reward for the trouble Equus and I used to cause. Now, it seemed, he was in trouble. Well, I was a Roman, by Jove, and if a Terra Novan savage could get into a scrape, I could bloody well get him out of it.

"There's more!" the telegraph boy said, becoming

rather agitated. "I think he wants some kind of ransom —and there's something about pyramid power."

The pole was puffing like mad, and the boy was struggling to translate it all. "Something about 'the heart of the great pyramid—mummies.' I'm really not getting any of this," he said sullenly. "Something about flying saucers, dinosaurs, and—"

"Never mind all that—where's Equus Insanus?"

"That's one of the things I can't quite figure out, sir," the child said. "The message sometimes purports to be from some kind of Green Pig—and sometimes it appears to be Equus himself who is speaking—oh, here's something I can understand! 'Don't come! It's no use! He's got me by the—' Can't make out the next word, and then it just says, 'Your friend, Equus Insanus.' Then there's more gibberish about pyramids and suchlike."

It all sounded like nonsense. But there was also a hint of high adventure in the enigmatic message. Obviously, I was going to have to travel somewhere, brave terrifying odds, kill dozens of enemies, and do all those other things we Romans do best. It sounded pretty bloody dangerous, by the maidenhead of Venus, but it had to be better than enduring another minute of the emperor's dinner party. Suddenly I felt invigorated, newly elated, I experienced a brief epiphanic moment as I remembered that I, too, had danced the sun dance in the New World, that I, too, had seen visions and gone on a spirit journey—and that I might yet do so again. Suddenly, saving the universe did not seem such a bad idea, after all, although I was not entirely sure how I could manage to take leave of my uncle.

I wiped the food stains off my cloak and tunic and started back inside, with the boy trotting behind me. He obviously wanted a tip, but I did not have anything on me except an Athenian dekadrachm and four gold pieces —I don't like to carry small change—and I did not fancy giving the boy enough money to live off for a whole year. "Call at the house of Lucius Vinicius in the morning, child," I said airily, "and my steward will give you a few coppers. Though the way you're holding your hand out, you'd think you'd just translated the *Iliad* into Latin."

"Yes, sir! Jolly decent of you, sir!" the boy said, scurrying off down the corridor.

I found myself walking down an endless hallway. There were busts everywhere—most of them my own ancestors—a god or two—and now and then a famous Terra Novan, such as the mystical Taurus Sedentarius, who had fought with Aquila in the famous Battle of the Flumen Pulveris, that is to say, the Powder River. I traded laurel wreaths with an old bust of Nero. Who was going to notice, after all? Then I took a turn into what I was sure was the triclinium in which we had been dining.

A sickly-sweet smell told me that this was no triclinium. I had wandered into the vomitorium by mistake. Enormous vats lined the walls, and a slave was busy fumigating the place with an incense burner while another scattered a solution of attar of roses over the vats —to no avail. Beneath the fragrance of incense and roses was the unmistakable stench of human vomit. I am a moderate eater even at the most prodigious of banquets and have never been forced to use a vomitorium. I was just turning my back to leave when I noticed a man bent over one of the vats—a man so tiny that he was forced to stand on a chair to reach the edge of the vomit jar.

Too late, I realized who it was. He looked up from his exertions and saw me, and declaimed heartily, "Ah, noble Lucius, I greet thee!"

"Ave yourself," I said, thankful that Euphonius's lyre was nowhere in sight. "Atque vale," I added, hoping he would not engage me in conversation. I had enough to think about, what with saving the universe.

"I say, Lucius, do you think you could help me? I think I've dropped my instrument into this vat."

"You want me to reach into that—"

"Well, I can't stretch my arm that far—and you, being such a patron of the arts, and an admirer of my poesy, will surely not begrudge me this favor, this sacrifice for the sake of the divine muse, whose beauty and grace inform the very texture of our lives..."

Pretty florid for a new realist, I thought. For the man

who wrote *Leda and the Duck*, he can certainly turn on the hoary clichés when he wants to! "Well, I—"

"I'll be glad to sing for your help!" he said eagerly.

"That won't be necessary," I said, hurrying to the side of the vat. The odor was abominable, and I nearly lost the contents of my own stomach, but luckily I was able to snag the lyre, which was bobbing up and down just beyond the poet's reach, with a twig of the laurel wreath I had just purloined from the marble head of Nero.

Eagerly he reached out to grab the lyre, which I had managed to bring almost to his hand. He began floundering about in tremendous agitation, and presently he fell into the vat headfirst.

I started to laugh.

The head emerged. Various bits of food clung to his hair; a slimy segment of entrail clung to one ear. He was sputtering. "Ah, the things one suffers for the sake of truth and beauty! And yet—" He went under one more time, and there were assorted gurgles before he emerged to complete the sentence, "—there is never any end to the anguish of the human condition."

"What anguish?" I asked angrily, thinking of my friend, embroiled in Jove knew what, perhaps suffering some vile torture at the hands of the Time Criminal at that very moment. "You have it easy, you insufferable old bore. Why, the very vomit you're floating in could feed a starving family in a Gaulish village for a week! You sit around snacking on larks' tongues and peacocks' brains all day—don't talk to me about suffering."

"Alas! No more nightingales' livers for me," the poet said, sobbing. "I've been exiled. The emperor doesn't like me anymore. He said, 'To be succinct, old thing, your verses suck.' I've got three days to gather my belongings and not be found within a hundred mille pas-suum of this city."

"Well, you had it coming! Leda and the duck, my arse."

"Yes, but the new realism's the best thing I've got going for myself. Do you want to hear the poem I'm working on now?" he asked as he flailed around, trying to get a purchase on the rim of the vat so that he could pull himself out. "It's about the labors of Hercules—except that Hercules is this washed-up old galley slave, see, and he gets a job working as a scribe in the public library of Alexandria, except that he can't spell very well—"

"No! No! Or I'll push you back in!"

"My *Ode to the Emperor's Eyelash* is pretty good—"

"That's probably what got you exiled, you idiot! You know how sensitive he is about his eyelashes. Anyway, I haven't got time for you. I've got my own troubles—I'm getting exiled myself, actually. In a manner of speaking."

"I say, help me out of this vat, what!"

I beckoned to the perfuming slaves. They shrugged. After all, it was the Saturnalia; they did not have to obey orders if they did not want to, and I could not blame them for not wanting to touch that despicable little man. I helped the tiny poet out myself, getting quite drenched by the vat's foul contents in the process.

"Ho, there," I cried to the nearest slave, the one with the bowl of rose water. I took the bowl from him and dunked it all over myself. Perhaps that would remove some of the odoriferous essences that were already seeping into my very pores and, worse still, into my expensive clothes. What would my tailor say? I shuddered. One could buy three or four decent slaves for what those clothes cost me—not that anyone can buy decent help anywhere in Rome these days.

At length, soggy, smelly, and disheartened, I wended my way back to the emperor's orgy. The frenzied fruit throwing had been the only activity of the evening, and now that the poet had left the room, they were all asleep once more. In a corner, some Nubian wrestlers were fighting to the death, but no one was watching.

In another corner, beside the bust of Homer, which was now liberally spattered with exotic fruits, jugglers juggled, Egyptian belly dancers wiggled their fat bellies and jiggled the priceless jewels in their navels; off to the side, a bevy of imported Esquimoi, extremely rare savages from beyond the northern fringes of the New World, were doing something my program notes referred to as a caribou mating dance—rubbing noses, butting heads that sported enormous antlers of solid gold, and grunting mysteriously.

My uncle was asleep; protocol demanded that he wake up so I could take my leave. He was snoring noisily, though, and I soon found myself sipping another goblet of the same aqua cocacola that I had brought to the party.

Presently, I saw that one of the wrestlers had the other in a death grip and was waiting patiently for someone to give him a thumbs up or down signal. His fallen foe was rolling his eyes; if the death grip did not get him, the boredom would.

Aqua cocacola can become dangerously addictive. But in small quantities it makes one feel master of one's destiny; one can do no wrong. "Enough of all this!" I cried, rising to my feet. "I'm bored!"

My uncle woke up.

"Bored? Who said that?" he asked, staring shiftily from side to side. All the distinguished guests immediately snapped to attention.

"Bored? Not me, your Divinity! Finest party I've ever been to in my whole life, by Mars!" and other comments of this nature began echoing from all sides of the room.

My uncle's gaze fixed itself on me. "Lucius Vinicius, old thing," he said. "Are you bored, by any chance, what?"

It was too late. He knew. And I was too carried away by the power of the aqua cocacola to care. My best friend was in the hands of an unspeakable alien; the world was about to come to an end, and no one could even be bothered about it; my clothes were ruined— there was just no point in beating about the bush anymore.

"Yes, Uncle, I bloody well am bored," I said. "I do wish you'd throw a decent orgy for a change. If only you'd put up the money for a decent spread! Even a lowly tribune could do better."

My uncle was sputtering with rage. "Biting the hand that feeds you, Lucius! How'd you like to have your hand bitten off for a change, eh? I've got a lion show coming up next month—and they haven't been fed in weeks!"

"Of course not—you can't even feed your guests, let alone your lions," I said.

"Off with his head! Off with his tongue! Off with his feet!" screamed Marcus Ulpius Trajanus, Caesar Augustus, White and Greatest Father, Pater Patriae, and so on and so forth, and picked up a mallet from beside his couch, with which he planned to strike the enormous Chinish gong that hung behind an arras between two life-sized statues of himself...

At that moment, the strains of an out-of-tune lyre reverberated through the chamber, and I heard the voice of Euphonius the bard squawking above the unpleasant twanging of his instrument:

> *Farewell, O Rome! Vale, o mea patria!*
> *I shall no longer waste my time in flatt'ry or*
> *Abase myself before th' imperial might—*
> *I shall be free! For I have seen the light!*
> *I shall not let thy punishments me vex;*
> *A cruel monarch is a nervous rex!*

I have heard the wheezing quasi-music of Terra Novan savages, the plangent ululations of the women of Arabia, the shrieking yowls that the Numidians call music—but never in my life had I encountered so painful a sound as that which assailed my ears at that moment. Apparently, everyone else thought so, too, because there was an immediate uproar. Fruit flew; crockery was smashed; even a few swords were being unsheathed. The emperor seemed as flabbergasted by the poet's effrontery as he was infuriated by his parting words, and his face was turning more hues than I had thought possible in a human being. Of course, my uncle is a god, so I suppose it should not have surprised me.

At that moment, the victorious wrestler, who had

been patiently awaiting the imperial gesture all this while, could wait no longer and snapped his opponent's neck; I am sure he was anxious to get home with his prize money. It was a perfect moment for me to make good my escape, so I slipped away and slunk off into the night.

CHAPTER
IV

MYSTERIES OF THE WEST

PICKING UP MY LINK BOY AT THE VESTIBULE, I LEFT the palace as quickly as I could. The news that Equus Insanus was in captivity would already have spread, considering the public nature of telegraphic messages. I was sure that tongues would already have begun wagging, and I wanted to reach Aquila with the news before some garbled version did.

But where could he be found on this night of all nights? I hardly had need of a link boy as I entered the Forum Romanum, where thousands of Roman citizens had congregated to celebrate the solstice rites. The sky was bright with the exhalations from other universes. A group of Romans and Lacotians performed a war dance around a roaring fire that was colored blue from copper dust; merchants hawked roast hummingbirds on skewers and peacocks' brains. A group of slaves was running after the master and mistress of their household, shouting imaginative insults; I knew that they'd be singing another tune after the Saturnalia was over. Clowns with enormous leather phalloi juggled and performed acrobatic stunts, and a little Mahicanus lad, with his mahau-

cum hairdo dyed purple, was attempting to unload an
armful of chariot wheel hubcaps onto some unsuspecting
Egyptian tourists. Drunks and homeless persons strewed
the streets; palanquins borne by Nubians passed by, with
now and then a curtain drawing open to reveal the over-
painted visage of some Roman matron.

Where would Aquila be on this night of nights? I had
an idea that he would be out carousing with Titus Papinianus among the stews of Little Lacotia. Or would he be
at the avenue of the prophets? It was so bright that I
decided to dismiss the link boy. I think I overtipped him;
he ran off joyfully into the throng without so much as a
"Farewell, O master."

Then I began walking downhill toward the slums. I
did not fear being attacked by brigands on this night of
nights, because I had a knife hidden in the sole of my left
moccasina, a short gladius concealed in my tunic, and a
dagger within the folds of my cloak. Besides, though it is
true that I was richly dressed, my clothes reeked of roses
and the contents of a poet's stomach, and one could
hardly tell that a few talents' worth of Tyrian purple had
gone into their making. And though I was reeling and
staggering from the effects of the aqua cocacola, I knew
that, if forced to fight, I would still be the equal of any
member of the lower classes.

I had not been to the house of Titus Papinianus for
some months, for since our captivity on Mars and the
subsequent disappearance of my half brother, we had all
drifted apart somewhat. But I was not displeased to see
the familiar walls of the old general's villa. Since it was
the Saturnalia, there was no gateman; it was Papinian
himself who admitted me into the foyer.

"Heavens! Lucius Vinicius!" he said. "What an unex-
pected surprise!" He wrinkled his bubble nose and
scratched his head. "Are there in Rome tonight no parties more decadent than the house of a retired general?
Come in, come in." He handed me an enormous krater
of wine, and I looked around. The house was much as I
remembered it, with the entrance to the atrium guarded
by twin totem poles and various statues of the gods dis-

porting themselves in the garden. But someone seemed to have been spending a great deal of money. There were murals depicting the various battles of the Terra Novan campaigns, with such famous scenes as the scalping of Publius Cladius the Younger by a gang of Manhattii, the flight of the Siosionian Princess Sacavazaea through the forests of the Montes Negri, the Battle of Cornu Parvum Magnumque, and so on; and murals depicting Jupiter Vacantanca, the composite Roman-Lacotian god, in various majestic poses. I noticed that parts of the totem poles had been redone in solid gold.

What I did not expect was the crowd. I was not aware that old Titus Papinianus had any friends, really, but the place was absolutely crawling with people—people, I may add, with money, for they positively reeked of expensive perfumes. Why, there was C. Lentulus Fortunatus, once the richest man in Rome and Papinian's archrival—whom I had never quite managed to forgive for his clandestine liaison with my departed mother—now merely the second or third richest, reclining in a couch and sipping from a beaker of rare glass; there was C. Pomponius Piso the Younger, gnawing on an unborn dormouse dipped in honey; and there was the Lady Deidameia, who was some sort of Egyptian aristocrat and who had a couple of live snakes attached to her gown by a gold chain; not to mention several real-live poets of the kind that Euphonius the bard could never aspire to imitate. In short, these were my kind of people.

"Make yourself at home, Lucius old thing," Papinian said. "Haven't had you over for quite a while, eh what?"

"Actually, I came over on rather serious business," I said. "Is Aquila, perchance, here?"

"In the back room," Papinian said, pointing vaguely across the atrium. There was no back room; it was, as a matter of fact, a gigantic tipi, not the usual single-family size but the kind that the Lacotii held meetings in—a chieftain's lodge. In the Roman fashion, some Ionian columns graced the tent flap, and the buffalo hides were painted with various mythological scenes. A slave stood at the tent flap with a bowl of scented water to wash the feet of those who would enter. "He's putting the finishing touches on the new religion, you know."

"Religion?" I asked.

"Yes, it's the only way to get rich nowadays. Everyone's doing it; ever since this whole end-of-the-world business, all those easterners have been getting in on the act. You've got your Cybelites, your Isis worshipers, your Adonis cultists, your Christianoi—"

"Who are *they*?"

"Who knows? I think they're a cult of carpenter worshipers from Judea. But they're the scurviest of the lot, seditious chaps, always corrupting the minds of the slaves and paupers, the poor helpless creatures! Aquila and I have cottoned on to something far better—a religion of the rich, full of modern technology, with arcane jargon, that appeals in particular to those who love reading *scientifictiones*."

"So are you planning to sponsor a big spectacle in the arena?"

"Heavens, no! Do you think I want our great and glorious emperor to know that I have money? He'd be over here in a moment, thinking of fancy new ways to tax me."

I followed him across the courtyard. Inside the tipi, several extremely rich people reclined. They were wearing, on their heads, what can only be described as copper copies of the Great Pyramid of Cheops in Egypt; to these pyramids were attached wires, which were all connected to a device that resembled a battered uranograph. You may recall that the uranograph, invented by the Sasquatius in the previous volumen of these chronicles, is used by high priests for determining in advance whether beasts of sacrifice have the politically correct entrails; it makes use of the radiation from a lump of the essence of uranium, which falls upon a silver-coated sheet—the stuff of *scientifictiones*, you may be sure, but it proved useful on a number of occasions in our adventures, since its emanations are also fatal to androids. Here, however, the instrument was being used for an even more mysterious purpose.

"What on Earth is going on?" I asked.

"Quiet!" said a wheezing, familiar voice. I saw that Aquila, in his senatorial robes and war bonnet, was sitting in the middle of the floor in a circle of pebbles. His skin was green, like that of all those who had traveled too long through other dimensions of time and space. Before him was the skull of an aurochs, around him were other magical fetishes; and in his hands was a peace pipe, from which he drew a few puffs before opening his eyes and seeing me.

"*How, até!*" I said, lifting my right palm in an attitude of blessing.

"Hail yourself, my wayward child," said the old man. "Are you hungry?"

"Aquila, we've got urgent business—"

"Be still. Let me finish smoking. Would you like a puff? *Na!*" He handed me the pipe across the sacred circle, and I took a puff, muttering the ritualistic word *ku* in response. It was an exceptionally strong tabaccum and did not mix well with the aqua cocacola I had imbibed.

"What is all this nonsense?" I asked, gesturing at the rich people, who all seemed lost to the world.

"I'm in the business of peddling the wisdom of the West, my son," the old Lacotian said. "I mean, all the other cults in town are from the East, so we of the New World might as well get into the act."

"I see a lot of pretentious, wealthy people attached to machines."

"Ah, yes, the encephalometron," Aquila said. "It doesn't do anything, but it has a certain placebo effect. These people, you see, are harnessing the power of ancient pyramids, which, as you know, are the creation of flying saucer people, and using it to enhance their mental powers."

"It sounds like quackery to me," I said.

"It's harmless enough," Aquila said. "And in these last days of the universe, people need something they can believe in. And why shouldn't we make a few sestertii off their burning desire for some control of their lives?"

"I see," I said, though I had to confess that there seemed to be something not quite ethical about what was going on. "But how can they believe all this drivel?"

"Why shouldn't they? I've been in a flying saucer, and they haven't."

"But you're Aquila the mighty, who routed General Pomponius Piso back in the days of—"

"Yes, but I'm an old man now, and Lacotia is a conquered nation. Why shouldn't I get what I can out of it?"

"Well, Aquila, you'd better gird up your loins and get ready for another adventure. I've received a message from Equus Insanus, and—"

"I know, I know. I saw it in a vision."

"He's been captured by—"

"Yes, yes, I know. Have some more tabaccum."

"A vision? What vision?"

He pointed at a man who was skulking in a corner of the room. I recognized him at once—it was the tall Gaulish telegraph operator, that drunkard who so frequently spied into my atrium! "The Great Spirit works in mysterious ways," Aquila said. "The universe is a great circle." I had heard all this, ad nauseam, from Equus Insanus during our school days. But somehow Aquila invested the words with a certain loftiness. The Lacotian chief rose, drew his toga tighter around himself, and tottered toward me. He was becoming very frail, I saw, yet his eyes held no weariness, no fear. "Has it rained recently?" he asked suddenly. "Perhaps I should do a rain dance."

"By the maidenhead of Venus!" cried one of the rich fellows tethered to the uranograph. "My mind—it's clearing up—suddenly I feel so—different—"

"Ah," Aquila said, lifting his hands in a posture of benediction.

"Thank you—oh, thank you," said the one whose brain had been so miraculously cleared, and tossed a bagful of gold at Aquila. It was conveniently retrieved by a serving wench, who tucked it into her bosom.

"Carry on," Aquila said, waving vaguely to the others, who continued to sit, their brows knit in expressions of bliss or puzzlement. He staggered up and put his arm on my shoulder and told me to lead him back toward the atrium. "We must confer with Titus Papinianus! *Hechitu welo!*" he said.

And he bade me escort him to another chamber of the house, the private bath, where Papinian was being massaged by a Chirochian woman. There was another tipi, a squat little one, in the bathroom, this one had steam pouring from its venthole, and I realized that it was for the *inichipi* ceremony—a sweat bath that induces visions among the Lacotii.

"There you are," Papinian said. "I suppose we'd better discuss our plan of action—you *are* planning to come with us on our mission to save Equus Insanus, are you not?"

"Yes, Uncle Papinian," I said. "But I couldn't help noticing—this fake religion you're plugging. Isn't that a little . . . unethical?"

"Listen, young Lucius," Titus said. "It's all very well getting on your high horse, but we've got worlds to save here, and if fleecing some of our aristocrats can give us the wherewithal . . ."

"But—"

Aquila said, "He's right, for once, Lucius. The last adventures we had were all funded by the emperor—in a niggardly fashion, to be sure—but this time we have nothing. We cannot even ask for help from the little green creatures from the other dimension, for they've declared a policy of noninterference—they don't want the Third Law of the Conservation of Multiplex Realities to snap back on itself, triggering the destruction of universes other than our own. They've essentially decided to cut their losses at one universe, and I can't say I blame them. I saw, in a spirit journey that I took within this very sweat bath, that we would be going on an odyssey ten times more dangerous than we dreamed possible. More than a spirit journey! You know that I worked for the Dimensional Patrol once. Well, a lot of unofficial 'peeking' goes on—so it's not surprising that I've already seen everything that's going to happen to us—and it's not pretty. I knew that we would be forced to hire mercenaries, buy ships, bribe officials—and for the past three years, while you have been acting the playboy, we have been amassing supplies for this trip."

"I know it goes contrary to the old Roman values, Lucius, old chap," Papinian said, grunting as the masseuse turned him over and began pummeling him on the chest, all the while sprinkling him with musk oil. "But what can I say? Alea jacta est."

"So what's the plan?" I asked.

"Egypt," the old chieftain said mysteriously.

"Egypt?"

"There's a ship docked at Brundisium right now; I've sent a telegram on ahead for the Egyptian and the Sasquatius; if we leave at dawn, and ride like the wind, we should be there in less than a week," Papinianus said. "This institution here will take care of itself; we'll find Equus, capture the Green Pig, deliver him up to the flying saucer people on Mars—and that'll be that."

I just couldn't help thinking that the two old men were being a little more blasé than they had any right to be. Of course, they had both been through far more of these adventures than I, but even so . . .

At that moment, a bloodcurdling racket burst upon our ears.

"Heavens!" Papinian cried. "Get rid of that cat—it'll upset the guests."

"That's no cat," Aquila said, frowning.

From the atrium came the twanging of a lyre and the cacophonous caterwauling of Euphonius the bard—and the sound of people fleeing in panic—screaming, trampling of feet—much as, I imagine, was heard thirty years ago in the streets of Pompeii during the disaster. A messenger ran in, his hands about his ears, and knelt in front of us.

"He's looking for Master Lucius, sirs—says he's been tracking him down all evening—wants to follow him to the ends of the earth—says something about how he saved him from drowning in a vat of vomit."

"What!" Papinian said, arching an eyebrow. "You saved that thing's life?"

"He exaggerates, Uncle Papinian."

The twanging came nearer, nearer . . .

"Quick!" Aquila said. "We must fight! It is a good day to die!" With astonishing agility, he whipped off his toga, to reveal a loincloth and buckskin leggings underneath. He pulled out a knife and, ripping his toga into strips, moved silently toward the archway. No sooner had Euphonius appeared than Aquila leapt and, with amazing alacrity, gagged the bard with the toga strips while holding a dagger to his throat. "Silence!" he whispered. "Else I shall silence your tongue forever!" Euphonius struggled, but Aquila quickly bound him hand and foot with the remnants of his toga.

"Bloody waste of a good toga, if you ask me," Papinian said.

"*Mmmm-mmm-mmm!*" Euphonius said.

"Oh, no, you're not!" Aquila said. "That is the last thing we need."

"How can you tell what he's saying?" I asked.

"Warriors are trained," Aquila said, "to be able to construe the utterances of the bound and gagged—pleas for mercy, cries of pain, and so on. In this, we are much like dentists."

"*Mmmmm-mm!*" Euphonius said, his eyes imploring me.

"Nothing of the sort!" Aquila said. "I don't care if you *have* been exiled; we shall proceed upon our quest without the benefit of your verses . . ."

"Tell the gate slave to boot him out the door, will you?" Papinian said. "You and I are going to have to pack if we're to make it to Brundisium." He watched as the masseuse and the messenger boy led the poet out of the bathroom. "But first—wine!"

CHAPTER
V

THE SENATE

WE PACKED OUR BELONGINGS IN HASTE. DEPART-
ing as we were in such a rush, and without the
emperor's blessing, it was unseemly to take more than a
dozen servants with us; the rest of the slaves were to
remain behind. We loaded the ill-gotten gains from the
encephalometric religion into several chests; they would
precede us to the ferrequus station, for we were planning
to travel to Brundisium by railway.

By dawn, most of the followers of Aquila's cult had
departed. But we barely finished throwing a few clothes
into a box when we heard a pounding at the gate. I hoped
it was not the Praetorian guard, sent to arrest me for
insulting the emperor. Instead, it turned out to be the
telegraph boy I had met the previous night. He was
ushered into the atrium; he gazed at me and the general
with a certain hero worship, but when Aquila entered the
room, his expression turned into absolute awe.

"*Tunkashila,*" he said, which is the Lacotian word for
"grandfather." Though this is a term of respect for the
aged among the Lacotii, it would not have surprised me
if it were literally true, for my half brother's father had a

woman in every town and dozens of children, if all the stories about him were true.

"Well, what is it? Another telegram?" I asked impatiently. I didn't want to miss the ferrequus to Brundisium.

"I want to join the expedition," the boy said.

"Join the expedition? What nonsense!" Papinian said. "This is a man's work. What do you know of our expedition, anyway?"

"Well," he said, "I'm a telegraph boy, and the lines have been puffing all morning; all Rome knows that you're off to save the universe. You owe me, Lucius Vinicius; I brought you the message."

"Perhaps," Aquila said, "you are unaware of the grave dangers, my child."

"I'm not called Lupus Ferox for nothing, O senator!"

"Ferocious wolf, eh what?" Titus Papinianus said. "A pipsqueak like you?"

"Might I remind His Bulbosity that Equus Insanus was only ten years old when he rescued you from a raging dinosaur?"

"Impertinence! Fifty lashes!"

"That's what you get for having your memoirs published, Uncle Papinian," I said, laughing.

"He can clearly read more than just smoke signals," Aquila said. "Perhaps we should—"

"No more extra baggage!" Papinian said, who did not need to be reminded, I am sure, of how my half brother had saved him from crucifixion at the hands of the Green Pig. "Let's get out of here before the whole town knows about it. It's already the second hour—the sun is rising."

"The second hour—by the great mystery—I have to go to the senate this morning!" Aquila cried.

"The senate? Who cares about the blasted senate?"

"There's a very important vote this morning—it's an appropriations bill to have a temple to the late Emperor Domitian dedicated in Omahopolis...I'm head of the committee, and I'll surely be missed if I don't go..."

"Ad infernum with your committees and appropriations!" Papinian cried. "We've worlds—"

"To save, universes to rescue!" Lupus Ferox said delightedly.

"Nevertheless, one must go about these things properly," Aquila said. "Look, I haven't even put on my war paint."

"War paint? I thought you had to go to the senate!" Papinian said.

"What is the difference?" Aquila asked, shrugging.

We did not reach the senate for a few more hours, while Aquila carefully painted his face with lightning bolts, white splotches, and other insignia. Then there was the pesky little boy to be disposed of; he finally went away after I gave him three or four gold pieces, probably enough to buy his freedom. At last the three of us were mounting the Capitol steps.

"I don't know why we're doing this," I said. "If I'm seen—with the emperor's displeasure known—"

"Oh, don't worry. The emperor never goes to senate meetings," Aquila said. "This will only take a second."

It did not take a second. One senator, Publius Pertinax, was holding forth on the relative merits of various methods of taxation. I and Papinian stood outside, walking to and fro impatiently, but we could hear the ancient senator's voice booming away. At length, unnoticed, we entered the hallowed hall itself. It was much the same as Trajan's party had been, videlicet, the noble senators all seemed to be asleep. Pertinax, his jowls quivering with righteous rage, was going on and on about the emperor's proposed tax reform. Of course, the senate's opinion was only academic, anyway. I longed for the old days—before my time, of course—when Caligula had been in power. He had made his horse a senator—or was it a consul? Probably would have raised the level of intelligent discourse to no end.

After an interminable wait, it was time for Aquila to make his speech. I marveled at how well he had learned the senatorial techniques of obfuscation, rhetorical sidetracking, and irrelevant apostrophizing.

"I can't believe the fate of the universe is waiting because of this!" I whispered to Papinian.

At last Aquila sat down beside us, and someone called for a vote.

Suddenly, bucinae blared, cornua trumpeted, and I could hear the tramping of military feet. The emperor!

"I thought he never went to senate meetings!" I whispered to Aquila.

"So I was wrong," he said.

Trajan stormed into the room, and I was so taken by surprise that I forgot to slither into the customary toadying position. That was why he noticed me right away. Several burly Praetorians were with him. My heart sank.

"Still in town, young man?" he said. "You still think I'm boring, do you?"

I started to stammer a response, but he went on. "I'll deal with you later. I'm here about the taxes."

Pertinax seemed to take it as a tremendous compliment and fell on his knees, gibbering his thanks. The emperor continued. "I have it on good authority that the purveyors of a certain new religion"—he pointed straight at Aquila and Papinian—"are planning to abscond with several thousand talents of religious contributions... without having paid any taxes on them!"

The senators began to babble "Shocking! Shocking! I say, what! Stealing our taxes, eh?" and other such remarks.

Pertinax rose from the marble bench. "That's precisely the sort of abuse I was talking about, O Caesar!" he said. "After all, the taxes on several thousand talents could easily fund, say, a few days of gladiatorial spectacles."

"Taxes!" Trajan said, gloating. "Plus late penalties, plus a fine for trying to leave Rome...shall we say, a total of one hundred and fifty per centum?"

"I'm ruined!" Papinian said, quaking.

"Ah, well," Aquila said. "It was a good idea while it lasted."

"Ruined, ruined!"

"Look on the bright side," Aquila said. "Other fringe

religions end up as spectacle fodder; we, on the other hand, are merely feeding the imperial coffers, not the lions."

Trajan said, "I've been jolly busy all morning, collecting; I've already seized your villa, O Titus Papinianus, and your slaves will be auctioned off next week."

Everyone who is anyone in Rome gets purged sooner or later; it was amazing that Papinian had lasted this long. He had actually lived through the reigns of six or seven emperors. It was bound to catch up with him. He would probably be exiled to one of those abominable country-club towns on the borders of the empire. As for Aquila, he would probably wriggle out of it somehow, and I supposed he still had ways of contacting the flying saucer people. I looked around. Most the senators were dozing through the whole thing.

"Arrest them!" the emperor said, and the Praetorians lunged forward.

At that moment, the entire senate hall started to fill with smoke. The emperor began to cough. The guards were sputtering. It was getting in my eyes; they watered; I could hardly breathe. I saw the emperor staggering about, still attempting to order my arrest. Then there was more smoke, and all I could see was Aquila's war bonnet sailing above the billowing fumes.

Someone pulled at my tunica. "Quick! Before we run out of smoke!" It was a child's voice.

"Lupus Ferox?" I asked, wondering what he was doing there.

"Don't ask any questions!" he said. "There's a palanquin waiting outside to take you to the ferrequus tracks!"

I saw a tiny hand poking from the fog. It clutched a little amphora. Next thing I knew, the amphora was flying through the air. I heard a *crash-tinkle-thud*, and then more smoke rose up. I felt another amphora being thrust into my hand. "For good luck," Lupus said. "Throw it as hard as you can on your way out!"

The hand tugged again, and I followed. I was choking. I collided with a column. Then I saw the war bonnet once more, negotiating the clouds of smoke with ease;

trusting to the gods, I followed the eagle feathers much
as a pilot follows the northern star. I paused only to
throw the amphora.

In a moment, Aquila, Papinian, and I were on the
Capitol steps, and there was, indeed, a palanquin waiting; ten oiled and muscular Nubians knelt, waiting for us
to climb inside. I saw that Lupus Ferox's war paint was
almost as elaborate as old Aquila's. The boy jumped in
behind us, and we were off, swaying hither and thither as
the Nubians negotiated the steps.

"Where'd all that smoke come from?" I asked.

"I'm a professional telegraph boy," Lupus Ferox said.
"You could at least give me credit for knowing where to
find the tools of my trade."

"I suppose you'll have to come with us now," Papinian said to the boy, sighing.

"Ditto for me," a voice said. A head poked upside
down through the palanquin drapes. "After all, I organized this whole escape route."

"Euphonius!" we all exclaimed, horrified.

"Oh, don't worry. I won't sing—not yet, at any rate,"
he said, clambering in beside us and hanging his lyre up
on the curtain rod. "And don't blame the boy—I bribed
him to tell me where you'd gone to. But I've become
even more convinced that I must follow you to the ends
of the Earth—all three of you." I noticed that he was
wearing a bronze pyramid on his head. "Ah," he said,
"the pyramid—I'm so happy I came to your house last
night, O wisest masters! I've been thoroughly and utterly
converted. Wearing this pyramid has made me the hap-
piest of men. I long to be wired to an encephalometron
again, for only then can I know bliss."

I rolled my eyes. "That's what you get for making up
a religion," I said.

"He's right," Papinian said. "I'm afraid the whole
thing is simply a load of twaddle—a joke—a way of
raising money for our journey."

"You cannot fool me, O wise ones, with your words
of obfuscation. I know it is only a test of faith. But I am
not the Euphonius you once knew. My mind is no longer

encumbered by such, ah, *encumbrances* as reality. Your religion has cleared the way for a more profound vision —an epic to end all epics—a final chapter in the story that began with Homer and continued through Virgil to ...ah, modesty prevents me."

Lupus Ferox said, "Shall I scalp him now, or do you want me to kill him first?" and pulled a little scalping knife from his buckskin tunica.

"Much as we'd like to," Aquila said, "we cannot let him be killed without becoming evil persons; after all, he has saved our lives. It would not be an honorable thing to do. So I suppose we must let him travel with us—"

"Oh, no!" said Papinian and I at the same time.

"—as long as he promises not to sing."

CHAPTER
VI

ALEXANDRIA

WELL, EUPHONIUS PROMISED, BUT YOU CAN IMAGine how long that promise lasted.

However, we were thankful for his bad verses when a detachment of guards began pursuing us down the Appian Way. For Euphonius merely poked his head out the back and burst into a florid recital, and the front row of guards stopped in their tracks, causing the second row to run right into them, whereupon the third row collided with the second, and so on—until all we could see, as we receded into the distance, was a pile of squirming scrap metal.

O reader! I shall not quote Euphonius's song to you. In the first place, I would not sully this papyrus with so hideous a composition. In the second... well, I would not want so powerful a secret weapon to become widely distributed. Who knows? With Euphonius as tactician and vocal instructor, some barbarian general might be able to slaughter an entire legion at a distance, and even bring about the fall of the Roman Empire... nay! Let the song with which Euphonius vanquished the Praetorian guard remain a mythic absolute, like the song that Orpheus sang to Persephone or the music that Odysseus heard from the lips of the sirens.

The above, an obligatory editorial apostrophe, was included lest the reader censure me for becoming slack in my use of rhetorical devices. Sometimes I fear that a natural love of storytelling blinds me to the art's higher purposes.

Of the journey to Brundisium and the voyage to Egypt, there is little to relate. With the ill-gotten gains from the new religion, Aquila and Papinian had outfitted us with a very fine ship indeed, one of the very few steamships in non-imperial hands. We traveled, if not in style, then without much discomfort, for the ship came equipped with dancing girls, cooks, wrestlers, singers, and other entertainers, and each evening we were treated to a rousing performance of one of the classic dramas of Aeschylus—spiced up a bit, of course, to suit the Roman taste. Clytemnestra's murder of Agamemnon, for instance, left nothing to the imagination, and the deck was awash with pig entrails and stage blood by the time the play was done.

I am rarely seasick, and I must confess that the only time was when Euphonius decided to give a command performance.

No sooner had we stepped off the ship than we saw Aaye the Egyptian and Abraham bar-David, the Judean sasquatch, our former traveling companions. They were gesticulating wildly to us. I was delighted to see them again, especially the Sasquatius, but not that pleased when he held me in a bear hug that nearly crushed me.

"Shalom," he said. "We must hurry—there's no time to lose!"

"Time to lose?" Papinian asked. "Oh, I say, what."

"The pyramids!" Aaye said. "They're taking off!"

"Taking off?" Papinian asked.

"Stands to reason," Aquila said, nodding sagely as though it were nothing out of the ordinary. "They have a habit of doing that."

"Habit, my arse!" Papinian said. "Or is this more of your flying saucer lore?"

"But you don't understand!" Aaye said hysterically. "What is Egypt without pyramids? We shall no longer retain our position as the most mystical, wise, and enigmatic people on this Earth if our pyramids keep deciding to walk out on us . . ."

I paid no attention for the moment; I was taking in the spectacle that was Alexandria. Indeed, the Egyptian Alexandria was much different from Alexandria in the New World. For this was a city both ancient and modern, in which thousand-year-old temples stood cheek by jowl with contemporary banks, apartment buildings, slave markets, and temples to Caesar. Camels hooted and grunted as they waddled by, laden with amphorae; dusky maidens from the dark south, their bosoms bare, carried vast oil jars on their heads; rich women, covered from head to toe with gold and pearl and faience, moved about the crowd, gesturing languidly to their maidservants while page boys fanned them with ostrich feathers. Statues of the ancient animal-headed gods stood here and there, and there was also a statue of my uncle the emperor.

The sound of the Greek tongue, the language of all cultured conversations, was strangely bent in this city, for the Egyptians, in their native language, have dozens of different coughing consonants, by which I mean a sound halfway between a *k* and a camel choking. This Egyptian-accented Greek, which sounds like the speaker is dying of consumption, came at my ears from every side, as did the native tongue (more coughing) and also the languages of barbarous un-Roman nations, some with weird lilting melodies, others with clicks and whistles.

Rome is grand and impressive and all that, and the Terra Novan cities are pleasantly quaint, but here one has the impression of a culture older than one's own, and one does not feel entirely welcome in it. Although I must say that they were taking full advantage of the tourist trade, and there were vendors all over the docks hawking miniature sphinxes, pyramids, and scarabs, and even such macabre souvenirs as the hands and feet of old mummies, which are prized by doctors, who grind them up and make various foul medicines from them.

I may add that Lupus Ferox, who was lugging a chest of my clothes, was staring in profound wonderment at the sights. Not the least of these sights was Euphonius, who was still wearing a bronze pyramid on his head and had been clearing his throat for some time. At length, after failing to attract anyone's attention, he pulled out his lyre and started to extemporize the following putrid stanza:

> *Hail, thou Magnificent City!*
> *Hail, O Celestial Abode!*
> *O Noble Domain! What a pity*
> *I'm subjecting thee to this Ode.*

Aquila whispered in my ear, "A rare moment of self-deprecation!" I heard Lupus Ferox sniggering.

Euphonius paused to retune his lyre and ended up snapping two of the strings. The Sasquatius had his fingers in his ears; Aaye the Egyptian, however, had assumed an expression of beatific intensity.

"By Osiris!" he said. "You must be Euphonius the bard! I am your greatest admirer—I've read *Leda and the Duck* fifteen times, and even had it translated into hierogylphics."

"You're joking, of course," I said. "Why, his verses neither scan, rhyme, nor make sense!"

"But that is all part of their charm," Aaye said. "Under the principles of the new realism, if a line of poetry should scan properly, it would be accounted too pretentious; it would lack the natural cadence of mundane speech."

"But poetry should elevate us," the sasquatch said, holding up his hands as though to ward off another stanza.

"Rubbish," Aaye said. "Aristotle's been dead for five

hundred years; it's about time for some new blood."

"We are just as elevated," Euphonius said solemnly, "whether the vehicle for that elevation be a ladder of gold or a pile of dung."

"Well put, O immortal songmaster!" Aaye said, his eyes shining with devotion. "Please, forgive my friends their lack of culture—sing again!"

"I've broken my lyre strings—" I breathed a sigh of relief, only to gag again when he continued. "—but I can get along with what I have." He fiddled with the two remaining strings; the third one broke. "Anyone have any harp strings on them?"

Aaye said, "Of course. I always carry a few on my person—" He reached into his robes and pulled out some. "—so I can perform spontaneous tests of Pythagoras's theories of music."

Euphonius was just about to start when I broke in with, "Shouldn't we be getting on with the order of business—trying to rescue Equus Insanus?"

"Don't interrupt the master!" Aaye said, furious. I turned to the Egyptian to tell him off, but when I looked back I found that Aquila and Lupus Ferox had managed, in a matter of seconds, to bind and gag the bard with the strips of cloth they now carried about for that purpose. Aaye *humph*ed and *harrumph*ed for a few minutes, but when he saw that we were not going to permit Euphonius to sing, he finally said, "Well, as I was saying before you fellows so rudely got me off the track, something strange has been happening to the pyramids."

Aquila nodded. "How frequent are the contractions?" he asked.

"About every day or two," the Egyptian said. "How do you know—"

"Good," Aquila said. "They're not pregnant, then."

"Pregnant?" Aaye said. "Pyramids? Preposterous."

"There's a lot you don't know about pyramids—a lot you wouldn't know, unless you'd had the deep philosophical conversations with the ancient astronauts that I've had."

By now we had wandered away from the docks—my

friends and I and the dozen slaves who were carrying our belongings—and we were walking down an avenue fringed with date palms.

The sasquatch strode furiously; he was clearly agitated. Aaye kept trying to undo Euphonius's gag, but Lupus Ferox guarded the bard well and would not let Aaye touch him.

"In any case, O General," the Sasquatius said, "we too have been receiving strange ransom messages involving Equus Insanus. And our friend is right; the pyramids have been acting strange lately, and we suspect the two are connected. That's why I've arranged, with the money you so kindly smoke-signaled me, to acquire some means of transport."

As we passed another of those endless temples of Isis, I heard an odd sort of wheezing, grunting sound from around the corner. I knew what it was at once, for the previous year there had been tremendous spectacle in the arena that featured pygmies on bicycles battling Nubians on camelback...and soon my nose told me that there were a whole lot of camels nearby.

"Good," Abraham said. "The camels are here. Let's be off."

As we rounded the corner, we saw some two dozen of the creatures in kneeling position, ready to be mounted; one or two had men already riding them, wild nomads in white flowing robes who I presumed were our guides. From not far off came the choral chanting of male voices. I knew from this that the Jewish quarter was nearby; doubtless Abraham's home was in the vicinity.

The sasquatch seated himself on the nearest camel, and I assumed it was no more difficult than mounting a horse. Lupus Ferox had no trouble, either; he sprang up easily, and even the Egyptian, who was in the midst of a long conversation with the gagged bard—a little one-sided, to be sure—on the finer points of car mummifying, managed to mount a camel with surprising grace.

"Oh, I say," Papinian commented, nonchalantly attempting the same feat. "Unsightly creatures, aren't they?" The camel was clearly displeased; it shuddered and sputtered and spattered us with a wad of phlegm, then rose to its feet abruptly, throwing the general ignominiously on his arse. "Damn these barbaric modes of transport!" he railed. "Is this not the modern age, and do we not have ferrequi, bicycles, even motorcars?"

"They won't get you across the desert," Abraham bar-David said, "and besides, these creatures, ungainly though they appear, are the fastest things on four legs you can imagine."

Some Judean youths, including a lumbering teenaged bigfoot, paused to jeer at Papinian, who was now trying to vault onto the camel's back from a running start. "I'll break this bloody creature if I have to use my flagellum!" he screamed, and began huffing and puffing his way toward the camel. The creature reared up at the wrong moment, and Papinian collided with its haunches. Then the camel broke wind, noisily and noisomely, settled back down on the ground, and refused to budge. Papinian drew a flail from his cloak and attempted to flog the camel into action, but to no avail.

All of us were ready; I had managed—with no little difficulty—in seating myself and was already getting a little blue in the face from the animal's swaying. All of us were ready, that is, except Papinian, who still could not get his beast to get up. I had my goad at the ready, for our nomad guides had told me that to get a camel to move forward, one need but tap it lightly on the neck and utter the words "hut, hut, hut."

"Time is running out!" Aaye said. "We must get to the great pyramids, for I am convinced that Equus Insanus is somehow involved with their strange behavior."

"Perhaps he has been imprisoned inside one of them," I said.

"That is all too possible," Aquila said darkly, "and if you knew pyramids as I do, you would not wish to contemplate such a fate."

"I still don't understand how he can know so much about pyramids," Aaye said, shaking his head. "After all, it is I who, as an Egyptian, possess the innate wisdom of the ancients, and who am, by my very nature, capable of understanding these deep things. Just as I'm the only one who appreciates good singing," he added, pointing at Euphonius, who, sharing a camel with young Lupus, was making muffled strangulated noises through his gag.

"Go on without me," Papinian said. I do not think he was too displeased at the prospect of abandoning ship. "I'll find some sleazy tavern to drown my sorrows in—I'll see you after the universe has been saved and all that. Don't want to be a spoilsport, you know."

"Oh, nonsense," I said. I had an idea. I carefully maneuvered my camel over to Euphonius, reached over, and yanked off his gag.

A bellow escaped his throat. It was the opening lines of some new epic, but he had been bottling it up so long that it fairly gushed out in one long high-pitched squeal, as though from the throat of someone drunk on aqua cocacola. Startled, Papinian's camel sprang into action and immediately began galloping down the street.

"After him!" Aaye screamed. "He's going the wrong way!"

My own camel was bucking, whinnying, and snorting. Euphonius's was going around and around in circles. I suddenly realized that I had precipitated a stampede. Dust rose on every side, and then we were off—all of us, a tremendous writhing mass of men and camels streaking through the streets of Alexandria at top speed.

I had not intended to see the sights of Alexandria— our mission was far too urgent to allow tourism—but we were nevertheless able to take in several temples, the marketplace, the fabulous lighthouse of Pharos, the imperial palace, a slave auction, and an embalming school. We received a crash course in the latter and emerged from the camel-shaped hole in the far wall all tangled up in mummy wrappings, pursued by a horde of angry embalmers.

"Fascinating, isn't it?" Aaye informed me (all this while we were racing through the streets at breakneck speed). "They remove the brains through the nose, you know, and insert them into a canopic jar, frequently made from alabaster, its lid in the shape of the head of the god."

"I know, I know! I just had one thrown at me!" I shouted. The city's eastern gates loomed up ahead, and I saw the centurion getting ready to demand our papers, but bureaucracy was thrown to the winds as our party raced toward the desert . . .

CHAPTER
VII

SHIPS OF THE DESERT

AFTER A FEW HOURS, WE SETTLED ON A MORE SE-
date routine. The camels, in single file, advanced
eastward. The sun burned and hot winds gusted, and
there was sand in our clothes, our hair, our mouths; even
Euphonius, whom we had, in our compassion, released
from his bonds, lost the desire to sing.

There was a certain monotony about our journey: our
guides in the front, Aquila striking a figure both comical
and magnificent as he sat, in full Lacotian war regalia, on
the hump of his beast, stern-faced, clutching a war lance
festooned with eagle feathers; Titus Papinianus constantly falling off his camel; the Sasquatius and the
Egyptian continually engaging in learned discourse;
the little poet looking more and more miserable—and
the ceaseless discomfiture of the high-backed saddle
upon our rumps, and the relentless heat.

Not surprisingly, the only person I ended up being
able to talk to was Lupus Ferox. He reminded me somewhat of a younger Equus Insanus, although of course,
unlike my half brother, he wasn't quite *our* kind of people. But I began to warm to him; he talked to me of his

50

childhood in Lacotia, of being torn from his parents' village in the middle of a retaliatory raid during the uprising of Cansapolis; of being sold to a telegraph merchant; of how he learned his trade; of his dreams of buying his freedom, going on a vision quest, performing the sun dance, and becoming a real warrior like his idol, who was—to my surprise—my own half brother. Of course, I was a little miffed at not being the child's idol myself, but I did not want to show it, so I merely said, "I've done the sun dance—did you know that? Beastly, savage custom, of course, but I suppose it does make a man of one."

He looked at me with a great deal more respect from then on. It is easy to impress the young.

Presently, our guides pointed out an oasis in the distance. That's what they claimed it was; to me it seemed like nothing but a smudge of green against the expanse of eye-smarting white. But within a few hours we saw that there really were trees there, and a little watering hole. There were also people—dozens of people, all wearing those pyramidal hats that betokened membership in the religion of encephalometry. They were squatting patiently beside the water, almost as though waiting for someone. One of them, seeing us approach, shouted out, "The exalted grand masters are here! The prophecies are fulfilled!" and they all rose up at once and began to swarm around us, falling prostrate, trying to touch the hems of our garments, kissing our hands, our feet, and even our camels.

"Goodness!" Papinian said. "I didn't expect to find any of *them* here."

"Actually," Aaye said, "there are a lot of encephalometrists in Egypt. After all, you did work in a hefty helping of pyramidology. In fact, your treatise has been absorbed into several of the local cults; I've actually heard your name taken in vain by a high priestess of Isis, Aquila. Some people think that you're really a reincarnation of the god Osiris but that Papinian, because of his prodigious nose, is more likely to be an aspect of Thoth, the ibis god."

"Maybe this cult-of-the-month thing wasn't such a good idea after all," Aquila said, beating off a particularly obstreperous woman with the butt of his war lance. "We never wanted to get ordinary people actually to believe in any of this stuff—just rich people."

"Don't listen to him!" Euphonius cried out to the faithful, who were looking at one another in consternation. "The noble Aquila is merely tempting us. Those who abandon their belief in pyramid power after so simple a test of faith will surely never achieve that mental clarity which should be the goal of every true encephalometrist!"

Much relieved, the throng pressed forward again, clamoring for attention. "They're getting in Aquila's way!" Lupus Ferox squealed, and spurred his camel on. He was brandishing a coup stick and was striking the faithful left, right, and center, but instead of moving away they began to kneel down in postures of adoration, muttering to one another in Greek and various Semitic languages.

"What are they saying?" I asked the Sasquatius, who was giggling.

"They seem to feel somewhat blessed by the lad's blows," Abraham bar-David replied. "There is some speculation that he may be the *kwisatz haderach*—a messiah!"

"Whatever that is," I said, shrugging.

"It's a Judean legend," Euphonius said. "Very quaint. Very ethnic. I've often thought of doing an epic poem about it, in fact. But instead of making the messiah a great military leader who will throw off the Roman yoke, I'd make him something very mundane—a carpenter, perhaps. And instead of blazing a trail of glory through the world as a messiah should, I was thinking of having him come to some ignominious end—getting himself crucified or something. Depressing, you might say, but a lot closer to life—one must have social relevance these days."

"I think there already is a cult like that," Aquila said, scratching his head.

Meanwhile, the adherents of our own cult never stopped clamoring. You could not hear what was going on—they all talked at once. Not surprising, since one of the tenets of the cult was that you could build self-confidence, and control the minds of others, by talking your opponents into submission.

"Well," Papinian said, "we better find out what they bloody well want. I suppose that being forced to listen to the prayers of one's suppliants is just one of the inevitable hazards of deifying oneself."

Aquila pointed at random to one of the pyramid heads. "You!" he said. Silence fell at once, and, trembling, the chosen one stepped forward. He started to grovel. "No, no," Aquila said. "Just tell us what is happening."

"The universe is a mystical circle," the suppliant began, and launched into a long series of encephalometric formulae before getting to the topic at hand. "But the fact is, we've just been at the site of the Great Pyramid and the Sphinx, drinking in the eternal vibrations of the universe—just like it says in your treatise, O Aquila."

Aquila raised an eyebrow.

"Well, we were expecting psychic vibrations, but we weren't expecting the Great Pyramid of Cheops to shake and shimmy like a belly dancer!"

"Quam spectaculum est!" Papinian said, awed. "Maybe there is something to all this rubbish. And to think we concocted it all over a jug of second-rate Aquitanian wine!"

"It's just as I said," Aaye sighed. "The pyramids have been acting very strange of late."

Aquila's mood suddenly seemed far more businesslike. He interrogated the encephalometrist in detail, asking about the duration, intensity, and frequency of the various vibratory episodes and whether any of the pyramids had actually taken to the air.

"Not really, although some of us *did* see the thing levitate about two cubits."

"So much for your precious pyramids flying off somewhere," I said to Aaye. "The tourist trade is safe."

"Don't be too sure of it," Aquila said. "I suggest that we hurry."

"I thought we were going to rest the night here," said Papinian, who I am sure did not relish the prospect of several more hours of coaxing his camel.

"Equus Insanus is definitely in danger," Aquila said. "I'm afraid that there is a spatiotemporal anomaly field surrounding those pyramids—proving beyond a doubt that the Green Pig has somehow managed to penetrate this holding universe, despite all the pains that V'Denni-Kenni and his were-jaguars took to render it impenetrable. I don't see how he could have broken through the barrier physically, but perhaps he has created some infernal device along the lines of the spatiotemporal bewilderizer, the one that brought those dinosaurs into our world."

As was usual when Aquila spoke of the superscience of the flying saucer people, he left us far behind. I could only marvel at the fluency with which all this arcane scientific jargon left his lips.

"Did you say dinosaurs?" the encephalometrist said. "I almost forgot. Those enormous reptilian creatures with the long necks?"

"Ah," Aaye said, not without a twinge of nostalgia, "brontosauruses."

"Yes, yes," the suppliant said. "There have been a lot of those hanging around the pyramids, too."

I looked at the others. I was remembering our past adventures; I knew that they were, too. Vividly I saw Equus and myself, fighting side by side, with brontosauruses hemming us in from every direction, with pterodactyls swooping down upon us from the sky...by Jove and Minerva, I missed the barbarian little bugger! I knew we would be quarreling the minute I saw him again, but...well, *if* I ever saw him again. What dastardly means had the Green Pig devised to enter our cosmos this time? Would it be androids that we faced, or minotaurs? I felt fear, real fear, for the first time since this adventure had begun. I realized that it must be because I hadn't touched any aqua cocacola in days . . . and the drug-induced false security had been sweated out of me by the relentless sun.

Grimly, Aquila said, "*Huka hey!* We must go on at once! Or my son will surely perish." He waved his war lance; feathers flew, camels bleated, and our followers cheered.

"Onward to Gizeh!" Papinian shouted. "We shall come, see, and conquer!" He fell off his camel. Several encephalometrists raced to succor him, tripping over each other in their haste to help one of the leaders of their movement.

As we rode through the night, our expedition had grown to some hundreds of people, for we could not shake off our followers, nor, after the initial shock, did we really want to. For, mindless though they were, they were most solicitous of us and were constantly giving us food and drink—and even more besides, perhaps. For, in the moonlight, I fancied I saw Aquila mounted upon something other than his camel, unless it was that the hump of his beast of burden had somehow acquired a woman's shape. But with the continual heaving of my own animal, I could not quite tell whether the old Lacotian, jogging rhythmically up and down upon that voluptuously expanded hump, was adding another conquest to his collection or was merely seasick.

Just before dawn, we could see the pyramids and the Sphinx. I had heard of their prodigious size, but no description could compare with the reality. It was bitterly cold before the sunrise, and the remnants of the ancient marble facing shone with an eerie rosy light; the Sphinx, her paws clasping the sand, stared into the desert with that sublimely enigmatic expression that every Egyptian endeavors to imitate.

Euphonius could no longer control himself and began singing energetically, but I did not care, for so tremendous was the spectacle that I barely noticed the assault upon my ears. It became slightly more tremendous when, as we neared the ancient edifices, a brontosaurus emerged from behind the Sphinx and began lumbering toward us, making the ground shake with every footfall. Our slaves and some of the encephalometrists began to scream and wail and make signs of aversion, but the dinosaur continued to shamble toward us, making funny little honking noises.

"Don't worry," I said to Lupus Ferox, who was cowering in his saddle. "It's a vegetarian. It won't eat you— just stay out of its way so you don't get trampled."

Lupus Ferox brightened. "If I count coup on it, do you suppose it'll count toward getting my first feather?" He had his little coup stick in his hand and was ready to whip his camel into a charge.

"Better hold on a moment," I said, noting with dismay that a flock of pterodactyls was wheeling over head. We were close enough to see the temple that stood between the Sphinx's paws now.

Suddenly a tyrannosaurus rex came strutting out, roaring, making straight for the brontosaurus.

"This is wasted on these people," Papinian said. "We really ought to find a way of putting this on in the arena."

"If inventing religions ceases to be a gold mine," Abraham bar-David said, "I suppose there may be something to be said for the profession of dinosaur wrangling."

The two beasts were going at each other tooth and claw now, when I suddenly beheld a sight even more startling—Equus Insanus, sitting on a kind of floating throne that seemed to hover in midair, about halfway up the Great Pyramid of Cheops!

"Michinkshi!" Aquila cried, and we all spurred our camels on, even though the brontosaurus and tyrannosaurus were battling it out just ahead.

Equus Insanus was a tiny figure. I could barely make him out, but I knew it had to be my long-lost brother. He wore the cuirass and plumed helmet of a Roman officer, but a buffalo robe billowed about his shoulders. He held out his hand as though to warn us away. I could not see his expression.

The two dinosaurs were directly in our path, and the pterodactyls were diving down toward us.

Suddenly the throne swooped down on the dinosaurs! Bursts of blue lightning sprang from Equus Insanus's fingers, and then the tyrannosaurus was instantly suspended in the air, a bemused expression on its face, floating as easily as if he had been a hot-air balloon! The brontosaurus, struck by the same blue lightning, flew upward, too, and in a moment all the dinosaurs were dissolving into thin air, as though they had been a mere vision!

As the encephalometrists all fell prostrate in adoration at this demonstration of pyramid power, Aaye started to explain the whole thing: "Just a mirage, of course. I've never seen one this realistic before, but—"

And Equus on his throne was again *whoosh*ing toward us. When he was almost right over our heads, I saw that the pyramids were all starting to tremble. I looked into my half brother's face, and it was indeed he, and yet something about him—a cruel twisting of the lip, a supercilious arching of the eyebrows—something was not quite right.

And Equus spoke! "I should never have let that telegram go out—begone! We're all doomed—nothing you can do for me—it is a good day to die—I go to the land of many tipis—*aiiieee!*" He writhed in agony, as though tormented by spirits within him. Then, abruptly, the throne changed direction and hurtled toward the Great Pyramid of Cheops, which was shaking and rattling like a jar of bones. Equus seemed to be struggling to bail out of the flying throne but was held in place by an invisible force.

"By Mars!" I cried out. "He's going to crash into the Great Pyramid!"

Abraham bar-David was reciting some ancient Hebrew prayer, and Aaye was praying for Osiris and Isis and Anubis to grant him a painless death. But just as the flying throne was about to smash into the solid rock—

The stone itself seemed to shimmer and blur, and the throne, well, blended into the sandstone and passed right through it!

I didn't have time even to gasp. For the very next instant, the entire pyramid began to rumble and seemed to be straining against its terrestrial confines—and suddenly, with a groan that set my teeth on edge, it pulled free of the earth completely and streaked up into the sky!

It wobbled about for a moment or two, zigzagged a couple of times, then began to sail off toward the sunrise. We stared at it, dumbfounded. Our faithful disciples, thinking we had somehow engineered this stupendous feat, were bowing down before us, a sea of human backs that stretched across the sand dyed rose by dawn. Their upraised voices regaled us with quotes from that silly treatise of encephalometry, that half-baked amalgam of Lacotian and Egyptian concepts. There were dire murmurings about astral projection, channeling, and telekinesis.

Then, as the pyramid vanished from sight, I saw another of those rifts in the sky that had been occurring with such frequency since our universe was destroyed. Through this jagged tear in the fabric of the universe, we could see stars, moons, myriads of worlds, whirling like children's tops through a dark miasmic abyss, and faintly, behind it all, a spectral apparition, viridinous of complexion and porcine of visage.

"The gods preserve us!" I whispered. "The face of Viridiporcus Rex—the Time Criminal—the mastermind —our archenemy!"

"What shall we do, O gods?" Papinian cried. "We are but a few mortals, and the were-jaguars of the Dimensional Patrol have decided not to help us, so we can't even count on being saved by flying saucers at the last minute!"

A burst of demoniacal cackling filled the air. In horror we gaped as the sky slowly closed up. Perhaps it had swallowed the pyramid whole, and my half brother with it, as a frog swallows a fly.

Then I felt Aquila's war lance prodding me in the

small of the back, and I heard the aged warrior shout, "Well, don't just stand there staring like a bunch of idiots!"

Aaye said, "The p-p-yramid—it's g-g-gone."

"Well, after it!" Aquila cried. "It can't have gone very far."

CHAPTER
VIII

MORE SHIPS OF THE DESERT

"RIGHT," PAPINIAN SAID. "THIS REALLY TAKES the cake, I'm afraid. You really have taken leave of your senses, O Aquila! It's not just Equus that's insanus—it's the whole bloody lot of you!"

"That's true, O imponderable and omniscient Lacota leader," Euphonius said. "Not even a master of super-science could fly after a levitating pyramid."

"And if you think that doing one of your infernal rain dances is going to bring that pyramid crashing down on our heads..." Papinian began.

"Enough words!" Aquila said. "We must storm the Sphinx!"

"What!" Aaye cried aghast. "That holiest of shrines? That most ancient of monuments? Whatever for?"

"No time to explain right now," Aquila said. He waved to the throng of pyramid-heads. "All of you, fol-low me—to glory!" They began cheering wildly and brandishing their weapons: here a gladius, there a pilum, over here a walking stick or a cloak pin.

I, too, was having some difficulty trying to figure out what Aquila was after. But I dutifully rallied; Lupus

Ferox, coup stick upraised, fell in behind me, and the
two Lacotians started in with their terrifying war cries.
They were soon joined by Euphonius, shrieking at the
top of his lungs, pausing now and then to pluck a chord
on his lyre, and we charged the pyramid all at once.
Never have I seen so much dust as that raised by the
hundred camels of the pyramid worshipers. As we
reached the steps of the temple, Aquila was out front, his
withered cheeks quivering as he shrieked out the war
paean *"huka hey!"*

We were all jammed into an anteroom just inside the
Sphinx, when a number of priests, shaven and wearing
those flounced linen kilts, came running out from an
inner chamber. They did not seem at all pleased at the
ruckus. Some of them seemed terrified and were trying
to offer us gold and jewels. The encephalometrists,
obeying Aquila's commands, started backing them
against the wall and tying their hands together, and I am
sure they feared for their lives.

There were also several curious animals running underfoot: sheep, an enormous ram, assorted gazelles,
even a Terra Novan armatillus. Lupus Ferox scurried
about, counting coup on everyone he could.

Presently entered a priest in flowing white robes, who
regarded us with a lugubrious expression. Lupus Ferox
flew at him and fetched him a smart rap on his bald pate
with the coup stick.

The high priest, who identified himself as one Nefer-
Kheperu-Sekhmet, addressed us in sepulchral tones:
"Who dares disturb the sacred sacrifices at this hour of
the morning?"

His aide, who carried a silver bowl of sacrificial blood
and a Terra Novan giant chicken under one arm, and
whose garments were drenched in gore, was looking
wildly at our group. "Master," he said to the other, "I
think it's a takeover bid—by a bunch of upstart encephalometrists!"

The high priest glared. "We, the priests of Amon-
Sekhmet-Ptah-Ra, the composite god-of-the-season,
have been in control of this temple for two years, ever

since we seized it from the priests of Amon-Vacantanca-Horus! You can't kick us out yet, not with the embalming season coming up—it's unethical!" I gathered that these territorial conflicts between different priests of different sects were commonplace among the Egyptians, and the current lot were not that secure about their position.

"At least let us finish sacrificing everything," the aide said. "I've only got—" He looked around, counting the animals that were chasing one another around the vestibule. "—about six, seven to go."

"Oh, go about your business," Aquila said. "What we're going to do won't interfere with your sacrifices."

"You're not going to—" The aide was so relieved that he dropped the giant chicken; it ran squawking about the chamber, and he pursued it, swinging his sacrificial ax and causing encephalometrists and Amon-Sekhmet-Ptah-Ra worshipers alike to duck in panic.

"I guess I'd better do something impressive," Aquila said, "to still the tumult." He plucked the bronze pyramid off the head of the nearest disciple, borrowed the coup stick from Lupus Ferox, and began banging wildly, jumping up and down, and singing in a wheezing, grunting sort of tone.

"What's he doing?" Euphonius asked, whipping out a wax tablet and taking notes.

I looked around. Lupus, Aaye, Abraham, and Papinian were all covering their heads with folds of their garments. "I think it's a rain dance," I said, and hastened to do the same.

The Egyptians and encephalometrists all stared at this curious sight for a few moments. Suddenly, we heard distant thunder from outside the temple.

Screaming, the Egyptians scattered. Encephalometrists cowered in the corners of the chamber. Aquila was dancing energetically, leaping up and down with more strength than a man his age had any right to possess, his face becoming greener and greener from his exertions. I was not surprised; I had learned to expect anything from the old man.

More thunder, nearer now. Emboldened, I shoved the high priest aside, and our little party stormed toward the inner sanctum, watched over by two painted eyes of Horus. Aquila was the last to enter the room, which had a burning brazier and a little altar covered with the remains of freshly sacrificed exotic animals as well as a statue of the composite god. In an effort to get all the various composite bits of the god into the same statue, the sculptor had been forced to be very creative; the thing had the beak of a hawk, the countenance of a lion, the double crown of Amon, the crook and flail of Ptah, the moon disk of Isis, the breasts of Hathor, and even the eyelashes of the Emperor Trajan. I remarked on this, and Aaye shrugged.

"They're all like this now," he said. "They never know when a new priestly faction is going to gain control of the temples, so they hedge their bets to avoid having to keep moving those heavy statues in and out with every coup."

The thunder was deafening; any minute now, I thought, the desert would be drenched in a torrential downpour. The sanctum had a great wooden door, covered with gold and inlaid with precious stones, on which were depicted various exploits of the gods, all explained in hierogylphics. This we slammed shut, and, not without effort, pushed the granite altar against it to keep the priests from getting in. There was blood over everything, and incense everywhere, clogging our pores, making it hard to breathe.

"Very well, Aquila," General Papinian said at last. "Now that we're trapped in this little room, with dozens of angry priests outside, with your son darting about inside a flying pyramid . . . how are we going to get out of this pickle?"

"Be quiet, my friends, and listen," Aquila said. He rooted around in the fascis medicinae that he wore about his neck, found a bit of old tobacco, and fished a pipe out from his tunica. "But first, we may as well light up, for we are about to enter into a sacred war council."

There is no hurrying a Lacota when he wants to explain something his own way, so we squatted on the granite floor, waited for him to get the pipe lit, and smoked. Then Aquila began one of those lengthy expository passages so beloved of old Lacotians and the writers of *scientifictiones*:

"Know then, O my friends—and do not think, Aaye, that you know better than I, for I have traveled the past and future and seen much that is beyond your comprehension—that there were in ancient times certain *astronautiloi*, id est, sailors from the stars; they were neither human, nor were they creatures such as those from our own future, the green were-jaguars, lobsters, and elephants with which we are all familiar, but a race of gigantic creatures, half-human and half-leonine in form. The ships in which these creatures sailed through space were pyramidal in shape, and appeared to be made from blocks of sandstone, for the bridge, living quarters, and power sources were all tesseracted *in alia dimensione*. Only he who possesses the secret of traveling between dimensions can find the entrance to the control room..."

I have spoken both Greek and Latin practically from birth, but the kind of Greek and Latin Aquila was spouting was quite incomprehensible to me, although the sasquatch seemed to understand, for he nodded sagely and responded, "And the pyramids of the world—both those of the Terra Novan Olmechii and these Egyptian ones— they are all spaceships?"

"A lot of them no longer work. But this one should— it is a model X-9000, built in the very shape of its original designers."

Aaye was getting very hot under the collar—not surprisingly, since he was wearing one of those heavy, bejeweled Egyptian collars, with beads of faience and little scarabs and effigies and gold trinkets all over the thing. "How dare you!" he said. "You impugn the honor of the world's wisest and most ancient race by implying that the Egyptians did not build the pyramids—"

Aquila shrugged and took another puff of the sacred

pipe. "If you know so much about spaceships," he said, "*you* fly the Sphinx."

"Fly the Sphinx! Don't be absurd," Aaye said.

Aquila shrugged again. Then he rose and began scanning the hieroglyphics on the walls, until he finally found the part he was looking for. It didn't make any sense to *me*, of course, but when Aaye noticed what he was reading, he paled and sputtered.

"You can't be serious—that's the sacred formula for opening the eyes and ears of mummies! If you start to read that aloud, the dead will rise from their sarcophaguses and start stalking the Earth!"

Aquila began intoning the words. Aaye buried his face in hands.

As Aquila read on, a strange luminescence filled the chamber. It emanated from the eyes of the god. Then sparks began to fly from the god's outstretched hands, and Aaye became rigid with fear, almost as though he had had himself mummified. Lupus cried out in pleasure. The lights danced, the chamber seemed to whirl about us, and the walls were melting away; the gods on the murals seemed to be wagging their fingers at us, and abruptly—

We found ourselves in a quite different chamber. Its walls were metallic and smooth, and control panels jutted from them. On two enormous screens one could see simulacra of the outside world; I recognized them for depictions and not reality, because I had ridden in one of the Dimensional Patrol's flying saucers. The screens were round and spaced like giant eyes, and one could see the outline of a sandstone nose jutting out from beneath. I gathered that the place to which we had so deftly been tesseracted was situated, in terms of the real universe, somewhere within the Sphinx's head.

In the middle of the room, quite incongruous, lay a sarcophagus such as was used to contain the mummies of ancient pharaohs.

"Good," Aquila said, "I must have read it right; I'm

not so old. Now we should jettison the temple unit, so our friends outside don't go crazy."

I hardly felt anything, but I saw plenty on those viewscreens. It was raining heavily; thunderclouds filled the sky. The sands were shifting, and a weird blue glow was issuing forth from the Sphinx, and then we were rising into the air, leaving the little temple far behind! As from a great height, I saw the priests and encephalometrists running around in the rain. Indeed, each group clearly blamed the other for the day's paranormal phenomena, for they were all trying to beat one another up—without much success, for the downpour made them slip and slide all over the place.

Aquila was studying the various buttons, levers, and dials on the control panel, rubbing his chin. "Vacantanca be praised," he said, "there is still some fuel—but not much. Lucius, hand me a piece of the mummy inside the sarcophagus, will you?"

"Sacrilege!" Aaye said indignantly, and tried to fend me off as I pried open the lid and saw the mummy within. "It is a sin of the direst sort to toy with the preserved remains of the great figures of the past."

"Nothing of the kind," Aquila said. "It's not a real mummy at all, just a rare isotope of . . . never you mind. It's *disguised* as a mummy—all ancient astronautiloi spaceships have them. These starfarers were very particular about blending in with the natives."

I pulled off one of the mummy's fingers. Unlike real mummies, which are hard as solid rock, the finger popped right off as though it were meant to, and I noticed that several more joints were missing, as was its right ear. I tossed the finger to Aquila, who inserted it into a slot. Immediately, we heard a thunderous roar, and this time I felt movement—in the ship and in the churning of my stomach.

"Is there a vomitorium on board this thing?" Euphonius asked, looking very unhappy.

"Relax!" Aquila said. "It's not every day you get to go for a ride in the belly of a Sphinx!"

Lupus Ferox was the only one who did not seem to be

getting airsick. He was running around the cabin, whooping gleefully as we soared up past the thunderclouds and into the upper reaches of the atmosphere, which was deepening in hue until it became a rich, star-spangled purple, like the color of the most expensive Tyrean dye. "Where are we?" I asked.

The Sasquatius squinted as he stared through the viewscreen. "By the positions of the northern star and the constellation of Orion," he said, "we appear to be heading in a southeasterly direction."

There was a city beneath us. I could see minuscule columned temples and statues of ancient gods and little white dots that must have been the white-walled houses of the poor. Aaye said, "That appears to be the city of Memphis," and pulled a very long face. "I must admit, O Aquila, that there appears to be something to this ancient astronautiloi business."

We flew for an hour or so before I had to pluck another finger from the mummy. There seemed to be no sign of any flying pyramid. Until suddenly Euphonius shrieked and pointed at a tiny dot in the center of the screen, a star that seemed to be streaking not Earthward like a meteor but up toward the zenith.

"I'll increase the magnification," Aquila said, and pushed a few buttons, whereupon the dot grew and grew—

And became the image of the Great Pyramid of Cheops, thrusting toward the stars, with plumes of rainbow-colored flame spurting from its base!

"It's pretty," Lupus Ferox said. "Do we have those colored jets, too, *tunkashila?*"

"Yes, my child," Aquila said, "but I don't think you need to know from which orifice of the monument they are issuing."

The pyramid did some acrobatic maneuvers, spiraling, corkscrewing clockwise and counterclockwise, nose-diving, and finally whizzing away in a tremendous arc—not made for something that probably weighed as much as the Circus Maximus in peak viewing hours. We *ooh*ed and *aah*ed, but not that much, for we knew that

Equus Insanus was imprisoned inside, in thrall to the caprices of the unspeakable Time Criminal.

"Heavens," Papinian said. "Do you think we can catch up with it?"

"I don't know," Aquila said. "It's heading straight for Mars."

CHAPTER
IX

ANTIQUITIES TO THE STARS!

As Aquila uttered those words, an indescribable feeling flowed through me. I thought at first that I was somehow enjoying the delayed effects of my last bottle of aqua cocacola, but I saw that all the others seemed to be experiencing the same thing. It was as though my weight were being drained from me—as though I was become light as a feather. I could almost float, and—

By the maidenhead of Venus, I *was* floating! In fact, my head had just collided with the ceiling, and I was face to face with a painting of one of those baboon-headed Egyptian gods. I tried to disengage myself, but I ended up flying gently across the chamber, narrowly missing Euphonius, who was swimming around in pursuit of his lyre. I rebounded off the wall, and on my next pass, Euphonius had found his lyre—indeed, he had become entangled in it, and his head was poking out from between two strings. Aquila was holding on to a lever, his legs twisting in the air, while the sasquatch and the Egyptian were holding on to each other and the mummy. The mummy's arm came off in the Sasquatius's hand,

69

and Aaye, Abraham, and arm all went soaring off toward the ceiling. Only Lupus Ferox seemed to be having a good time, as usual; indeed, his constant good humor was starting to get on my nerves.

"Giggle one more time, young man, and I'll—" I attempted to fetch him a clout on the ear, but he dodged, and, propelled by the force of my errant blow, I found myself heading straight into the arms of the statue of Horus-Sekhemet-Ptah-Ra.

"It's all very simple," Abraham bar-David said. "We have just passed the moon, have we not? And all that is above the moon is composed of quintessence, the fifth, most perfect element. Though we ourselves are tainted by the four sublunary elements, there is within ourselves a soul, made of the same quintessence as these universal spheres and this quintessence within, naturally attracted to the quintessence without, is causing us literally to become elevated—a most fascinating corollary to Aristotle's thesis on the nature of matter..."

We all listened to this lecture with but half an ear, for it was interrupted by the sound of Euphonius the bard retching. The poor little poet simply didn't have any good old Roman stamina—that is what you get for being one of those effete Greeks, I suppose.

"Ah," said Aquila, who was drifting serenely around and around the chamber, still puffing on his pipe, "you must give yourself into the ebb and flow of the universe, feel the rhythm of the stars—then you will be able to move about in this condition of weightlessness without effort." He put his hand out to touch the wall and, with a precise flick, sent himself sailing off toward me. I marveled at his accuracy, though I supposed it required no more practice than being able to fell a running buffalo with a bow and arrow. "I must apologize," Aquila said, "that the artificial gravity doesn't seem to be operational; you have to expect something to go haywire after a few dozen millennia, you know. Actually, I am surprised we managed to get the Sphinx airborne at all. But had we crashed into the sand, it would have been a good day to die."

"The pyramid!" Lupus Ferox shouted, pointing through the Sphinx's left eye socket. "We're gaining on it!"

Gaining on it and more. We had shot past the moon, and—for we were traveling at inconceivable speed, using something Aquila offhandedly referred to as the lost inertialess drive of the ancients—the planet Mars could already be seen, three-quarters full and ruddy against the starscape. The pyramid was plowing full speed ahead. An irregularly shaped rocklike object— something like our own moon—hung in the sky. The pyramid was making straight for it!

At that moment, Aquila managed to fix the gravity, and we found ourselves on the stone floor, rubbing our arses. Except for Euphonius, who had somehow become entangled in the entrails of some sacrificial beasts on the altar.

Though I was relieved not to feel weightless anymore, I shall always bear a certain nostalgia for those moments. There was a euphoria in being able to drift about through the air. It is said that the gods do things like this all the time, but I had never observed my uncle Trajan doing anything of the sort. It occurred to me that he would probably give anything to be able to float through the air. It would certainly liven up those ennui-laden orgies of his.

I stared through the eye as Aquila brought the Sphinx —or the X-9000, as I suppose I should properly call it— closer and closer to the pyramid. The pyramid rounded the chunky little moon, and we started to nose-dive toward its surface, when—

"Per magnum spiritum!" Aquila cried. "A trap! They mean to head us off at the asteroid!"

Indeed it was. For, concealed within the craggy formations on the moon's surface and now emerging one by one to confront us, were other pyramids. Large ones, small ones, pyramids of the Olmechii of southern Terra Nova as well as the Egyptians.

"Isis protect me," Aaye said in agitation. "That's the Step Pyramid of Zozer, the most ancient monument in

Egypt. This is most humiliating, to discover that it's just some extraterrestrial public conveyance—oh, why did it have to be the pyramids?"

"What's that thing?" I asked, pointing at something that looked like a mountain with four faces carved into the rock, four of the ugliest human beings I have ever looked on, uglier even than the last few emperors of Rome. This thing was even now bearing down on us, with two or three pyramids in its wake.

"Fascinating," Aquila said. "I didn't know that was one of them, too—it's Mount Rushmore, a monument from a different dimension in which—never mind, there are limits to what you can humanly be asked to believe."

"We'd better get out of here fast," I said. "Before—"

Zap! A bolt of bright green lightning shot out of the mouth of one of the heads on the flying mountain, and I could see part of the Sphinx's nose shear off and flutter into the void!

"We appear to be doomed," Aquila said.

"Well, don't just sit there!' Papinian said. "Do another rain dance or something. Drown the buggers out." He drew his gladius from his scabbard and was waving it about, striking swashbuckling poses, doing the entire big, bad Roman general bit.

"I'm afraid I can't make it rain in outer space," Aquila said. "It's just not done."

We sustained several more hits and were thrown about the cabin a little. We were running low on mummy parts, too, for all this fancy flying used up plenty of fuel.

"Doesn't this thing have any catapultae, scorpiones, or any other good old Roman weapons?" I asked.

"I'm looking, I'm looking," Aquila said, trying all the buttons on his control panel until—

Bolts of lightning streamed from the Sphinx's eyes, and the four-headed mountain was riven in twain!

"How clever!" Aquila said. "Mount Rushmore split along partisan lines." He rambled about transdimensional complexities for a moment, but no one knew what he was talking about, so he summoned me to his side, showed which buttons to push, and said, "You do it, my lad, I'm getting old myself; my aim's shot."

The controls were easy enough to manipulate: There was a sort of rudderlike lever with a knob on it that one clutched and moved about in a circular motion, which activated these missile projectors—glorified catapultae, actually, which apparently sent out beams of pure energy instead of rocks or boiling oil, in keeping with the quintessential nature of the superlunary spheres in which we were traveling. There was also a rod for controlling the movement of the Sphinx; it operated much like the reins of a chariot, for it caused the X-9000 to move in whatever direction one pulled it. All in all, these superscientific devices were child's play to operate, far simpler than the elaborate machines described at such length in the works of the writers of *scientifictiones*.

In short, I was presently at the helm, and, with the help of Lupus Ferox, who manned the controller for the other energy-beam turret, I was soon causing the ship to weave in and out among the pyramids and other monuments. I dodged an obelisk, dashed around the moon, blew up a building that resembled the theater of Dionysus in Pompeii, though I knew the original had been destroyed years before. Faster and faster I flew the device, but we were one and the pyramids were many, and the Great Pyramid of Cheops was firing lightning bolt after lightning bolt at us, forcing us into a bewildering pattern of evasive action. Moreover, we were entering a swarm of enormous flying rocks, which Aquila called asteroids—even though they did not resemble stars in the least—and we could feel them smashing into the flanks of the Sphinx, making our teeth rattle whenever they collided with us.

"We're surrounded," Aaye said. "We're all going to die—no thanks to you, O Aquila, for stripping away all my illusions about my ancestors, the gods, the afterlife, sarcophagi, mummies—"

Papinian put his hand over the Egyptian's mouth. "Silence! Can't you see that the old chap is thinking of a way to get us out?"

Aquila did indeed appear to be thinking—or asleep.

Suddenly, though, he popped into consciousness and said, "Yes, yes, the transformer gambit—assuming that this ship is fully operational and not one of those older models."

Although I was firing as rapidly as I could, we were being assaulted from all sides. Lines of blue light criss-crossed the starfield as more and more pyramids converged on us. I only caught a sentence here and there of what Aquila proposed.

"This ship is cleverly constructed so that it breaks up into three smaller vehicles, videlicet: the head, the front torso, and the buttocks. What we must clearly do is split up, break apart, fight our way out of this whole thing, and rendezvous at some preordained location."

"Oh, thank you very much," Aaye said. "First he destroys my cherished beliefs, tells me my pyramids are really glorified motor-cars from outer space—now he wants me to get down from my exalted intellectual pedestal and actually drive one—like a common charioteer, a camelherder, a—"

"O glorious adventure!" Euphonius cried. "Ye muses, give my tongue flight and my voice wings, that I may sing future generations of our odyssey through the lambent flame of our destiny's end."

"Yes, yes, future generations, very well," I said, pushing a button to repel the attack of a convoy of pyramids that flew in perfect formation, like a flock of geese. "As long as you leave the present generation out of it—"

Another direct hit! We all fell to the floor once more; I leapt back to the controls.

Aquila said to the Sasquatius: "Abraham, have you been observing how this thing works?"

The furry Judean nodded sagely. The Lacota chief continued. "You go with Aaye, then, through that wall there—don't worry about it, it'll dissolve to let you through. You'll find a tesseracted control room just like this one, with a sarcophagus full of fuel. I will go with Titus Papinianus to the other room and—"

"I refuse to control the Sphinx's buttocks," Aaye

muttered as the sasquatch started to lead him away.
"Anything but the buttocks."

"As soon as you hear my war cry, prepare for the
three segments to detach themselves from each other!
We'll be able to maintain radio contact unless we're
more than two A.U.s apart." He did not stop to explain
any of this, but I fancied I would learn by doing. "We'll
meet back on Earth in a few horus—I'll set the automatic homing mechanism so that the different sections
seek one another out and we'll all be one big happy
Sphinx again."

We had no time for questions. We were about to be
rammed by three pyramids that were bearing down on
us, points aimed straight at us. I had no wish to be a
cosmic souvlaki, and Lupus Ferox and I were firing as
rapidly as we could when we suddenly noticed that
Aquila, Papinian, Aaye, and Abraham were all gone.
The only one left was Euphonius, who had been too
busy tuning his lyre to notice.

"Ah!" he said at last. "That alpha string is always the
hardest." He twanged it a couple of times. His instrument sounded just as out of tune as when he started, but
then again, I am no judge of tonal precision—I just know
what I like.

"Prepare for three-way split!" Aquila's disembodied
voice boomed through the sacrificial chamber. I felt a
queasy sensation, and then I saw the torso and the buttocks of the Sphinx, each complete with jets of rainbow
flame, break off and begin to draw some of the pyramids'
fire. With a wild shout of *"Huka hey!"* Lupus jerked the
steering rod sharply taut, and we were whizzing off in a
new direction, leaving the three pyramids to skewer one
another and rupture their hulls.

"By the eye of Horus!" came Aaye's voice, disembodied also. "You did give me the buttocks, you savage!" The buttocks were sailing across the face of the
Martian moon, rather erratically, like a chariot with a
drunken driver. Then came the torso, soaring, arcing,
darting in and out of the hordes of enemy pyramids with
astonishing skill; this I knew to be piloted by the intrepid

Aquila. But I had no more time to admire their skill, for I had my hands full fending off Mount Rushmore, which had miraculously patched itself together again and was charging at me, spewing lightning from all four of its mouths.

"Duck!" Lupus cried, and we brought the Sphinx's head down low so that Mount Rushmore missed us and went barreling into the moon. "This is splendid!" the boy cried as he fired the scientifictive catapultae at what appeared to be a Babylonian ziggurat.

It was a tremendous spectacle—the three segments of the Sphinx, holding their own against these starfaring monuments—and we were actually managing to beat them off. The Great Pyramid of Cheops was hovering far off, on the other side of the moon—or was that a second moon?—suspended against the surface of Mars. I was beginning to think that we might emerge victorious when—

A writhing, glowing cloud appeared in front of us. Aaye and his buttocks were careening around, and abruptly they seemed to get sucked into this nebula. I heard Aquila's voice. "Aaye! Aaye! Do you read?" and then, in a disappointed tone, "What a nuisance—a spatiotemporal anomaly field!"

"A spatio—" I said. "What in blazes do you mean?"

"By the time I explain it to you, we'll all be dead. Just look out for yourself—don't get sucked in at all costs—if we lose each other, look for me at the—whoaaaaaaah!"

And the torso was gone, too.

We were being bombarded on all sides. On the control panel, buttons blinked, lights flashed, levers toggled themselves madly. The nebula loomed closer and closer, a whorl of rainbow-fringed light. "Maybe there's a button that'll get us out of this," I said.

I turned to see Euphonius, who had put on his pyramid hat and had wired himself to the statue of the composite god; doubtless he was trying to get us out of this jam by the judicious exercise of pyramid power. I turned to Lupus. The buttons were all labeled in hieroglyphics.

"Can you read any of this stuff?" I asked the boy. He just shrugged. Then he turned away from me and started to sing softly to himself. I knew that it must be a death song. I was surprised that so urbane a child, torn from his Lacotian roots at such an early age, had managed to learn such a song, yet it came easily to his lips. "We're all going to die anyway," I said as the nebula extruded a sort of luminous pseudopod that seemed to be making straight for us and as our vehicle received several more glancing hits from our assailants. "I might as well just try pushing all the buttons."

I did so.

Suddenly—poof!—we were somewhere completely different!

In fact, we were rapidly plummeting toward what appeared to be the Earth, and I could see Terra Nova clearly through the veil of clouds!

"We're falling too fast!" I screamed. "Lupus, throw me some more fuel so we can steady our descent."

Lupus Ferox ran to the sarcophagus to grab another piece of mummy. He tossed it to me. "Last piece," he said.

It turned out to be the mummy's virile member—swaddled in mummy wrappings, to be sure, but nonetheless recognizable. I threw it into the device. It fizzled for a moment, but we gained no more power. We were still falling. I raged at the impotence of the situation. "By the gods! Far from saving the universe, we cannot even save ourselves!" I apostrophized. "We are but the playthings of fate." You see, I was so convinced that these moments were my last that I was determined to squeeze in every possible rhetorical device before I—figuratively speaking—breached the womb of eternity.

Another voice—I did not recognize it and thought I might already be hearing the voices of the gods—rang through the room. "Nine seconds to impact," it said. "Automatic seat belts will now be activated."

Immediately, lariats came flying down at us from the ceiling, and we were bound fast and pulled up into the air! And the altar, the statue of the god, and various other pieces of furniture were all expanding as though they were being inflated like hot-air balloons! Soon Euphonius, Lupus Ferox, and I were wedged into place by air cushions that had once been temple furnishings, and my stomach seemed to be flipping over and over. I could see from the corner of my eye that Earth was rushing toward us in the viewscreen, and I began to scream.

"One second to impact," the voice said.

Before I lost consciousness, I saw a sight that filled me with both fear and hope.

There was another object shooting Earthward alongside us. Even though it appeared to be on fire, it still looked remarkably like the Great Pyramid of Cheops.

My half brother was in there somewhere. Had he managed to break free of his captors? Was he, too, flying toward our meeting place? I thought of my other friends, stuck in a nebula somewhere, perhaps no longer even in this universe... and of Equus Insanus, waiting to be saved... and of the Green Pig who was pulling our puppet strings, drawing us toward some as yet inconceivable confrontation.

And it was all up to me now—me, a hopelessly aristocratic youth, used to having everything done by slaves—to save the universe with the help of an untrained boy and a tone-deaf bard.

What an insensate spectacle, I thought as everything went black around me.

THREE MEN IN A SPHINX

CHAPTER
X

THE MIDDLE OF NOWHERE

OUR PRIMARY ENERGIES NOW HAD TO BE DIRECTED at one of the fundamental questions that have plagued philosophers since the dawn of civilization. "Ubi sumus?" I found myself gasping, forgetting in my distraught state to speak Greek.

"Good question, very well put." I heard Euphonius's voice ringing unpleasantly in my ears long before I could see anything but blackness. "Where, indeed, are we?"

We were not moving, anyway. Presumably, therefore, we were no longer in imminent danger of dashing out our brains upon the face of our beloved Earth.

We looked out of the viewscreens that simulated the eyes of the Sphinx. Desert . . . stark, rocky, uninhabitable. I pronounced the mystic formulae that detesseracted us into the dimensio terrestrialis, and we exited from the Sphinx's mouth. The heat was almost unendurable, and I could not see any water anywhere; nor was there provender of any kind inside the Sphinx. Strange rocky outcroppings dotted the sand, and in the distance there were reddish mountains.

81

"Maybe it isn't Terra Nova, after all," I said. "Maybe it's—"

"It wouldn't be Egypt, would it?" Euphonius asked. "With any luck, we might have landed exactly where we took off from, in which case, dozens of solicitous encephalometrists will soon manifest themselves, ready to obey our every whim—unless they've all been sacrificed by the priests of Amon-Sekhmet-whatchamacallit, of course."

"No such luck," I said, pointing to a nearby cactus. "This is definitely the New World, but from my knowledge of the area's geography, I don't think that this is within the territory where the Pax Romana holds sway. In fact, I would venture to guess that we are in hostile territory."

"Hostile?" Euphonius asked. "To what, I pray? Are you not the nephew of the emperor of almighty Rome itself? And am I not the world's most accomplished lyric poet? And as for the boy"—Lupus Ferox had been watching us all the while, sniggering to himself—"he's just a telegraph boy, and hardly likely to have enemies in a foreign land."

"You certainly suffer from a few illusions, old chap," I said. "Lupus, do you see that cloud of dust yonder?"

The boy squinted where I was pointing. Between two distant buttes, there was a smoky smudge on the horizon. "Per spiritum magnum!" the boy cried. "It's a war party—twenty, thirty Apaxae—or perhaps Comanxae. We're done for, I'm afraid. Good day to die and all that, sir! Sorry we couldn't save the universe! Permission to sing death song, O Lucius Vinicius?"

"Heavens, child!" Euphonius fretted. "They are positively *miles* away, and we have many weapons at hand, even though we are out of fuel for the Sphinx. The power of music, for example. Remember that Orpheus tamed the wild beasts with the exquisite beauty of his singing."

"But you don't understand, you silly little bard!" the boy said. "These Apaxae are ruthless! Why, they make a habit of raping women to death!"

"Then we are quite safe, my boy, since none of us happens to be a woman."

The boy raised an eyebrow, and indeed, as the poetaster minced around in his gold-bordered tunic, arranging his unattractive form into an endless series of far from fetching poses, one had to agree that our uninvited companion was not the most virile of specimens.

"If you are a man, O poet," the boy said, "the Apaxae, I have heard, inflict the cruelest of tortures—cutting off your eyelids and staking you down on top of a butte, that sort of thing. And screaming won't help. A proper Apaxa endures such torture without a word, and if you scream you will only earn, in addition to your death, his undying contempt."

"How very unsporting of them," Euphonius said.

I had to agree. Judging by the fact that the Apaxae were right at the horizon, I reckoned we had but a few minutes to think of a way of beating off those savage forces. "We'd better get back into the Sphinx's head," I temporized. "Perhaps there's a weapon we've overlooked."

"What a fine plan," Euphonius said haughtily.

"Well, think of a better one, then."

"Tush! I shall stand out here with my lyre and subdue their savage breasts with one of my epic poems, much as Orpheus tamed the wild—"

"Orpheus, Orpheus, Orpheus!" I said, kicking the little man back toward our X-9000. "You dare compare yourself to Orpheus one more time . . ."

We were soon huddling inside the Sphinx's head, looking out through the viewscreens that appeared to be the Sphinx's eyes, wondering how soon it would be before the Apaxae flushed us out.

It was a matter of a quarter of a hora. We were gazing out of the viewscreens, watching as a couple of dozen brutish Apaxae, long-haired, wearing headbands, rode around the Sphinx head, shooting fire arrows, whooping and shrieking various war cries, and generally making a thorough nuisance of themselves. Some stood on horse-

back and made faces; some shot their arrows as they
hung by their feet from their saddles; some leapt from
horse to horse in a bewildering display of equestrian
prowess. These particular desert savages lacked the ele-
gance of the Lacotii or Sianii, for their faces lacked
paint, and they did not wear feathers or colorful beads;
indeed, there was an uncompromising hardness to their
features that lent credence to Lupus's lurid descriptions
of their methods of torture, of which, at that moment, we
were hearing more than we needed to.

"Then they tie people to anthills and—"

I gritted my teeth and tried to squeeze some reaction
out the controls of the energy catapultae that had worked
so well out in space. It was no use; there was simply no
fuel.

Euphonius was kneeling in front of that funny old
statue of an Egyptian god, offering up assorted dithy-
rambs, hymns, and odes; Lupus and I watched grimly,
for though we could not be harmed—the engine room of
our vehicle was, in effect, not part of these Apaxae's
universe at all—the savages did not seem to tire; nor
was there any food in the chamber—oh, a few sacrificed
animals, which would sustain us for a day or two in a
pinch, but who knew how long we would be besieged
for? And besides, there was no water, and we were in
the middle of a desert.

"Perhaps we should surrender," Euphonius said as
one Apaxa somersaulted past the viewscreen, his
demeanor pitiless.

"Maybe he's right," the boy said glumly.

I realized that he had been living in Rome too long.
"What's the matter with you, O Lupus Ferox?" I said.
"Are you just a telegraph boy—a Roman lackey—or are
you a true Lacotius?" I was becoming quite startled at
my own sentiments. Maybe the influence of my half
brother had been more profound than I thought. "You've
spent your whole life away from the wide-open spaces of
Lacotia. You've never hunted an aurochs or gone on a
vision quest—you've just hung around at orgies waiting
for someone to toss you a slice of larks' tongue. Why, I

may be a decadent, comfort-loving Roman rich boy, but at least I've jolly well done some of those things. And I know a good day to die when I see one!"

Lupus Ferox gulped. Then he said, "You're right. Let's fight them to the death."

Euphonius said, "I don't like the sound of this. I think I'll just sit this one out." He took out his pyramid-shaped helmet, attached it to the statue of the god by a few wires, and launched into a recitation of the ritual formulae of the cult of encephalometry.

"Well, my boy," I said to the young Lacotian, "it looks like this is it."

"I'd better put on my makeup," he said. I was surprised that he could think of such a thing at this hour, but though the boy had lost many of the qualities of his people, he still had their insufferable vanity; since there was a distinct possibility that he might die, he did not wish to enter the Land of Many Tipis looking like a pauper. I watched in some amazement as the boy, with singular resourcefulness, scraped some of the pigments off the freshly painted murals—Aaye, I'm sure, would have had a fit—and, using a little spit, mashed them into a paste. As the Apaxae continued to hurl their insults and themselves at our ship—zeugma here, lest I forget my rhetorical devices!—and to thrust their war lances against the Sphingean jowls, Lupus Ferox calmly straightened his feather, made sure his moccasinae were bound tightly, and found a sacrificial wand to use as a coup stick. I had brought few weapons with me, but there was a gladius to hand, and I gave Lupus a tomahaucum so that he could at least fend off a few attackers and a scutum to ward off their blows.

"Alea jacta est, and all that," I said at last. *"Huka hey!"*

"Huka hey," the child responded a little faintly.

"Louder," I said.

We both screeched the war cry at the top of our lungs, and then we noticed that there was no one out there anymore.

Euphonius said, "Ah! Just as I thought! Pyramid

power to the rescue! By a proper exercise of mental clarity through the focusing of superlunary energies, I've managed to control their minds, and they've all gone home!"

I looked. So did the boy. The desert seemed quite barren. Perhaps—no, it seemed so improbable. Euphonius sat there, crowing.

At last I decided to try going outside. With Lupus crouching beside me, I whispered the words that released us from the tesseract, and we crept outside.

The sun was scorching; sweat poured down my brow, into my eyes. I kept my gladius drawn and ready. I strained to listen. I put my ear to the ground as Equus Insanus had taught me, and I could not hear a thing. Where had they gone? Had Euphonius indeed wished the buggers into limbo?

I looked around for a few moments. We retreated into the shadow of the Sphinx head; even there the air was so hot, it seemed to bury my lungs. Suddenly I heard Lupus scream. "Look out! Above you!"

I looked up. Too late! There was a wiry old fellow up there, knife in hand, squatting on what was left of the Sphinx's nose and poising himself to spring. I was transfixed. I could not get out of the way. And the savage leapt, howling out a horrifying war cry as he swooped down upon me—

"Hieronymus!"

CHAPTER
XI

HIERONYMUS THE APAXA

As the bloodcurdling cry rang out, he was upon me, thrusting me to the ground, sitting on my chest, wielding a nasty-looking scalping knife. I struggled, but he had me pinned fast. I looked into the face of my assailant: He was an old man, wiry, his face parched and wrinkled like a cabbage. His breath reeked of some inferior wine—I think it was Falernian, and not one of the better vintages—and he was making remarks in his rough speech, spitting all over my face.

I was clearly about to die, I decided that it was time to do the whole Roman thing—you know, stiff upper lip and all that—so I did not say a word; I just lay there and waited to feel that blade on the top of my forehead. Around us several Apaxish braves had gathered, jabbering away in the Apaxian tongue, which is, as I understand it, of the Athapascan family and bears no relation to the language of the Lacotii at all. I could not tell what they were saying, but I would not have been surprised if they were discussing the means of my death. I wondered whether, like the Lacotii, they had the singularly distasteful custom of practicing *onze wichahupo*, that is to say, of violating their fallen enemies *in culo*; indeed, my rear end quivered at the prospect, and I almost beshat myself.

I was lying there, O reader, in a most abject state, concentrating with a kind of frantic intensity on the strict maintenance of my stiff upper lip—for I did not want it said that I had shown fear in the face of an attack by one so barbarous as this—and attempting at the same time to rein in my bowels, and the withered old man, who easily held me pinned down by the simple expedient of jumping up and down on me, was singing a mystic chant in a wheezing monotone, the words of which appeared to be something like:

> *O wi yo ho wi yo ho wi yo*
> *Ho howeyo aah ee*
> *O wi yo o ho o wi yo.*

Not much of a set of lyrics, you might say, but in the mouth of this Hieronymus, it seemed interminable. Luckily for me, it appeared that he had to get through the entire song before he could kill me—doubtless one of those strange Apaxa customs. I had squeezed my eyes shut tight, waiting for death, but when I peeked, I saw that all the other Apaxae were crowding around, shouting words of encouragement, and joining in the refrain of the song. Another of these savages appeared to be using my stomach as a drum, though I could not see past the one sitting on my chest, so I was not at all sure what was going on.

Presently, though, little Lupus Ferox rushed at Hieronymus and began pummeling him with one fist, with the other grasping a coup stick with which he bashed the Apaxa on the small of his back. "Take that, you horrible man!" he was squealing. "Don't you know that the entire universe is going to be destroyed if we die?"

To my surprise, although it could easily have been done, the Apaxa did not turn around to snap the child's neck like a chicken leg. He laughed uproariously and relaxed his hold upon me a little. I could breathe—

barely—and I could see that two of the Apaxish braves were holding the lad by the arms.

Hieronymus got off my chest. I was too weak to move. He kicked me a few times in the ribs and then bade two more of his braves pin me down; then he approached Lupus Ferox, brandishing his scalping knife.

"You fool!" I gasped. "He'll slice you to pieces!"

"Never mind!" the little pipsqueak said. He was clearly frightened, but I'm afraid that his stiff-upper-lippedness far outdid mine, for he laughed at the approaching Apaxa and tried to spit in his face. The old man towered over him, though, so he only managed to hit him in the navel.

Hieronymus grabbed Lupus Ferox by the hand and made a great gash in his palm with the knife. I could not bear to look, especially since the other Apaxae were all watching with interest and making appreciative comments, which I could only assume were discussions concerning the finer points of torture.

The next thing that happened, however, was that Hieronymus made as big a slash in his own hand and, firmly grasping the boy's hand in his own, raised it up high while his men cheered.

"It's all right!" Lupus Ferox cried. "Apparently he's made me his blood brother!"

"Jolly good!" I said. "I suppose these damned savages have come to their senses, then?"

Hieronymus turned to me. He regarded me with the contempt one normally reserves for a piece of merda. Then he said, in passable Greek, "Damned savages, eh? You Romans are all alike. You see a breechclout and you think we can't understand a word you say."

I gulped. "Oh, you do speak Greek! Frightfully sorry, old chap, I didn't mean to imply that you were uncivilized or anything—but you did give me rather a scare, jumping up and down on me like that."

"A worse scare is in store!" Hieronymus said. "Are you surprised I speak your language?"

"Well, yes." Surely he was not going to kill me—not after exchanging these pleasantries!

"Beneath this savage exterior," the old man said, crossing his arms, "beats a noble heart, I'll have you know. And anyway, I spent ten years studying rhetoric in Alexandria. That is why I go by the name Hieronymus, with its Judeo-Hellenistic implications."

"Oh, I say," I said. "Awfully clever of you."

"I didn't have much choice. I was a slave, in the forcible employ of one Abraham bar-David, a sasquatch. I picked up my knowledge of rhetoric, oratory, and dramaturgy while cleaning the latrines of His Hairiness's school for the pretentious, and—"

"You know Abraham bar-David!" I said. "A personal friend of mine! Why, I was there when he invented the uranograph!"

"How nice! Well, I didn't much appreciate his floggings. For that, I think I'll double the amount of torture you're going to undergo before you are mercifully taken into the bosom of the magnus spiritus."

"Actually, I hardly knew him at all," I said, trying to back out of that one. "Besides, Roman citizens always flog their slaves—it's really nothing personal, it's just a custom, you know, like...well, you know...eating larks' tongues for breakfast."

"I should have suspected something when I noticed the head of the Sphinx whizzing around the sky. But who pays any attention to these things? The skies are always full of flying stone heads these days—it's very much the rage."

I was about to make some flattering remark about his brilliant imagination when, indeed, I noticed that an enormous stone head was crossing the zenith at that very moment. It had to be an illusion, surely! I blinked. No, it was still there. It was perhaps half the size of the head of the Sphinx, carved out of stone; it had a certain negroid quality to its features, as though a Briton had mated with a Nubian to produce such a visage. As I watched, the head vanished behind a cloud, and I saw that it was suspended from a number of bulbous round objects...hot-air balloons!

I began to see a glimmer of hope, for I knew that

hot-air balloons were the provenance of the Roman army. In my previous adventure, when Equus Insanus and I were battling the androids to the death, had not the cavalry come rushing to our rescue, borne aloft by hot-air balloons on which was blazoned the legend SPQR?

I strained to catch another glimpse of the balloon. But it was gone. I resigned myself to being hideously tortured.

At that moment, however, Euphonius the bard emerged from the Sphinx head, pyramidal hat on his head, wires dangling, waving his lyre. What an idiot! I thought. Surely this would be the last straw.

But when the Apaxae saw him, they immediately released me. And the chieftain said, "You didn't tell me you fellows were encephalometrists! That changes everything."

The Apaxae proceeded to go to their horses and to retrieve their own pryamidal helmets; all of them put them on and squatted in the sand, and then there arose a caterwauling the likes of which I had never heard before. Apparently this communal wailing was a local variant of the religion. There was another big difference, too—we all had to consume great quantities of a certain *fungus magicus* that causes one to have peculiar visions.

Sitting on the ground among the strange new friends, who seemed to have completely forgotten that they had planned to kill me just moments before, I was handed a portion of fungus magicus myself, and it was not long before I was plunged into a waking dream.

It seemed to me that the real world was fading away. I was rushing around the parallel dimensions at top speed. Buildings, flying machines, dinosaurs, whole armies whirled about, and mingled with these images was the face of the Green Pig. I was running or flying or swimming. The air was like water, wet and streaming—and like fire. This was far more interesting than the imbibing of the aqua cocacola. In the case of the one, you feel all-powerful, as though your mind were filling the entire universe—which is all very well if your mind is all you're interested in. But the ingestion of these fungi magici produced a quite opposite effect. I felt like a tiny strand in the fabric of the universe; it seemed that all things flowed through me. The one disharmony was the image of Viridiporcus Rex, who seemed to taunt me at every turn. I knew that somewhere Euphonius was singing away lustily, but through the power of the fungus magicus his cacophony was transmuted into the most exquisite melody, and his trivial poesy was transformed into the utterances of the very muses.

I passed from dream state to dream state and finally to another world entirely, or so it seemed, a world within a magical circle circumscribed by the skulls of aurochs. The world was fragrant with sage. Blood flowed all about me, as though the River Oceanus had become my own life force. A searing pain tore at my chest, and I knew that I was dancing the sun dance...and I saw Equus Insanus beside me, and Lupus Ferox, dancing in joyful agony.

Equus turned to me. He did not speak as such. None of us spoke, for we had wooden whistles in our mouths and our hands grasped bunches of sage flowers, so that we could not even signal with our hands. But I heard his voice in my mind.

"Lucius—Lucius—"

"By the maidenhead of Venus!" I responded, using some kind of mental telegraphy. "What are you doing in my dream?"

"Lucius—if you don't find me soon, the circle of the universe will be broken—"

"I already know that," I telepathized in some annoyance, for here I was, dancing away in some vision, my chest pierced with rawhide strips—this was not pleasant, let me tell you—and what was I learning from this hocus-pocus? Only stuff I knew already! "You've really landed us in a royal pickle," I said, "by running off like that—and hijacking the pyramid—and trying to nab His Viridiporcitude all by yourself! Now Aquila and the general have all been sucked into some kind of vortex, and I'm bumbling through the cosmos searching for you and being bombarded with bad poetry—I've lost a few pounds, let me tell you, from not being able to eat whenever that bloody bard opens his mouth—and—"

"Calm down, calm down," Equus said. "It could be worse."

"Worse! Ha!" I said, and returned to the sun dance, staring all the while into the sun, my ears burning, the pain exploding in my chest every time I jerked around.

"I can't talk long," Equus said. "I'm almost completely under their control..." His voice was fading in and out, and the face of the Green Pig was somehow weaving itself in and out of the fabric of the vision. "I'm reaching out to you across the transdimensional anomaly gap—disjunctive nodes within the framework of the Fourth Law—"

This was the way people always ended up talking when they spent any time with the were-jaguars from the Dimensional Patrol. I shouted, "Can I reach you through the fungus magicus ceremony?"

"Yes, the drug creates a right-brain-directed null consciousness state that allows increased receptivity of—"

"Never mind!" I interrupted. "Where are you? How can I rescue you? And where is the Green Pig?"

"Everywhere! Nowhere! And I *am* the Green Pig—that's what I've been trying to tell you—*aaaaaah!*—" I felt an intensity of anguish that surpassed even the pain of the wounds on my chest as I danced and the flesh tore free.

There was another voice, a childish voice that cried out my name again and again. Suddenly, I snapped out of my vision. I looked into the face of Lupus Ferox, and I heard the insensate twanging of Euphonius's lyre, and I screamed, "Let me dream again!" I also realized that I was shaking all over and that sweat was pouring down my face. And the sun was going down, so I must have been in this state for several hours.

"The vision has ended." It was the voice of the old Apaxa, Hieronymus, as he handed me a gourd filled with refreshing water. "Wouldn't really do to give you more than one vision a day—you might get confused, you

know. By the way, why didn't you tell me you were the
half brother of Equus Insanus, son of the Lakota Chieftain Who Rides the Night Sky? I took you fellows for
just any old Romans—and we're not in the empire
around here you know; we've orders to kill Romans on
sight."

"Orders? The noble chieftain of the Apaxae takes
orders?"

"Well . . . this country you are in, known because of
its desolation as Zona Arida, is technically within the
confines of the Olmechian Empire. Normally we don't
pay much attention to the Olmechii, but at the moment
we are allied with them, since we're at war with Comanxae, Caddones, and Anasazii, although we have a
truce with the Seminolii and the Siosionii."

I knew that there were tremendous differences between the various tribes of savages, but I had no idea
how they all managed to keep each other straight. "And
what tribe are those?" I asked, pointing skyward, for
that enormous stone head, dangling from a fleet of hot-
air balloons, was once more hovering overhead.

"It looks like the Olmechii are out and about," Hieronymous said. "That's a surveillance head; they fly back
and forth from the city of the Olmechii to make sure that
the various treaties are observed."

"And we're at war with them right now? Rome, I
mean." That would not be a pleasant prospect, since the
head seemed to be slowly descending into our midst.

"You are indeed," the Apaxa said. "Well, old chap,
it's been nice knowing you, and it was a lot of fun doing
the fungus magicus ceremony and all that, but I'm afraid
I'm going to have to torture you to death after all."

"Good heavens! Why?" I asked, as I saw Euphonius
quaking and the telegraph boy looking defiantly on.

"Oh, I shall spare the boy, of course—he's my blood
brother now, and honor dictates that I must protect him
—and as for that bard, he is somewhat parvuli potatii, if
you see what I mean; besides, with a voice like that, he
could be useful, say, in resurrecting recently dead
braves. Anyway, he's just a Greek. But you're the ring-

leader, and a true Roman besides, and we have sworn an oath of fealty to the Olmechii, and, well, we're supposed to kill Romans on sight, you recall."

"What a damned nuisance!" I said. "Not a very good day to die, and all that; can't it wait?" For although I was about to wet my tunica in my terror, I was not about to unstiffen my upper lip in the least.

"Look," he said, eyeing the sky warily, for the Olmechian head was scarcely a hundred cubits above us, and one could see Olmechian high priests in their gaudy plumed garments looking down at us, "I'll make you a deal. I like you, so I'll kill you with the highest honors."

"What does that entail?" I said.

"It's a slow death," he said, "but if you don't scream, and spend the entire time taunting us, we'll all feel deeply honored. And I have been assured that, after the burning of the soles of the feet, the chest flaying, the drilling of the skull, the release of fire ants into the nostrils, the slitting of the genitalia, and the carving of the arms to ribbons, one ceases to feel much, and the last ten or fifteen hours are a breeze."

"How comforting," I said as the Apaxish braves bound me fast once more.

CHAPTER
XII

OLMECHII BEARING GIFTS

THE OLMECHIAN HEAD MADE A SOFT LANDING IN the sand, about half a mille passus from where I was about to be brutally manhandled by the Apaxae. My fate was a rather novel form of crucifixion, for I was tied, spread-eagled, to a cruciform cactus that chanced to grow nearby. My garments had been stripped away so as to provide the maximum access to every region of my body, and various implements were being readied for my excruciation: daggers, branding irons—doubtless traded from the Romans, for the Apaxae did not possess the secret of smelting—and arrows, both the regular and the fiery variety. However, my erstwhile companion in hallucinogenic voyaging, the turncoat Hieronymus, had not yet commenced the torture. He explained that he wanted me to get into a suitable mental state and that furthermore he wanted the Olmechii to be present, so that they could see that he was obeying the letter of the pact between them and his people.

"You're very thorough," I said ruefully. "Your clarity of thought is remarkable—you could almost be a Roman general."

"I owe it all to encephalometry," the Apaxa said proudly. He had donned his pyramid helmet once more, as had the other braves. He tapped the helmet proudly.

"What a fascinating example of cultural syncretism," Euphonius said. "The wisdom of the Terra Novans was coupled with Egyptian mysticism to create encephalometry, and now that it has been adopted in the New World, it has adopted native qualities unforeseen by its creators."

"Cultural syncretism!" I said furiously. "I'm about to be killed, and all you can do is intellectualize!" Though the torture had not begun, the thorns of the cactus pricked me all over. Hieronymus was overseeing the lighting of a fire. The sun was setting, and the desert air had become pleasantly cool; had it not been for my imminent demise, the desert's stark beauty would have made a greater impression upon me. For in the rosy light the sand was stained a hundred shades of crimson, scarlet, vermilion, russet; cacti cast long shadows and in the distance the buttes loomed, dark and bleak and pervaded with mystery. "If only," I said to Euphonius, "you would pay attention to the beauty of the surrounding landscape instead of to the sleazier aspects of contemporary life, you might have a chance of being a decent poet."

"Oh, Lucius . . . I pity you," Euphonius said. "You're so hopelessly old-fashioned—so dreadfully banal in your tastes—you epitomize everything that's decadent in Rome today."

"Oh, shut up," Lupus Ferox said.

I was not exactly in the mood for literary arguments. But there suddenly came a bleating sound in the distance, and I looked up and saw that a party of Olmechii was approaching. The bleating came from conch trumpeters who were leading the delegation. There were slaves bearing torches, followed by a few scantily clad women prancing about with feathery anklets and golden ornaments in their noses, beating on tambourines, singing, and strewing the sand with petals. Behind them came Olmechian soldiers, almost naked too, except that they carried spears and shields of leather and wore cloaks made from the pelts of jaguars; behind these walked an impressive fellow, at least a handspan taller than most men, his height exaggerated still further by an enormous assemblage of garish plumes upon his head. His features resembled the enormous stone head's, an odd admixture of the Northern and the African races. He was covered from head to toe with feathers—on his cloaks, in his ears, dangling from necklaces and bracelets; there were gold ornaments in his earlobes, which weighed them down and made them descend almost to his shoulders. An enormous jewel was embedded in his chin, and his septum was pierced by a golden circlet. All in all, this was a spectacle such as I had never seen before, not even in the Circus Maximus, and my mind was racing with notions of transporting this whole troupe to Rome and my subsequent fame—if only I could extricate myself from the present predicament.

The Apaxae paid me no heed, but began to address these newcomers in a strange tongue. Hieronymus was telling them all about us, now and then pointing to me and fixing me with a look of utter opprobrium; I could not tell whether he actually hated me or whether it was merely out of deference to his treaty with the Olmechii.

Presently, this chief of the Olmechii approached me and eyed me curiously all over, not hesitating to scrutinize my private parts in the way one might examine a slave in the market. I was distinctly uncomfortable—after all, I did not know how much longer I was going to be able to hold on to those selfsame parts—and became even more unnerved when the fellow began talking to me in his native tongue.

"I'm afraid I never bothered to learn any barbarian tongues in school," I said.

He began scratching the ornament that depended from his left earlobe. When he spoke again, it sounded like: "*Bzzthp* . . . jolly decent of you . . . *blapawhatl quatmzll* . . . torture, eh?" When I stared blankly, he yanked the thing from his ear, screaming, "Blast these translating devices! Nothing's worked since the little green ones took off!" in quite passable Latin—trace of a

Neapolitan accent, but it's not the end of the world to have been born in Neapolis.

I responded in Greek—I wanted to die a patrician, not a peasant! "Now look here," I said, summoning up my last reserves of strength, "these fellows are about to torture me to death, and I suppose you're here to enjoy watching. I have enjoyed seeing people tortured to death often enough myself—I love spectacle as much as the next man, and I go to the games whenever I can—so I won't begrudge you a bit of sport. Moriturus te saluto and all that, as we say in the vulgar tongue." I gritted my teeth, waiting for the pain to come.

He raised an eyebrow and said, "My name is Ketzal-kouatoulos—in your language, Serpens Plumatus. You arrived in a flying head, did you not?"

"Yes."

"Then you must be the savior of the Olmechii whom we have been awaiting. I thank the gods!"

I didn't know what he was talking about, but I was not going to let such an opportunity be wasted. "Then release me, O Serpens Plumatus!" I said. "For I cannot save you from anything whilst still in this cruciform state."

He waved to his attendants. Gold ornaments tinkled as he clapped his hands, and slaves ran forward to untie me from the cactus. I slumped onto the sand.

"Bloody good show," the Olmechius said, switching to Greek after fiddling with the device some more, though I must say that the movements of his lips did not match the sounds that I was hearing. I realized that the thing in his ear must be something left by the little green were-jaguars from the future and that—if I remembered the memoirs of General Papinian aright—the Olmechii had been masters of superscience once, enjoying the favor of the Dimensional Patrol until the flying saucers departed from their land.

Serpens Plumatus then proceeded to kneel down and prostrate himself, along with his entire retinue. What a spectacle! I thought as I struggled to assume a more dignified position and at the same time unobtrusively scrape the sand from my arse. A slave threw down a rich tapestry and beckoned me to sit upon it; another threw a blanket over my shoulders to shield me from the cold. I called the poetaster and the telegraph boy to sit beside me and then said—for I appeared to have the upper hand again—"Speak."

"We have been searching for you for some time. Since the departure of the little green masters, our empire has fallen on hard times. The loss of our high technology, coupled with the encroachment of the Roman Empire . . . but I'm sure you know all about those things. Nevertheless, we were able to control our own dominions adequately, for our pyramids and magical stone heads were still capable of channeling the energy of the universe, and our fleet of hot-air balloons was still at our command. But in the last year, our pyramids and stone heads have grown increasingly recalcitrant and have taken to just flying off for no reason."

"Good heavens!" I said. "We were battling those pyramids somewhere in the vicinity of Mars, ere I crash-landed in this Zona Arida."

"This is the only stone head we have left, and we are forced to guard it constantly to prevent it from departing. The last pyramid in town flew off last month, and we've become the laughingstock of our subject peoples. We've sacrificed, of course—about half the population of our capital city has willingly gone beneath the obsidian knife —but, far from accepting the food we offer him, the sun god seems to be out to lunch. But now you have come in your own flying head." I saw that in the middle distance some workmen were attaching hot-air balloons to the head of the Sphinx and were preparing to tow it away. "The gods have clearly sent you to us, and—Roman though you are—I must welcome you."

"So take me to your leader," I said. This was more like it. This was how the nephew of Caesar was supposed to be treated.

"Actually, you *are* our leader. For a while, anyway."

"Well, then, find us some decent lodgings, fetch us some food, and a bit of wine wouldn't hurt."

"We don't have wine, but there *is* an amphora of aqua cocacola somwhere around here, O Divinity!" This was sounding better and better. "And we intend to escort you, with due honor, to your palace—this very night!"

Lupus Ferox looked quizzically at us. He seemed dubious. I said, "Come on, child! It's time we had a decent orgy for a change."

"I don't trust these Olmechii one bit," he whispered in my ear.

"Look, in the past few hours I've been snatched from the jaws of death at least three times. I'm not about to question Olmechii bearing gifts."

Later that evening, the three of us were bedecked in full Olmechian regalia and escorted to the nearest hot-air balloon. I had no misgivings as our convoy took off into the night sky.

Except . . . was that not the silhouette of a pterodactyl against the full moon? I blinked; it was gone. Perhaps it was merely a hallucinatory flashback to the fungus magicus episode, I thought, as I clutched my cache of the mushrooms, for Hieronymus the Apaxa had given me some with which to contact Equus Insanus.

Surely I would not have to face the Viridiporcine One just yet. I could live like a king among these friendly natives until I figured out a plan. Perhaps I could even get the Olmechii to help me. I had visions of going against the Evil One with a fleet of top-notch pyramids.

No. I refused to be pessimistic as our hot-air balloons drifted. I allowed myself the luxury of a deep sleep, disturbed only once or twice by the raucous heavings of Euphonius the bard as he vomited over the side of the basket.

CHAPTER
XIII

BREAKFAST OF CHAMPIONS

I**T WAS OUT OF THIS PROFOUND SLUMBER THAT** I **WAS** awakened by the following words, punctuated by the strumming of that infernal lyre:

> *O Moon.*
> *That shinest on both boatman and buffoon.*
> *On lout and lawyer, goat herder and goon.*
> *Toilet and temple, sparrow and spittoon.*
> *That shinest in November as in June.*
> *That shin'st at night, but never shin'st at noon.*
> *O Moon.*
> *That shed'st thy light on this hot-air balloon*
> *That hang'st in heaven like a silver spoon.*
> *And listen'st as these verses I do croon—*

The singing broke off just as I became completely awake, and I heard the voice of the poetaster: "By the nine muses, I can't think of anything else that rhymes! Let's see...goon, loon, dune! I haven't done *dune* yet..."

Rubbing my eyes, I looked around. Serpens Plumatus

102

paced back and forth, grinning smugly the whole time. I could not fathom why. He had enormous plugs in his ears, though; perhaps he was familiar with the tale of Odysseus and the sirens. It took Euphonius some fifty-seven more lines before he exhausted all the conceivable rhymes. I think that rhyme is a ghastly device—one of the worst new inventions in poetry, taking all the subtlety out of it. Think how monotonous the epics of Vergil would sound if there was this constant vulgar pounding to announce the end of each line! And yet, perhaps rhyming will catch on, for it makes verse so easy to remember that even a member of the lower classes can recite long passages from these silly faddish new poets. Of course, only Euphonius would take this fashion to such an extreme.

Finally, I could not stand it anymore. "Shut up," I said, "or I'll throw you overboard myself."

Euphonius sighed. "Perhaps I should perform an excerpt from my masterpiece, the one I've been working on all my life. It's about the labors of Hercules, you see, well, actually, it's about *one* labor in particular, the Augean stables...after all, *anyone* can empathize with having to shovel shit! It's ever so relevant, a profound metaphor for the human condition."

We crossed mountains and forests; so much I could see by the faint light of the flames that were used to keep the hot-air balloons aloft. As a glimmer of dawn dyed the treetops blood-red, breakfast was served; I was most surprised that mine consisted entirely of a raw heart. I did not particularly care to inquire about its origin but in my hunger devoured the whole thing, while Serpens Plumatus studied me.

In fact, he was staring at me and taking notes. Well, not exactly notes—he appeared to be drawing on an old hide with a little paintbrush. In fact, when I spit out the aorta—it was very stringy—he dashed to retrieve it before it could touch the floor of the basket. "Excuse me, Divinity," he mumbled as he retired to the far corner.

I felt rather like Apis, the sacred bull of Egypt—you know, the one they give the sacred grain to, and whichever one he chooses is analyzed to predict the year's harvest. Not as reliable as the entrails of sheep, to be sure, but then if their stochastic methods were better than ours, this might well be the Egyptian Empire and not the Roman, and wouldn't it be dreadful to live out one's life in perpetual fear of involuntary mummification?

I remembered that it is the wont of the Egyptians to examine even the merda of the sacred bull for clues as to the future, and I wondered as my stomach rumbled from the motion of the balloon and the unusual victuals whether each little faex of mine would be scrutinized with the same precision by these Olmechii.

Both Lupus Ferox and Euphonius seemed to have been given real food. There was even an ample supply of aqua cocacola; from this I knew that we were heading south, where the coca plant grew in profusion. Sure enough, as the sun climbed higher in the sky, I saw our destination, a city in a jungle clearing.

Wide-eyed, Lupus Ferox watched as we floated over the city. The Sphinx's head dangled about half a mille passus away. "Look at the tiny little people!" he said, pointing at the throng that had gathered to gape at us. Thousands of thousands of brown-skinned natives crowded the avenues, each clothed in plumage gaudier than the next and one or two wearing the skins of exotic jungle cats. This was no city of a thousand years, like Rome, built without a plan, streets running into streets, twisting and turning, insulae piled on top of insulae, palaces here, slums there; from our vantage point we could see that this city had been created from the mind of a single artist. The streets met each other at right angles and were broad; trees lined them at regular intervals.

As we came closer, though, I saw that there were many squares and plazas that must once have contained pyramidal structures but were now empty. The vast public edifices, the temples, had been ripped out by the roots; only the houses of the common people remained.

"We shall be landing shortly," Serpens Plumatus said. "I hope you enjoyed your breakfast." He and his companions were eating now, off gold and silver plates, no less. Serpens was gnawing on something. The Olmechii were all squatting around a huge covered platter. The whole operation smelled strongly of roast pork.

I thought I had better be polite, so I said, "Delicious, quite delicious; might have been better a little less rare, though."

Suddenly Lupus Ferox gave a little squeal of fright. I looked at what the Olmechius was eating. It was a human hand, and he was sucking on it and spitting out the bones, as matter-of-factly as though it had been a calf's brain omelet or an unborn dormouse dipped in honey or some other common-or-garden variety dish that a normal human being might eat.

"H-he's eating a—" he said as a few metacarpals whizzed by and landed on my lap. I got up in a panic. The hot-air balloon rocked.

"Cannibals!" I said.

"Does it surprise you, O champion of the gods?" Serpens Plumatus asked, wrinkling his brow. "But you yourself..."

He lifted the lid of the enormous platter at his feet. It contained a human torso—that was what smelled so much like roast pork. Its chest cavity gaped, and even I, with my limited knowledge of anatomy, could tell that it contained no heart.

"My brother-in-law," Serpens said. "Just sacrificed him a while ago while you were asleep."

"Good god! How barbaric," I said.

"Barbaric indeed! You should be jolly grateful we did; the sun's risen right on schedule, as you can see." He pointed triumphantly at the sun, which shone so brightly that the balloon was awash with light. Sweat was pouring down our faces, our backs; my woollen tunica stuck to my skin and to the cheeks of my arse, and the knowledge that I had been breakfasting on a raw human heart was not the most stomach-settling news.

I remembered that these Olmechii believed that the world comes to an end every night and must be revived by constant human sacrifice. I had not known that they then proceeded to eat the slain, but I supposed, in a land where meat was scarce, that it was a pretty conservation-minded thing to do.

"Of course, we haven't been getting enough victims lately, what with the collapse of civilization and all that," Serpens said ruefully. "That's why you're here. You're going to be the incarnate god—the all-wise incarnation of the sun—and you're going to get all our pyramids back for us so that our peoples will return to the city once more instead of hiding out in the jungle, quaking for fear of the end of the world."

"But the world has already ended," I said, "and if you don't release me, I shan't be able to bring it back again."

"Well, at least we agree on something," Serpens said. "But you'd better get some rest. We've got several weeks before your grand ceremony of deification, and you'll need energy to enjoy the constant supply of wine, women, and song that we aim to provide."

"That doesn't sound too bad," I said. "There's got to be a catch somewhere."

"Catch? What sort of catch?" said Serpens Plumatus as he bit off an enormous chunk of his brother-in-law's thigh.

CHAPTER
XIV

THE CATCH

I CAN BE DENSE SOMETIMES, AND IT WAS NOT UNTIL about the second week that I cottoned on to the fact that being the living god of those people meant having to get sacrificed in the third week—which did not leave me much time.

It was a little difficult to think of our new palatial surroundings as a prison, but that was about the truth of it. Our quarters were enormous chambers of stone, full of motifs not dissimilar to those of Egyptian temples; the place of our confinement was within an enormous courtyard surrounded by an impregnable stone wall topped with gilded human skulls. Our clothes had been taken from us, and instead we were forced to wear these astonishing assemblages of plumes and jaguar pelts, all lined with enough gold to buy half the dancing girls in Rome; our wants were attended to by a woman who, I gathered, was a sacred priestess of some kind. Her name was about as unpronounceable as you can get, something like Tlatlaclatlaklatloc or Titiclataclatlic, but we soon named her Callipygia, because whenever she came to attend upon us wearing a cape of brilliant green feathers, I was always struck by the comeliness of her buttocks. Her face was not bad, either—her nose well arched in the Roman fashion, her skin a subtle reddish-brown hue, and her large eyes brown and somewhat bovine, like the goddess Juno's.

She spoke no Greek, of course, but with the aid of sign language and one of those translating devices we managed to understand each other well enough.

Apart from serving us food—the human heart episode was not repeated, thank Jove—they left us pretty much alone, and we would wander around in the courtyard, the three of us. The head of the Sphinx had been returned to our custody, but of course it was useless without fuel; it rested on the flagstones, staked down with great weights, for though it could no longer fly, the natives still feared that it would take off. As for the Olmechian head, that occupied a place beside our Sphinx, and every few hours the high priest and his retinue would perform their barbaric rites in front of it. These invariably included killing someone, but it was far less fun to watch than, say, criminals being torn apart by wild beasts, for those who died seemed resigned, nay, eager, nor did they scream, protest, or carry on—it was bloody unsporting of them, if you ask me. Took all the spectacle out of it; the whole human sacrifice bit, once you got used to the idea, was really a bit of a bore, actually. And the sacrificers were so mechanical about it all; they did not seem to enjoy it one bit, for all that they were ripping out people's hearts and holding them up for the sun god to drink!

I pointed this out to my two companions as we strolled around the courtyard in the humid afternoon. Priests and acolytes bowed to me as I approached, and scurried about with their eyes downcast.

Another sacrifice was occurring just down the way from us, and the victim, a young man no older than I, was lying down on the bloody altar to have his heart ripped out. Serpens Plumatus was officiating himself and was brandishing the obsidian knife, which glittered in the brilliant sun. "Another of those interminable sacrifices,"

Euphonius said. "It'll be our turn soon—and then ad infernum with all your promises that we were going to save the universe and Equus Insanus and everyone else."

"I didn't promise," I said.

"I've been eavesdropping on the guards," Lupus Ferox said, "and the way they're going to kill you, O master, is singularly disgusting. They're going to flay you alive, and then that little priest yonder"—he pointed to a chubby fellow officiating beside Serpens Plumatus —"is going to wear your skin until it rots off. Something to do with the renewal of the universe. As for Euphonius and me, it's just the old heart-ripping routine—nothing fancy."

"Surely, O Lucius Vinicius, you have a plan!" Euphonius said. "Even I have a plan, and I am only, ahem, a humble bard."

"Let's hear it," I said.

"Well, I thought we might arrange for one of the local scribes to translate my verses into Nahvatish, the local dialect, and arrange for some kind of public performance, perhaps at a local orgy or whatever they have here that passes for an orgy...and once they hear the affecting tale of the ugly duckling, they'll realize how valuable we are, and what a supreme loss to world art our demise would precipitate."

"I don't think your poems...ah...translate very well," I said. I did not want to offend him too much, now that we three were the only island of decent Roman values in this sea of barbarity. Actually, I was so desperate that even so harebrained a scheme as this seemed to contain a modicum of feasibility.

As I was mulling this over, the exquisite Callipygia came to find us and to summon us to dinner. It was the usual fare; by then I would have given anything even for a humble old peacocks' brain stew. We sat in an enormous throne room, with augurs on every side making copious notes on the way we ate everything.

I never found out whether, as I suspected, they examined our feces for signs and portents; all I knew was that the chamber pots—which were solid gold and embellished with bas-reliefs of skull-faced gods—were spirited away every night as we slept and returned to us empty each dawn. I was about to ask Callipygia that very question, in fact, when an astonishing thing happened. The high priestess, who until that moment had been the epitome of decorum, drew one of those obsidian knives from her bosom and began waving it at us, ranting and raving the while in her native tongue!

She was flinging herself about, and her breasts were heaving and her eyes were flashing—I found her performance most erotic, I must confess, barbarian though she was; she wasn't nearly as self-conscious as the senators' wives and languid patrician bitches who are really the only thing one can get in Rome, unless one has a taste for fornicating beneath one's station. I had no idea what she was saying, but eventually the translating device was able to keep up, and I gathered that she was angry at me for not yet having performed the act with her, and what's more, if I did not do it, she was going to be sacrificed anyway, so she might as well kill herself now!

"By Jove," I said, "what a predicament! I daresay I'll have to remedy the situation without delay."

"Apparently you're some kind of living god," Euphonius said, "and part of your living god's duties seems to consist of impregnating the high priestess; something to do with the renewal of the earth and the cycle of eternity or something—quaint, isn't it?"

"So it's a choice between a fate worse than death—or death, eh?" I said. "By Venus, I know what *I'd* pick."

The device translated—although she had finished talking and had collapsed, panting from her exertions, upon the stone floor at my feet. "Take me now! Take me my lord! Else I shall perish!" she said, and many other such remarks in the same vein.

"Oh, very well," I said. "But you can hardly expect me to perform my divine duties in front of all these!" I waved my hand, and sure enough, there were dozens of Olmechii in attendance—from the guards at the portals, reminding us that despite our luxurious surroundings we were still prisoners, and on death row at that, to the priests with their tall plumes and the serving wenches who were already ogling young Lupus Ferox and loud Euphonius.

She looked up at me from the floor whereon she had prostrated herself, and gazed at me with that look of abject vulnerability that is a surefire aphrodisiac to any red-blooded Roman patrician; I had to confess that she was not undesirable. Indeed, so long had I been without the companionship of a woman that it seemed to me the only thing in the world that mattered. Saving the universe was of little consequence, could I not prong this paragon of beauty *instanter*!

"Isn't there somewhere we could go?" I said. It is one thing to indulge one's lusts at a Roman orgy, to lose one's decorum in the company of one's social equals, but these were barbarians, and I did not much care to have them gaping at the virile member of Caesar's nephew. As those of you who have followed this tale will know by now, I am really a very liberal-minded sort of a person— but there *are* limits.

Callipygia giggled and took me by the hand, and we left the huge chamber. Two guards followed us at a respectful distance, though I was hardly planning to escape at that moment.

There were various twisty little corridors. I wished I had had the presence of mind to bring the proverbial ball of yarn, as Theseus did when he battled the Minotaur— but I had pulled that trick in our previous adventure, and it never occurred to me that I might need it ever again.

We passed long hallways decorated with bas-reliefs of Olmechian deities. The green were-jaguar images were omnipresent, as were depictions of the cruelest tortures. What an unfortunate stroke of fate that the Olmechii and the Romans were forced to live as enemies, I thought. For had they but conquered the world together, instead of on separate continents, who knows what spectacles we would be watching in the Flavian Amphitheater. As I walked hand in hand toward the consummation of my passion for this dusky wench, I fantasized about such spectacles. Imagine! Relay human sacrifice races! High priests mounted on ostriches battling Amazons swathed in anacondas, having at one another with obsidian-tipped knives! So thrilling was the thought of such bloodshed that I almost forgot that I was about to pierce the pleasure portals of a priestess who might, for all I knew, be the one chosen to pierce me on the altar. When I reflected on this irony, however, it merely added more piquancy to the proceedings.

At length, the guards who had accompanied us reached a particular portal, where they planted themselves on either side like guardian statues. Callipygia beckoned me through, and I realized that there would be no escape from this particular tunnel of love.

"Where are we going, by the way?" I said. I noticed that the artwork in this corridor was somewhat different, was, in fact, remarkably familiar-looking. That figure perched on a chair in front of some kind of console was almost reminiscent of Aquila at the controls of the Sphinx! But for the pierced earlobes and the heavy gold ornaments, could that not be . . . surely not. It must be one of the ancient astronautiloi of whom Aquila spoke.

The priestess spoke to me through the translating device. "Does it matter where we go, so long as I am impregnated, O Divine One?"

"I can't guarantee results, you know."

Her face fell. "But you're a god," she said.

"So's my uncle," I said, "but I've yet to see him predict the chariot races, let alone who's going to give birth to what." Apparently this woman suffered from the astonishingly primitive delusion that being a god actually had to do with something other than political expedience. Of course, she did not have the benefit, as my friends and I did, of knowing that the universe had already ended and that the gods she believed in were all pretty much old petasus.

"Your uncle is a god?" she said, confused.

"Yes, he's the emperor of Rome," I said, "and it's a jolly sight better being a god there than here, let me tell you! Over there, it's parties every night, debauchery on every corner, and tax and tax and spend and spend. Everything of every gender, age, and species is only too happy to present themselves for an amatory encounter at the drop of a wreath; you can have peacocks' brains for breakfast whenever you want, and every mealtime is an eat-all-you-want festival! And orgies—oh, you should see the orgies!" Though I did not remember the last one as being much fun. Well, my dire straits lent my speech wings, for frustration is the tenth muse, and I waxed poetic. "Being a god here, on the other hand, is just about the most boring thing one can do. You can't pick your mealtimes, all they ever feed you is human hearts, and to top it all, they flay you alive once a month! What kind of godhood is this?"

She said nothing for a while, mulling it all over, all the while removing assorted pieces of jewelry and feathers. This was all very thrilling—until I noticed where we were.

We were standing in a small chamber whose walls were carved out of naked granite. There were more familiar-looking images there. Indeed, there was a whole row of hieroglyphs—or what passes for hieroglyphs among these people—and inscriptions in what appeared to be other scripts: a Parthian cuneiform, a Phoenician, an Aramaic. Nothing I could understand, of course, but still disturbingly familiar. Lining one wall were some mummies. These were not the elaborately posed, bejeweled mummies of Egypt; they were a somewhat lower class of mummy, without any wrappings, arms and legs akimbo—evidently they had been somewhat hastily preserved. They came in all ages, sexes, and sizes, and vestiges of clothing clung to their emaciated bodies. They all had the hollow cheeks and hideously gaping eye sockets that characterize mummies, and it was a little unnerving to see them and to know that one was expected to impregnate a woman in front of them. I must confess that I found my manhood wilting at the prospect. Luckily, since I had not yet doffed my tunica, Callipygia had not yet noticed any cooling of my ardor, for she continued to poke, tug, and tickle me and to utter lengthy imprecations in her native tongue, of which only one or

two words seemed to make it through the translator intact, rather like this: "nudity—ah—*xyzzy*—passion!—
mxyzptlk—"

At last, a burst of garbled pseudo-Greek came
through on the device, followed by a clear and unmistakable "Take me—I'm yours!" She then began, with the
apparent ferocity of a tigress in heat, to rend at my garments, which was all most exciting, until I fell panting
into her arms and at that precise instant, came eye to eye
with a particularly desiccated mummy. My priapic organ
shriveled in an instant, and Callipygia, eyes widening,
said, "Is it me?"

"No, it's—" I pointed.

"Ah, the sacred gods of the past," she said, nodding.
"Doubtless you're in such a transport of joy to see those
Divine Ones with whom you will soon be united that
you've been rendered temporarily incapable of performing the more prosaic functions to which your mortal flesh
yet condemns you." It was the clearest sentence the infernal device had ever translated, and it brought home to
me with the utmost clarity the fact that this was not the
kind of situation I would be able to get out of by telling a
few jokes. No, this was serious as all infernum. She was
importuning me again, lying down on the stone floor.
"You're not getting any younger," she said, "and if you
want a painless death, you'd better get this over with. I
haven't got all day."

"Painless?"

"Well, the priests do have the option of numbing you
before they kill you, using a potion made from the juice
of the coca leaf."

Aqua cococola! I would have gladly died for a sip of
that wonder drink. But then again, I was going to die
anyway. I thought about death. It was not entirely pleasant. I mean, I know that a good Roman patrician is supposed to welcome death, be able to fall on his sword at
the slightest disgrace, and so on, but that was the one
aspect of the upper classes that I had never quite managed to swallow. In any case, dying here, in an exotic
land, with no one to witness my glorious death except

for a few superstitious savages, was hardly my idea of a
proper death. If one must die, at least let it be a spectacle—let many members of one's social milieu be present
to remark on the nobility of one's bearing under pain; let
poets be present to serenade one and cosmetically con-
ceal one's dying groans; let it, in short, be appreciated by
those with the taste and education to appreciate dying
properly. Since this was not to be such a death, I re-
jected it. Not that I fear death, mind you—my upper lip
can be as stiff as the best of them—but I digress.

The purpose of the above is to show that I had come
to a kind of epiphanic moment. It was time to stop taking
all this lying down. I sprang up, started rewinding my
loincloth, and shouted "I shall fight to the death! Alea
jacta est! Delendi sunt Olmechii! Bonum est, haec die
mori! Moriturus te saluto! Vale, O Roma!" and various
other classical platitudes.

Callipygia jumped up in astonishment. "I haven't had
this job very long," she said, "but I've seen enough to
convince me that the gods must be crazy."

"Enough chatter, O wench!" I said. "I am returning to
Rome!"

"Good heavens! Am I about to witness some kind of
divine miracle?" she said, awestruck, staring at me with
the large round eyes of a lovesick puppy. "Ah, happy
me! I die fulfilled!" She pulled an obsidian knife from
what remained of her clothing and was about to plunge it
into her breast.

"What nonsense," I said, grabbing the knife and tossing it into the gaping maw of the nearest mummy. "Now,
how do I get out of here?"

"Are the orgies of Rome truly as decadent as you described them to me, Divine One?" she said.

"Yes, yes. Now leave me alone so I can battle those
guards out there to the death."

"Then take me with you! I've had enough of these
Olmechii. I'm not even a real Olmechian. I'm a member
of the Toltechii, captured and sold into slavery at birth."

"Olmechii, Toltechii . . . you all look alike." I pushed
her away from me. She put her hand out to steady her-

self and decapitated the nearest mummy. Its head scud-
ded across the floor, a necklace snapped, and we were
sprawling about on gold beads.

I watched the mummy's head bouncing about. Something about it was not quite right. I mean, mummies are
normally stiff as rocks—and suddenly I knew what the
matter was! This was not a real mummy's head at all. It
was—it was a fuel unit for a vessel of the ancient astronautiloi! What a spectacle! "Quick!" I said. "Are there
any—" I looked around, trying to find the bas-relief on
the wall that depicted the ancient astronautilos at his
console. "—any of *those* things anywhere around here?"

"Oh, *those* things. I think there's one behind that
mummy yonder," she said, pushing it out of the way.

There was just a wall there, and she said, "Funny, I
could have sworn that the last time I was here, the high
priests chanted something and—" The wall was covered
with familiar-looking inscriptions, including one in
Greek! I began steadily to recite those words, and the
room began to whirl about madly, and I knew that we
were being tesseracted into another dimension, and I
wondered whether it was just this room, or whether all
my friends—nay, the entire temple in which we were
incarcerated—were being tesseracted along with me.

CHAPTER
XV

DOUBLY DEIFIED

I T SOON BECAME APPARENT THAT I HAD BITTEN OFF A little more than I could chew. Not only was the entire room ablur, with mummies swirling madly as Callipygia clutched at me with fervent and ferocious ardor, but I could see that, down the hall, guards were running madly about, a high priest was vainly invoking some deity, and the murals and bas-reliefs were shifting in a wild frenzy of rainbow colors. And emergent from the kaleidoscopic madness was a control panel such as I had used to chart the Sphinx's course through space and to fire the energy catapultae at the ancient monuments that had attacked us!

"Let's get back to the throne room," I said to the priestess, "and see whether it is part of the astronautilic vessel, or whether we have been detached, podlike, from the temple matrix."

I took her by the hand, and we ran down corridors that seemed to melt as we passed them. Soon we found ourselves back at the desultory orgy, where Euphonius was holding forth about the Nature of the One to an assemblage of sacerdotes. Young Lupus Ferox was reclin-

117

ing on the floor, being alternately titillated and confused
by a pair of dancing girls. I shouted, "We're getting out
of here!" to the two of them.

"How?" Euphonius asked.

No sooner had he spoken than we felt the entire building tremble. All the natives fell instantly prostrate at my
feet. I shrugged. "About time," I said. "But don't just lie
there worshiping all day. You've made me your god, and
by god, there are going to be some changes around here.
You—" I pointed at one priest, who had these delicate
golden wires piercing his septum, which quivered as he
trembled before me, making him look like an overgrown
rabbit. "Go and fetch me some decent food: toucans'
tongues, armatillus gizzards, anything but human
hearts!" He got up, quaking, and went to obey, but
ended up walking smack into a wall, for the building had
shot up into the air!

"Come on, friends," I said, "let's find out how much
of this thing can fly." Lupus, Euphonius, and I went out
onto the parapet. Far from being stopped by the guards,
we were subjected to more bouts of cringing adoration.
When we looked out over the courtyard, we could see
that it, together with our Sphinx's head, had risen along
with the building. The parapet on which we stood was
rising at a more rapid rate than the rest of the courtyard;
it seemed to be set on metallic stilts, so that the palace
was both levitating and changing shape at the same time.
Soon we could see the entire city, which in fact was also
slowly rising into the sky. One could hear the surprised
cries of the citizens coming from every quarter. Men and
women were rushing out of buildings, pointing, shrieking; some were falling over the edge into the rapidly
shrinking sea of jungle below. It was an unmitigated
spectacle.

"I feel an ode coming on," Euphonius cried out as the
wind whipped at our faces. It was cold, and I was wearing only a loincloth. Fortunately, Callipygia had seen fit
to wrap her sultry form about me, generating a satisfying
heat from her person that put me in mind of my favorite
couch back at the villa in Rome. It was her proximity

that enabled me to endure the song of Euphonius without becoming airsick:

> *Aloft we hover, atop this topless tower,*
> *Above the clouds that o'er the crass clod glower;*
> *Mellifluous muses! Set my tongue aflame,*
> *That burning, it may not thy name defame!*
> *Set fire to my heart! Ignite my thighs!*
> *Make of my nose a tinderbox! Mine eyes*
> *Transform to glowing coals! My stomach stoke!*
> *Yeah, let my very anus belch forth smoke!*
> *For I do yearn to sing thee words of fire,*
> *And for that boon, would willingly expire.*

"I'm afraid he really will," Lupus Ferox said. "Have you seen how red in the face he's become?"

Indeed he had, for having selected the Lydian mode in which to sing this song, Euphonius had failed to allow for the fact that his voice could not quite reach the highest notes of that scale. Such a scale is more suitable for the eunuchs of Asia, who give up the joys of love in exchange for the more ethereal benefits of music. Euphonius, yearn though he did for those words of fire, had not seen fit to make the ultimate sacrifice, so his voice cracked at every climax, much like the sound of a cat being crushed under a Corinthian column.

"It serves him right," I said, "for trying to extend a metaphor for longer than two lines."

At that moment, Serpens Plumatus approached us. He was somewhat less dignified than he had first appeared, for his feathers were in disarray, and he glanced about him fearfully and eyed me as though I were almighty Jove and could strike him down with a thunderbolt whenever I wanted.

"Forgive us, O—" There followed the name of a god so long that I have not the wit to set it down. Indeed, after he uttered it, he looked sheepishly at the ground; I took it that this was one of those unmentionable gods, rather like the Judean god, which has neither name nor form. Now, unmentionable gods are always a lot more unpredictable than mentionable ones, so I was not surprised at his behavior. I gathered that they had originally captured me to take the place of one living god, only to discover that I was in fact another, more powerful one— as witness the fact that we were now suspended in midair and racing through the skies at an average velocity of over twenty mille passuum pro horam! I had been elevated from a mentionable to an unmentionable, and this had to mean that my word was now law—and none of the old rules applied.

Well, it was about time to make some new rules, and the first one I laid down was that I should have a decent meal served to me on the instant. "No more of this blasted human flesh. Not that it isn't exotic, but it does get a trifle monotonous, and the purpose of food is to entertain, not to bore. Now, peacocks' brains, if you can get them, but I suppose I'll have to settle for those of some other brightly colored bird," I demanded of the bewildered Serpens Plumatus, "and roast prime rib of boar—or its nearest local equivalent."

"The local equivalent of roast boar—that would undoubtedly be *longus porcus*," said the high priest, nudging and winking at another of his kind; I gathered that I did not really want to know what species of viand that might be.

"How can you worry about food," Euphonius said, "when we are soaring in the air in a flying city, like creatures from ancient mythology? Surely your mind should be on more elevated things."

"We're plummeting!" Lupus Ferox squealed.

He was right. The lower levels of the city were skirting the treetops. You could hear people screaming. Ahead, a dense rain forest stretched, and the air had changed from bracingly chilly to hot and humid.

"I'd better go and man the console," I said, and with the bard, the boy, the priestess, and old Serpens Plumatus trailing behind me, I hastened back inside. Soon we were once more within the whirling room of mummies. For some reason, Callipygia had gained the impression that we were going there for the purpose of

resuming that coitus that had perforce become inter-
ruptus.

"Whee! I know what to do!" Lupus said, for the room
had now transformed completely and was a cockpit similar to that of the Sphinx. He broke off a piece of the
nearest mummy and prepared to stoke the reactor, while
I busied myself trying to find whatever device it was that
would enable the windowlike apertures to appear before
us and afford us some view of what was going on below.

At last I managed to find the control for that. It was
disguised as the beak of a sculpture of a sacred bird—
and when I pulled, portions of the walls were replaced
by images of the world beneath. To the south, a mighty
river; to the north, more forest. There were also views of
the panic in the city.

"Miracle upon miracle," the high priest cried.

"Just the wonders of technology," I responded, and
the priest seemed much taken with my utterance, not
knowing whether to take it as a joke or as some incon-
struably godlike profundity.

At length, he responded with, "To you, such wonders
must indeed seem nothing out of the ordinary, but to
such as we—"

I raised my hand for him to stop. "Why don't you go
down and try to stop the panic in the city?" I said.
"That's what you should be doing, not standing around
gawking at miracles." For we had already lost several
members of the populace of the Olmechian city; not only
had many fallen off the edge of town, but I now saw,
through the magic of the image-projecting walls, that
many had pulled out obsidian knives and were voluntar-
ily immolating themselves. Whether they were doing so
to try to bring their city back down to earth or whether
they were simply so exhilarated at being airborne that
they no longer felt it necessary to go on living, I could
not tell, for these were by far the least scrutable natives I
had ever encountered in all my travels. "You must prevent those people from committing suicide," I said, "or
there'll be no one left in the city to serve me."

"Why? They know what they're doing," Serpens said,

"and if we run out of peasants, you can always create more."

It almost made me long for the homespun casuistries of encephalometry!

"Well," I said, "go and do *something*—you're making me nervous, hovering over me like this."

For in truth, now that we had an entire flying city at our disposal, I thought it best to have a private discussion with Euphonius and Lupus Ferox about how best to get on with our mission, which was, in case you have forgotten, to become reunited with Aquila and his merry geriatric warriors, rescue Equus Insanus from the Green Pig, and, of course, save the universe.

"There's nothing for me to do anymore," the high priest said, "now that you're here. I mean, my function as your mouthpiece has been rendered redundant by your graciously consenting to be incarnated amongst us mortals."

"Well, go and make dinner," I said.

"Very well," he said huffily, "though I don't see why you can't create it yourself."

"It's a test of your devotion," I temporized.

"Well, if you're going to put it like *that* . . ." he said, and departed, snapping his fingers so that the guards and sycophants who hung about his person went with him. Only the priestess Callipygia remained, but I thought it was safe to take her into our confidence, since she had already shown me how little she thought of her Olmechian overlords.

Lupus manned the secondary console—formerly some kind of sacrificial slab—while I sat in front of the main one. Euphonius was restringing his lyre and was therefore, luckily, too deep in concentration to try to help us navigate. I put Callipygia to work watching the image windows for anything dangerous: flocks of birds, mountain ranges, anything that might get in our way.

We had been in danger of crashing, but now the city seemed to steady itself.

Now, you may recall that Aquila and my other friends were last seen somewhere around the planet Mars, falling into some kind of nebulous force field. Obviously, my best bet was to try to go to Mars. I was not quite sure how to do that. Nevertheless, I remembered the levers for up, down, starboard, port and a few other simple controls. They did not seem too different here, even though some of them were shaped like terra-cotta phalloi, and one was in the shape of a turquoise death's-head. After all, the ancient astronautiloi had been attempting to make their structures seem to blend in with those of the local natives—camouflage is camouflage, as I always say when I am sneaking into the Temple of Hestia for a quickie disguised as a vestal virgin. I pushed the *up* button, which happened to be shaped like a jade were-jaguar.

Nothing happened.

I tried starboard.

The city shuddered a little, dipped for a second, and then ploughed on as though nothing had happened.

"The controls don't work," Lupus said ruefully.

"How exciting!" Euphonius said. "We're actually in the ineluctable hand of fate—nothing we do can avert its stern decrees!"

"Yet another platitude from the lips of Euphonius," I said, rolling my eyes.

"Of course it's a platitude! How else, except by clichés, is one to reach the lame intellect and minuscule brain of the common man? It's part of the subtextual framework of the new realism."

I ceased listening. Watching the jungle roll by, powerless to control the flying city in which I had accidentally become deified, I despaired of ever finding my friends again.

CHAPTER
XVI

THE SPHINX'S ARSE

FOR THREE LONG DAYS WE DRIFTED. SINCE I WAS now infallible, I did not dare let on that I had no idea what was going on. I merely informed the high priest that just as those who were daily sacrificing themselves in my honor knew what they were doing, I bloody well knew what *I* was doing, and he should just spend all his time preparing banquets and spectacles to amuse me.

So he did.

Meanwhile, in between bouts of tempestuous love-making with the fair Callipygia, I was endeavoring to form some kind of strategy. It was difficult, since I had only Lupus Ferox to rely on to make any kind of sense whatsoever; Euphonius, alas, had become so inspired by our celestial flight that he had thrown himself into the composition of his epic poem about Hercules cleaning the Augean stables. Daily, he would recite the latest tidbits for us as we sat at breakfast. Unfortunately, he was at work on Book XXXVII at the time, which consisted mostly of a long speech by Hercules, giving an exhaustive account of what appeared to be every single *hipposkaton* in the stables.

Now, even at the best of times I am not particularly partial to horseshit, but when individual feces are described to me over breakfast, with all sorts of rhetorical devices and fancy figures of speech, it is all a little hard to swallow. Even this *longus porcus*—whatever it was— that they were serving to us every day, delicious as it was, failed to entice my tongue.

On the third day, we passed the last of the mighty forests and began flying over terrain more similar to that of the Zona Arida; indeed, the more of it we covered, the more convinced was I that we were fast approaching the country of Hieronymous and his Apaxae, who had given me those samples of *fungus magicus* that had allowed me a fleeting contact with my half brother Equus Insanus.

This was breakfast on the third day:

Sitting on the couch, dining on a paté of the ears and livers of *longi porci*, having my feet gently massaged by the voluptuous Callipygia, talking to young Lupus Ferox while Euphonius intoned in a far corner of the chamber:

Of the eighth faex our hero saw that day—

The throne room, you will recall, abutted on a large veranda that overlooked the courtyard in which the one remaining stone head and our own Sphinx's head were parked; beyond, and past the limits of the flying city, one could see nothing but an endless desert. The terrain resembled nothing so much as the rocky deserts in the vicinity of Carthage or perhaps some of the more desolate areas of Judea. Strange rocky outcroppings and buttes and now and then a fuzzy green clump that might have been a cactus—that was about it.

I was relating to Lupus the whole story of how I thought I had had a meeting with Equus Insanus through the medium of the magic mushrooms. But I suddenly noticed that he was not paying attention to me anymore. He was looking way past all of us, at the distant scenery —he seemed transfixed.

"Lupus? Lupus?" I said. "Surely the odes of Euphonius have not caused you to turn to stone! I've little use for a petrified little boy on these adventures."

No answer. I waved a hand in front of his face; to my surprise, he brushed it away. "Quiet, I'm reading," he said.

I squinted. Then I saw what he was looking at—a narrow tendril of smoke, no fatter than a hair, projecting skyward from the top of a cliff in the middle distance.

"If this is what I think it is—" he said.

"Surely there's no telegraph in this Jove-forsaken place," I interrupted.

"Oh, but you're wrong, O Master Vinicius," he said. "Remember, it was the Terra Novans who invented the principle of smoke signals. You Romans merely applied the mysteries of high technology to it!"

"Well, what's it say?"

"It appears to say, 'Sphinx's arse to larboard,' sir."

"Is it some kind of joke?"

"I doubt it. For one thing, we are rapidly nearing the land of the Apaxae, and they are highly adept at the art of smoke signaling."

"But whom are they signaling to?" I said.

"I can't quite tell—us, maybe?"

"Come, come!" I said. "Surely there can't be any Sphinx's arse in the neighborhood." Then I realized what it might be. "Could it possibly—" Without another word, I ran from the throne room to the larboard veranda of the palace, leaving Euphonius singing to the servants.

And there it was! Not five hundred paces above us, the hindquarters of the Sphinx floated! They were somewhat the worse for wear—they had developed a few nicks and scratches, perhaps from passing meteors or something—but there they were, exuding a pale blue jet of propulsive smoke.

On the veranda, the high priest was already busy worshiping it, it seemed, for there was a kind of altar set up, with the half-burnt torso of a young woman upon it, beneath a statue of some kind of idol, and old Serpens Plumatus was raising up his arms and reciting a series of mystical formulae doubtless designed to propitiate the flying arse.

"What a relief!" I said. "It's another section of our very own Sphinx—and if the back end is here, the torso can't be far behind."

"Oh, no!" Lupus said. "That means that old scatter-brained chatterbox Aaye is going to be joining us soon!"

"Believe me," I said, "compared with these Olme-chian mystics, I welcome the old bugger." The smoke signals were still continuing in the distance. "Who's signaling, anyway? Can you find out?"

"I'll need smoke," said the boy.

"No problem," I said. "Not for nothing am I a god."

I stalked over to Serpens Plumatus. "Clear the altar of those superstitious sacrifices!" I said. "We have greater need of it now—in the interests of science!"

"Sacrifices?" Serpens said superciliously. "These aren't sacrifices. Why would I bother to sacrifice to a bit of airborne masonry when such things are a common-place in our land of ultimate technology?"

"Well, what were you doing?" I asked, for the female torso roasting in the flames jolly well looked like a human sacrifice to me.

"What you told me to do—cook breakfast."

It was thus that I discovered the identity of the longus porcus I had been devouring with such gusto. Without further ado, I raced over to the veranda wall and vomited over the side. There was a crowd of natives staring curiously at me. They did not scatter as I heaved but instead began to prostrate themselves in the direct line of fire, taking the contents of my bowels as a benedictive outpouring of the essence of my being—just another thing one has to put up with when one is a god, I suppose.

Serpens Plumatus quickly pulled me from the wall. "Are you quite all right?" he said. "I mean, Divine One, I'm sure the populace is very grateful for any small token of your love for them, but enough is enough." I think he was starting to suspect that I was neither omniscient nor omnipotent, but it was now politically expedient to keep up the fiction. After all, if *I* was not responsible for the city taking off, who was left?

I saw that Lupus Ferox was at what I had thought to be the altar but now knew to be a kind of barbeque. He was fanning the flames with a device of bright green plumes and controlling the smoke with a wet cloth he had fashioned from his own tunic. Olmechian priests looked on, mystified.

"Any luck?" I asked the boy. The Sphinx's arse was now nearer and looked as though it was going to land in the courtyard.

"I'll say!" he said. "The message is from our old friend Hieronymus. They've just concluded a treaty with the Anasazii, seceded from the Olmechian Empire, and he now has a job as an air flight controller, whatever that is."

"Perhaps Hieronymus will enlighten us—watch out!" For the Sphinx's arse was now very close to us indeed— no more than a cubit or two from the topmost turret of the palace—and I feared that some of the frieze-reliefs would be knocked off.

"If Hieronymus is supposed to keep us from colliding, he's not doing a very good job," Lupus said as the thing I feared occurred, and a gold and turquoise representation of a human skull fell off the roof and almost brained me.

We were now coming up to a kind of sandstone plateau, and it was my earnest hope that whatever force had us in its power would not allow us to crash into the side of the cliff. Between the Scylla of the cliff and the Charybdis of the Sphinx's arse, things were getting a little frightening. A short distance from the cliff, we were dramatically plucked into the air, and the flying hindquarters took a simultaneous dive toward us. I did not know whether to run or duck.

Then the arse landed in the courtyard right behind the Sphinx's head, leaving just enough room for the missing torso, and at the same time the flying city rose above the cliff, bringing a new landscape into view—one so astonishing that I was quite overcome by the spectacle of it.

Below us was a vast plain of surpassing smoothness. It looked as if the plateau had been blasted smooth by some divine force. Drawn on the face of the plateau was

a complex design of sandy ridges that seemed to repre-
sent some supernatural creature, not quite human and
not quite feline. I realized from Aquila's description of
the ancient astronautiloi that this must be an actual representation of a member of that eons-dead race. The design was huge enough to swallow two or three of the
seven hills of Rome, yet it was evident that it could only
be seen from the air, and therefore it had to have been
created by forces other than human. I could discern no
purpose for it.

There were so many questions I wanted to ask. Perhaps Hieronymus could answer them, for his column of
smoke still beckoned to us in the distance, from atop an
obelisklike butte. "Ask him what it is!" I said, turning to
Lupus Ferox, who had been manning the altar-cum-
stove that was now our makeshift telegraph pole. But he
was not there—indeed, I was all alone on the veranda.

I saw them all in the courtyard, clustered around the
Sphinx, of which we now had two-thirds. I ran to join
them. And there they were, wriggling out from the interdimensional interstices of the impenetrable rock: Aaye
the Egyptian and Abraham bar-David the Sasquatius!

On seeing me, the sasquatch said, "Shalom" and
made as though to crush me in his arms. Though I knew
this was but a token of his affection, it did not look that
way to the Olmechii, who immediately surrounded him,
waving spears and bows. Abraham turned and growled
at them; they slunk back. As they waited uneasily for the
visitors' next move, there came from within the throne
room the distant screeching of Euphonius, like the stri-
dulation of a swarm of hungry locusts:

"*O Zeus!*" quoth noble Hercules. "*I plead, I grovel
For thee to magically cleanse this hovel—
That I no longer needs this shit must shovel!*"

"Hmm," the megapus said. "Word order's a tad
strained, isn't it? I suppose that's what they call poetic
license."

"The golden voice of Euphonius!" Aaye exclaimed,

closing his eyes and almost fainting away with rapture. "How I have longed to hear him sing again. Through all our travails, I dreamed of nothing but this moment—indeed, the memory of his dulcet yet abrasive singing kept me from despairing totally during our lengthy sojourn in the vortex of despond."

"Where have you fellows been?" I said. "And where is Aquila?"

"He's not with you?" Aaye asked. "But your vessel and his and ours were all together only a minute ago!"

"A minute?" I said. "Some kind of minute that must have been! Why, in that minute, Euphonius and I have journeyed all over the incognite continents of Terra Nova—have feasted unknowingly on human flesh—have come near to getting ourselves sacrificed several times . . . and but a second ago you spoke of your lengthy sojourn within the vortex."

"Well," Aaye said. "It certainly felt like forever! Never again will I suffer the indignity of being transported in a Sphinx's arse!"

The sasquatch said, "While you were complaining, Aaye, I was reading the hieroglyphics on the walls, and I saw something that may explain this little paradox of duration. You see," he said, settling into the expository mode so beloved of academics and the writers of *scientificitiones,* interspersing his remarks with Latin phrases that he offhandedly glossed in Greek, "Aquila set the three segments of the *Sphinx* (or sphinx) to a homing device that should have allowed the segments to find one another—no matter where they were in space and time —and reunite. Unfortunately, the spatiotemporal anomaly into which we were sucked caused us to be flung about at speeds close to the *celeritas lucis* (that is to say, the speed of light) and the resultant retardation of the *flux temporis* (id est, the flow of time)—as a result of which we are all going to arrive at the same *locus*, but at *tempora* different relative to one another."

"What?" I said.

"I don't understand it myself," the Sasquatius said, "but it does sound awfully good, doesn't it? I think it means that Aquila might turn up at any time—but it could be a millennium hence—so we'd best to try to save the universe without waiting for him."

Quickly I explained to the newcomers what had transpired in their absence; the two academics were particularly interested in the fungi magici, and I assured them that I still had plenty of them lying around. "Perhaps," I said, "we can all get together this evening, partake of the fungi, and all commune with Equus Insanus."

At that moment, Lupus Ferox called out to us. He had been watching the smoke signals with care. He was jumping up and down. "We'll be landing soon," he said. "Those ridges down there are a landing strip, according to the signals."

"But who is controlling us?" I asked, for I still resented the fact that we could not get the city to go where we pleased.

"I don't know, but the signal says something about 'remote autopilot,' whatever that is. I'd best go put on some makeup. If we're to meet important aliens, I don't want them to think I'm just a kid." And Lupus dashed off to put on his war paint.

We were getting closer and closer to the ground. As we descended toward the ridges that were laid out in stylized images of starfaring sphinxes, I saw that the surface of the plateau was covered with Olmechian heads, pyramids, and ziggurats, all parked in neat rows. In the midst of all this was the Great Pyramid of Cheops itself —and my heart fairly leapt into my mouth at the sight, for I had last seen my half brother and occasional friend vanish into that very pyramid!

Far from having to seek out Equus Insanus, we were being ineluctably drawn toward him! I sputtered, I trembled with impatience. Soon we would meet Equus Insanus—soon, perhaps, we would be forced to confront the Green Pig and his minions. In the meantime, I had to deal with Serpens Plumatus, who was on his knees, gibbering away in Nahvatish.

"So you see, old chap," I said, "I have restored all

your flying heads to you—and a good many more besides."

"I see, your Divinity, but when can we take them, and our city, home?"

"In due course," I said, waving my hand in the languidly imperious manner I had seen my uncle Trajan use so effectively so often.

In the midst of all this excitement, I suddenly felt an unwonted tranquility in the air, a quality of serenity that struck me as strange until I realized that it was only because Euphonius had stopped singing. In fact, he was shouting to us from the throne room. I went to see what the matter was, clutching the very perplexed Callipygia by the hand.

When we got there, he was jumping up and down and pointing at the starboard side of the city. "It's our friend the Sasquatius!" he was screaming. "He's returning to us—he's trying to climb aboard the city!"

"Nonsense," I said. "Abraham and Aaye have arrived and are already with us." I indicated the sasquatch and the Egyptian, who were standing right behind me.

Euphonius saw Abraham bar-David and did a double take so dramatic that he got his head stuck between the strings of his lyre. "But you've shrunk!" he said.

The city suddenly began to shake. Thinking it was an earthquake, I dived for cover under the nearest couch. The others all had the same idea. The entire building shifted to an angle, and the couch began sliding out toward the starboard veranda. Aaye was shivering and mumbling about how his father had been buried under a heap of rubble in Pompeii. "And we didn't even have time to mummify him," he moaned.

"This can't be an earthquake," I said. "We haven't landed yet."

Nevertheless, the couch, with me and the Egyptian under it and the Sasquatius perched on top, was still rolling inexorably toward the edge of the veranda—until it lurched to an abrupt stop against something big and furry.

I heard people screaming from somewhere beneath

us, the kind of elemental mass scream of terror that you might hear from, say, a crowd of criminals about to be devoured by lions. It was with some amazement that I saw that the couch had been stopped by what appeared to be a hand, except that that hand was approximately the size of one of the Uncle Trajan's treasury vaults and was covered with dark brown fur.

The couch was lifted into the air, exposing us to the full gaze of the creature to whom the hand belonged. It did indeed appear to be a Sasquatius, except that it was about the size of the Sphinx. Although we were still a few cubits short of landing in the pyramidal parking lot, we had been stopped in midflight, and this giant ape was attempting to climb into the city, using the veranda of the palace as a handhold.

Panicking, I looked around. There was Serpens Plumatus the high priest. I called to him, but instead of responding he fell dead onto the flagstones.

"Good heavens," I said. "He seems to have committed suicide." An obsidian knife protruded from the breast of the hapless priest, and one of his assistants was nonchalantly engaged in plucking out his heart and proffering it to the giant ape, who did not seem very interested.

"It was the least he could do," Callipygia said disdainfully. "He was due to get sacrificed days ago. What a hypocrite! The gods are clearly not amused. That's why they've sent the giant ape."

"What a fascinating creature," Aaye said. "Since I have discovered it, I demand the privilege of naming it. What about 'gigapithecus'—videlicet, 'giant ape'?"

Abraham bar-David had been staring at the creature for some time. Suddenly he gave a bellow of recognition and began shouting. "By the Tetragrammaton! By the Unspeakable and Unutterable Sacred Name of the Singular Deity!" It was the worst profanity I had ever heard from his lips.

"Why, what's the matter?" I asked him, for he looked as though he were about to explode with joy, which seemed an inappropriate sort of emotion, to say the least.

"That creature—though he's grown somewhat since I saw him last—happens to be my long-lost cousin Joshua, stolen by brigands from his mother's side when he was but three years old!" The Sasquatius then proceeded to regale the giant ape in Aramaic.

The creature looked at Abraham in disbelief. With his free hand he scratched his head. Then he started scratching with his other hand.

In the process, he let go of the flying city, and we finally landed—none too smoothly, for one of the outlying streets was impaled by an obelisk that happened to be parked in the wrong space.

CHAPTER
XVII

GIGAPITHECUS

I F FLYING AROUND IN SPHINXES AND EATING LONGUS porcus in levitating palaces and being constantly on the verge of having oneself sacrificed was not excitement enough, being shaken out of one's dwelling place by a giant ape was a spectacle without equal. I felt like one of the knucklebones that soldiers use for dice as the entire city crashed onto the plateau, doubtless crushing to death any armatilli in its path.

We all slid—for we had all been clinging to the same couch—to the far edge of the veranda. Joshua bar-Joseph (for that was the name of Abraham's enormous cousin) sat down beside us, in the process flattening some huts and, presumably, their inhabitants. We attempted to converse with him, but his ears were too far away to hear much until he actually crouched down and placed one ear to the flagstones of the courtyard. His ear was not a pretty sight, for we spotted, hidden among the forest of hairs, tics and lice the size of puppies. Though he was not someone one would normally invite to dinner, I reflected that he was, after all, Abraham's relative, and thus must be treated with a modicum of courtesy, even if his breath could knock a vulturem de vehiculo merdae.

"My, how you've grown," Abraham said. He spoke Aramaic, but Aaye the Egyptian was kind enough to act as interpreter amid all this, else the conversation of the two Sasquatii would have sounded like the morning sickness of recalcitrant she-camels.

"It's not my fault I've turned into a giant ape," Joshua said, and launched into the ensuing pathos-ridden expository lump. I shall omit the particulars of his birth and lineage and dive straight in in medias res.

"When you last saw me, O my cousin, I was a blithe young infant, happy and innocent, doing nothing each day but sleeping and eating salmon that my dear mother pulped for me. I little knew the wicked fate that awaited me! For—as you know—I was abducted by members of the Quaquiutii, who traded me by potlatch to a tribe of Tlingitii, who passed me on to a village of Nutcae, who sold me to some Esquimoi traders as a slave."

"You must forgive my cousin," Abraham whispered to me. "It seems to have been a long time since he spoke his native tongue, and he's trying to get as much in as he can."

Joshua shifted his buttocks, doubtless squashing a few more peasants, for we heard a strangulated gurgling coming from his nether regions that did not sound quite like the kinds of things one usually hears from that region of the anatomy. "At length, I was taken into captivity by a certain Green Pig, who called himself Viridiporcus Rex."

A collective gasp escaped the throats of all who had encountered this nemesis in previous adventures; those who had not stared, baffled, at those who had.

"The Pig did not treat me very well. He kept me in a cage, in a menagerie along with divers prodigies of nature, both natural and artificial: on the one hand dinosauria and obscure flora, and on the other chimaeras, minotaurs, and hippopters. At length, there came a day when some struggle was taking place. A shattering spectacle, for the Green Pig was most agitated, and we could hear battles raging everywhere in our citadel—and it was whispered among us creatures in the menagerie that the end of the universe was at hand. And so it was that the Pig disappeared from the palace, everything stopped working, and all was in disarray. We were all wandering wildly about the grounds of the citadel, waiting for something to happen. A cerberus, one of Viridiporcus's genetic experiments, was something of a visionary, and he told us that a Lacotian prince in shining armor would come and liberate all of us from our captivity—a story not unlike that of the *kwisatz haderach* in which I, as a proper member of the Lost Tribes of Israel, have been taught to believe since childhood. And indeed such a prince did appear—one Equus Insanus—riding to the rescue from the distant east. Not every detail of the cerberus's vision was true—for example, Equus wasn't riding a white horse but an appalusa—but it was close enough to inspire us all with profound spiritual feeling, and we were convinced that Equus Insanus was the Messiah. Unfortunately, our hero worship seemed to have gone to his head. For in the months that followed, Equus Insanus began to act increasingly as though his mind were divided in two, the second mind being not dissimilar from that of the departed Green Pig! And as the second mind began to possess him more and more, he began to indulge in bizarre experiments . . ."

"Aiieee!" said Aaye. "His soul has been taken over by an alternate intelligence—his *ka* and *ba* are in woeful jeopardy!"

"But how did you come to be a giant ape?" Lupus Ferox asked. I had been meaning to ask myself, but I did not want to be thought rude. After all, it is not nice to make fun of people because of their size.

"Alas, that happened only the other day, when I accidentally fell into a device that Equus Insanus is perfecting—a device designed to shrink or expand objects to any size."

"And where is Equus now?" I asked, for I feared to think what could have befallen him.

"He has set up his quarters in a city of the Anasazii—an urbs hollowed out of the living cliff face, right beneath this pyramid landing pad on which we now stand," the gigapithecus said. "O my friends, if you could but rescue the size-changing device and return me to my normal shape—I feel so awkward!"

"Well, I suppose it's labyrinth-crawling time again, isn't it?" I said, remembering our previous adventure with the minotaur.

He shifted his arse again, knocking a small temple of some Olmec deity into its moat and causing the deaths of more Olmechian innocents. "And I feel so guilty about killing all these people, for I am a gentle, compassionate creature who wouldn't so much as hurt a fly," he added as he scratched at a louse in his ear. It landed at our feet, and I saw that it was about the dimensions of a good-sized chicken and that its meat did not look half-bad— with the texture of lobster.

"Dinner!" I said, and we all concurred that a giant louse, roasted over charcoal, would probably constitute a tastier meal than the longus porcus we had been sub-jected to these past few days.

At that moment, we noticed that Serpens Plumatus, the high priest, was with us once more—only it was not quite him.

"But you're dead!" I said. "And you smell awful."

Well, it was not exactly Serpens Plumatus, and when he opened his mouth to respond, his lips sort of *slipped* and there was a lot of blood.

"Eek!" said Euphonius.

Suddenly I remembered the fate that was to have awaited me, the particular great honor that had been re-served for me when they were about to sacrifice me—to be flayed alive and to have my skin worn by the high priest.

"Anything wrong?" the priest who was wearing Ser-pens Plumatus's skin asked. "You look like you've just seen a ghost."

I could not quite meet his eyes. It was all very well to contemplate the barbaric customs of the natives when reading them in battered old one-denarius thriller papyri, but it was quite different being confronted with the real thing. Indeed, it was Lupus Ferox who saved the day by exclaiming, with profound admiration, "How bravely the old priest slew himself, O new high priest! And how snugly the skin fits! You will be wearing it for a while?"

"Oh, until it rots off," the high priest said, shrugging.

"Let's eat," I said, indicating the giant louse. "I feel like insect flesh tonight."

The high priest looked at us glumly. "But so many people have been standing in line for days for the sublime honor of feeding your august divinities," he said. "How can their souls attain the proper level of enlightenment if they are not slain in the supreme sacrifice of their flesh for the feeding of the gods?"

"I'm hungry, too," Joshua bar-Joseph said, "and the pickings have been pretty slim these past few days."

A glint came into Serpens Plumatus's eye. "Are you a god?" he asked. "If there were some way to call you a god, perhaps you could see your way to giving these poor souls their chance at paradise."

"Well," the giant Sasquatius said, "I could crack 'em in my teeth and—"

The high priest's eyes lit up. "Alive?" he asked.

"If you want."

"Is it very, very painful?" the high priest asked, wringing his hands in glee and jumping up and down.

"I imagine so," the gigapithecus said.

"Done! For it is only by offering their pain that we mortals can properly be assured of our place within the eternal sun disk," the priest said, and turned to give instructions to his underlings to have the sacrificial victims brought hither. As the gigapithecus deloused himself and the high priest led the giant insects away to be roasted on a spit, a makeshift staircase was built on a wooden frame that resembled one of the Olmechian pyramids, and the citizens lined up to be eaten, their arms spread wide in adoration, singing mystical chants as they entered the crunching maw of Abraham's cousin.

"It's none too kosher," Abraham said, wrinkling his nose in disgust as his cousin spit out a few bones, "but in this world of increasingly secular Hellenism, I suppose it's all right." The bones landed all around us. Lupus Ferox was particularly impressed by the gigapithecus's voracious appetite and almost did not get to eat any of his louse liver paté.

"What a spectacle!" I said. "This is better than the lions in the circus! Although, of course, these victims are all too willing, which tends to ruin the fun a bit."

"They're very brave," Lupus said with profound admiration, for the ability to endure unspeakable pain is a prized trait among the Lacotii. "I only hope I can learn to die that well."

I, for one, preferred to contemplate my roast leg of louse.

CHAPTER
XVIII

THE PYRAMID PARKING LOT

OUR FIRST GOAL, OF COURSE, WAS TO RETRIEVE the device that had caused Joshua's unfortunate condition. "Find the shrinking ray," he said, "and I'll—"

"Shrinking?" Abraham asked. "Didn't you say it was designed to shrink or expand?"

"I think it's *supposed* to be a shrinking ray," Joshua said, "but I somehow had the wrong end pointed at me. I surmise this from all the miniaturized cities he had in bottles."

"Cities?" I said, astonished.

"Yes—Jerusalem, Alexandria, Tachyopolis—"

"But we were just *in* Alexandria," I said.

"I fear that you will find it changed next time you visit it," Joshua said. "Right now it's about the size of a camel's hump."

"O horror!" Euphonius said. "Perhaps Rome, queen of cities, is next; perhaps our beloved eternal city is even now being reduced to the size of an amphora of wine!"

"Bah," Lupus Ferox said. "No one in Rome would even notice—there's just too much spectacle in the air as it is."

"It does lend a certain urgency to our situation, doesn't it?" I said. I could not quite figure out why Equus would want to turn Rome into an ant farm, but on the other hand, he was a Lacotian, and all Lacotians are crazy; then again, maybe he was just rebelling against all the civilizing he had had to suffer under Papinian and the lash-happy Androcles.

Then, Joshua promised us, he would be able to show us the way to Equus Insanus himself, and we would find out whether he had somehow become possessed by the soul of Viridiporcus Rex—whether, indeed, there was anything left to rescue.

"We can't all invade the stone city of the Anasazii," I said. "That would cause a ruckus, and we wouldn't get far. How many are we up against?" I asked the gigapithecus.

"Well, he's managed to control the minds of the Anasazii in much the same way that you've managed to conquer the Olmechii—the old 'superior beings from the sky' trick—we've all done it. But there are some Anasazii who don't believe that Equus Insanus is the incarnation of the great spirit; rather, they think he is a manifestation of some trickster deity and, as such, not to be believed in."

Sort of like a used-chariot salesman, I thought. "But we've been sitting here for several hours," I said, "and we haven't attracted anyone's attention. Isn't that a little bizarre? I mean, it's not every day that a flying city lands in one's neighborhood. And what of Hieronymus and his Apaxae? Whom are they working for?" For it was hard to imagine the fearsome old man taking a retirement job as what amounted to a lighthouse keeper.

"Alas," said the gigapithecus, "poor Hieronymus and his band have been reduced to abject slavery. Though they formed an alliance with the Anasazii for the purpose of defeating the Olmechii, the Anasazii turned on them and chained them to the butte, where they do nothing all day but send smoke signals to tell pyramids where to land; the Anasazii themselves have taken the cushier jobs of pyramid pilots and fly about the entire continent doing the bidding of Equus Insanus—leveling mountains, terrorizing villages, all that sort of thing."

"Heavens," I said. "But that's the job of the Romans. I mean, hasn't the Pax Romana been in effect long enough?"

"I'm afraid the Anasazii don't see it quite that way," Joshua bar-Joseph said ruefully, spitting out a human skull that he had skillfully cracked between his teeth so as to suck out the brain.

Dinner was continuing apace, and the temple girls, emboldened by the fact that we were now on terra firma of sorts, were dancing up a storm, hips thrusting, eyes ogling, waving wands tipped with the plumes of jungle birds. The one thing I did not terribly enjoy was the odoriferous attendance of Serpens Plumatus—for the new high priest insisted on being called by that name, the title being hereditary—and the occasional whiff of him was enough to put me off my food. Nevertheless, the dancing girls were not bad, though a tad bony by Roman standards, and my goddess-consort was massaging me as I ate and popping tidbits into my mouth, which did much to mitigate Euphonius's performance of his Herculean saga.

It occurred to me that we were making quite a racket and that nobody had noticed—I was a little surprised that we were not already being attacked from all sides. In fact, although the plain on which we had landed was crowded with spaceships-cum-monuments, there was not a peep to be heard from a single native save our own.

"That," the gigapithecus said, "is because most of them are out on a raid at this very moment, a mushroom-gathering raid."

"Mushrooms—!" we all said at once.

"Don't ask me to fathom the mind of Equus Insanus," he said. "But I know they plan to be gone for some days. They go off mushroom hunting every few moons; they've got a thing for them, and everything comes to a standstill until the quota is met."

* * *

We decided to take advantage of their absence to attempt to liberate the Apaxae. Of course, having the gigapithecus traipse around in our wake was hardly
conducive to the element of surprise, so beloved of the
divine Julius Caesar; it was agreed that he, the Olmechian high priests, the Egyptian mage, the sasquatch academic, and the fair Callipygia should remain behind.
Our party, then, was to have consisted only of Lupus
Ferox and myself, except that Euphonius refused to be
excluded.

"The divine Nero," Euphonius said, "was a dreadful
poet because, from his godly height, he never deigned to
taste real danger, nor did he choose to dwell among the
abject offal of the lowly—as I, in my compassion, have
done."

"But you're a dreadful poet, too," I said.

"I listen to your remarks with the humility proper to
one nobly called," he said. "I know you do not yet per-
ceive the light, else you would know that the so-called
dreadful aspects of my verse—the failed rhymes, the
bathetic climaxes, the overblown and inappropriate met-
aphors—are all part of my cunning ploy to imitate the
rhythms, the colors, the intensity of life itself."

"Hear, hear!" Aaye said, deeply moved.

"Yeah! 'Tis true that Vergil was content to sing of
arms and the man; well, I want to sing about sausage
vendors and sewage collectors, of prostitutes and politi-
cans, of fleas and flatulence—in short, of the common
man. *That* is the creature to whom these trite clichés are
addressed, not the aesthete in his chryselephantine
tower!"

"Common man, my arse!" I said. "Fat lot of good it
does to the common man when you use words like
'chryselephantine'!"

"Oops! Sorry." He looked around nervously, cleared
his throat, and launched into a second tirade. "All I
meant to say is that in order to sing of terror and degra-
dation, I must experience it—therefore, I *must* come
with you if I am to preserve my artistic integrity."

"Well, if you put it that way," I said, reluctant to

waste any more time, for it was getting toward evening, and at this rate we would not be able to rescue the Apaxae before nightfall.

We began walking toward the butte across the plateau littered with pyramids. The landscape was desolate, void even of the cacti that bloomed, in a desultory fashion, on the plain below. But to my amazement Euphonius did not complain much. I realized that despite his wretched lack of accomplishment, he was actually fairly serious about his craft, and he was willing to suffer gratia artis.

I moved with care, staying within the shadows of monuments wherever I could, remembering the lessons I had learned from Equus Insanus in the forests of Lacotia. I crouched, I darted, I thought myself into the body of a forest creature, for these rows of pyramids seemed indeed to be like particular unshapely trees, and I could, with some difficulty, imagine us being enveloped in the darkness of the forests of the Montes Negri. I saw that Lupus, too, was attempting to assume the spirit of a forest animal. But he had been a slave too long and was too long civilized; to my surprise, I had a lot to teach him about his own native ways. "Bend your body to the shapes of nature," I said as we ran, and I attempted to make use of what Equus Insanus had taught me. A Terra Novan could become invisible whenever he wanted; that was one of the reasons the empire had had so much trouble conquering them.

The ground was rocky; my moccasinae had long been worn to ribbons, and the sharp stones chafed my feet. I tried to imagine them sinking into the moist soil of the prairies. The memories came flooding back, more and more vivid. As I ran, I was shedding civilization as a snake sheds its skin. Lupus ran behind me, his footsteps in my footsteps' shadows. He was starting to keep up, falling into the rhythm of our running. Euphonius did not sing at all; he needed all his breath just to keep going.

In the distance, the pillar of smoke rose. Lupus said, "He's not saying much right now—probably because there aren't any flying things in the sky to talk to."

"Why is he saying anything at all?" I asked.

"It's the 'stand by, ready to broadcast' signal," Lupus Ferox said.

Luckily, we did not have to climb the butte at all. There was a sort of basket, similar to those of hot-air balloons. At ground level, there was a device of cogs, wheels, and whistles, all operated by a steam engine, which was kept alive by a couple of slaves; this sent the basket up and down by a system of pulleys.

"You take the one on the left," I told Lupus, "and I'll take the pug-nosed one."

The lad grinned. At last he was going to get to count coup properly! Then we sneaked up on the slaves in suitably Lacotian style, quite silently, using Euphonius as a diversion. The slaves were Anasazii and, having lived in cities hewn from rock instead of the forests of Lacotia, were relatively easy to sneak up on. I bonked mine on the head with a rock, and Lupus used my victim to trip his.

"Oh, *skatá*! Didn't bring my scalping knife," he said.

"We'll take the scalping as read," I said, "as long as we get out of this mess alive."

We climbed into the elevator. Presently we reached the platform at the peak, and we gazed down into a shallow depression in which sat Hieronymus and several members of his tribe, tending the flames of a telegraph machine.

"Look at them!" Lupus said.

"They don't seem terribly happy," Euphonius commented, the litotes falling from his lips with enviable naturalness. For the Apaxae were chained to posts, the chains having about ten paces of play, which allowed them to reach bowls of food, an eliminating trench, and the tools of their telegraphy.

We crept up closer, but the Apaxae did not even seem to notice us. Indeed, they did not appear entirely conscious.

"Hieronymus!" I whispered, crouching behind the old

man as he fed himself from a terra-cotta bowl of corn mush.

He looked dazed; his eyes were like glass pebbles, and he stared straight forward. He did not lift a hand in greeting. His breathing was a continual wheeze; indeed, he seemed so far removed from the lean, eagle-eyed man I had encountered previously that I thought he must have caught some deathly illness.

I looked around at the other Apaxae; they, too, stared ahead with glazed eyes.

"Yoohoo!" I said. No response.

I glanced at Lupus Ferox, who was trying to rouse one of them by tickling his feet with a feather from his hair. "Not a peep," he said.

"Let's go for the secret weapon," I said. "Euphonius, give 'em a few stanzas, will you? Something that'll *really* wake them up."

Euphonius cleared his throat. "I shall perform the call to arms from my historical epic, *The Caliguline Grain Riots*. He then launched into the ensuing strophe:

> *Then Caesar spake: "They haven't paid their*
> *taxes!*
> *'Tis time, my men, to hone your lethal axes!*
> *Awake, Praetorian guards! 'Tis time to crush*
> *Those foul, fell, filthy peasants into mush!*
> *Stampede their huts! Ravish their cattle! Burn*
> *Their women's flabby flesh from stem to stern!*
> *Cut off their heads! Yank out that stuff that passes*
> *For genuine brains amongst the lower classes!*
> *Yeah, crack their skulls like eggshells; nay, impale*
> *Them on our spears; ah, torture them in jail*
> *Ere they are summarily to lions thrown,*
> *That they may have their flesh gnawed to the*
> *bone."*

The Apaxae stirred a little, though Hieronymus's face was still buried in his bowl of corn mush.

"Rejoice, O Hieronymus!" I said. "We have come to rescue you!"

At last he looked up at me, his eyes full of pathetic, intolerable longing. "Vinicius?" he asked, as though he had seen a ghost.

"Yes, yes, we're going to cut your chains and free you."

He considered for a long time, then asked at last, "Do you have any magic mushrooms?"

CHAPTER
XIX

IN THE HALLS OF THE ANASAZII

LUPUS FEROX SAID, "THAT EXPLAINS EVERYTHING,
Master Vinicius! These poor Apaxae are suffering
from mushroom withdrawal!"

I looked from one Apaxa to the next. Each looked so
listless, so devoid of any desire to live, that I was surprised they had not all sung their death songs and faded
quietly into the desert sands.

"The fungi magici..." I said. "They have some undesirable side effects?"

"I'll say," the boy said. "Haven't you ever seen some
old Terra Novan derelict in the streets of Rome, withered
and impotent, holding his hand out for a brass *as* so he
can go buy a mouthful of vinum? Well, these fungi magici must be just as addictive as your Roman *mniwakan*."
He used the Lacotian term for intoxicating beverages,
and well I knew that a stoup of wine had been the down-
fall of many a stouthearted Lacotian brave. I could well
believe that one could become addicted to the vision-
inducing mushroom—why, I had seen the same happen
with those who overindulged in aqua cocacola. If you're
not careful, the temporary *altus* can get shorter and

149

shorter, and the depression longer and longer, until you're selling your slaves, your villas, your children, and your wife to support your habit. Not that I'm not careful, understand. But there are those who are not averse to enticing others to destroy their brains, the better to be divested of their worldly possessions. Indeed, my uncle the emperor himself has employed such a strategem of carefully controlled temptation—a "just say yes" policy —that last year netted him seven latifundia, four villas, and a silver mine in Attica. So I knew exactly what Lupus meant when he said that Hieronymus was suffering from withdrawal—and I knew, also, that whoever had managed to hold the fearsome Apaxae in thrall must have tricked them into a state of addiction to the fungi magici. Now I had an inkling of why Equus Insanus and his cohorts would be off on a quest for mushrooms.

Desperately, I shook Hieronymus by the shoulders. "Don't you remember me, old friend? I almost got scalped by you."

"Scalped?" He blinked rapidly, then closed his eyes and remained motionless for several minutes. I could barely tell he was alive.

"He's not going to be very coherent," Lupus said, "unless you can somehow give him a fix—"

"Fix?"

"You know—tether his camel, stridulate his cricket, dissemble his jowls," Lupus said, using some prime samples of slum slang such as had never been uttered in the presence of a patrician such as myself. I got his drift, however, and I remembered that I still had a fair quantity of the magic mushrooms Hieronymus himself had given me.

I rooted about until I found a piece of one, stuck in a fold of my tunica. I pulled it out, whereupon Hieronymus immediately went into a frenzy, rolling his eyes, frothing at the mouth, and generally flapping about. His compatriots, too, were all edging closer, glaring at one another, snarling—a pack of dogs, and me the only bone! Quickly, I popped the fungus into Hieronymus's mouth, and he slowly began to calm down. At length he recognized me and greeted me. "Ah, you're the fellow whose life I saved," he said.

"And I am about to save yours, O Hieronymus, so try to stay sane for a few moments while we try to break you loose of these chains!"

"But I can't leave my station—my duty—or else I won't get any more mushrooms."

"We've far more important work to do! You have to help me steal the shrinking ray from the secret hideout of Equus Insanus before they all return, so we can get Joshua bar-Joseph down to his proper size, get Rome out of its bottle, and bring the Green Pig to the Dimensional Patrol!"

"That's got to be the silliest speech I've ever heard," Hieronymus said. "But you gave me mushrooms—and, for all I know, you may have many more, so—" He yawned. "—I guess I'll help you."

Lupus and Euphonius were hacking away at the chains, and presently we managed to free Hieronymus from his bonds. Luckily, these were not strong fetters such as can be found in any decent Roman dungeon—nay, rather, they were makeshift devices, for the Anasazii know little of metallurgy and their master had not trifled to instruct them, relying instead on the power of drugs to keep the Apaxae under control.

At length, we had ourselves a small army of emaciated, dissipated-looking natives. I did not want to run out of mushrooms—I only had a couple on me and a small cache back at the Olmechian city—but I managed to break one fungus into a dozen little pieces, and we contrived to revive the Apaxae enough to get a bit of the old fight into them.

"Rape! Kill! Slaughter!" they were all shouting as they prepared to perform one of those interminable war dances, pounding on a drum with a human thighbone that happened to be lying in the debris of their smoke-producing apparatus.

"Enough!" I said hastily, fearful that the mushrooms would wear off before they ran out of steam.

* * *

"Now," the gigapithecus said after we arrived safely back in the flying citadel and were once more partaking of a splendid feast of giant lice, "before I can lead you to the lair of the Evil One himself, you must first find the shrinking ray. There is, within the city of the Anasazii, a certain warehouse where Equus Insanus dumps the detritus of his failed scientific experiments..."

This was how we found ourselves—that is to say, Lupus, Euphonius, myself, and Hieronymus—disguised as natives, attempting to infiltrate the stone city built into the side of the cliff. Luckily, the Anasazii mode of dress consists mostly of wrapping huge blankets around oneself, so that my most un–Terra Novan countenance could not be seen very well. We were armed with nothing but a few obsidian daggers borrowed from the high priest; indeed, I was not at all certain that it was a good idea for four people to try to invade a whole city, and was not terribly amused when Lupus Ferox and Hieronymus both sat around singing their death songs before we climbed the stone steps that led to its portals.

The city resembled nothing so much as one of the insulae in the slums of Rome, where thousands of assorted riffraff are crammed, dozens to a room, in apartments that are stacked one on top of the other so flimsily that the shit from each dwelling drops easily onto the heads of those in the dwelling beneath... or so I've heard, for I would not be seen dead in a place like that.

None of us could speak the local language, which resembles to some extent the Nahvatish of the southern climes; even Hieronymus had but a nodding acquaintance with it. Our cover story was that we were visitors from the northern Great Plains, desirous of obtaining examples of the famed Anasazian pottery. Luckily, all the locals had a smattering of the Terra Novan sign language, which, though properly only a lingua franca among those who inhabit the plains, had begun to spread southward beyond the borders of the Imperium Romanum.

How impressive the city was! Chamber upon chamber, hollowed out of living rock; some chambers

were private houses, others were meeting places, and
still others appeared to be mercantile establishments.
The similarity to Roman slum dwellings was more and
more uncanny. I caught a glimpse of potters at work,
fashioning their wares from long strands of rolled clay,
for the potter's wheel was not known to them.

"How ironic," Euphonius said, "that we should be
pretending to be impressed by these miserable pots when
back home we would be drinking from red and white
wine kraters, finely painted with bucolic, sacred, or
erotic scenes..."

We were not noticed by many people. And indeed, we
were far from an exotic sight, for here and there among
the natives were some very strange beings indeed. I
spotted a minotaur, perhaps the very one Equus and I
had fought in our last adventure. He did not look terribly
bellicose, though; he was wearing a headband and a
woven blanket and was dozing in a corner, leaning
against the rock face. In one of the pottery shops, I saw
what appeared to a mermaid, sitting in a trough of water;
she was fashioning a large water jug with her hands,
while her tail, protruding from the other end of the
trough, was painting another pot with a stick dipped in
some yellow pigment.

"These must be some of the chimaeras that were liberated from Viridiporcus's menagerie," I whispered to
Lupus, who was staring at some young women who appeared to be doing some kind of ritual corn-husking
dance. Although a three-headed cerberus was dancing alongside them, none seemed to think it was anything out of the ordinary.

Nor did any of them seemed particularly spirited; indeed, all the natives we had encountered looked very much
out of sorts. I surmised that they were all, by and large,
being kept in line by their dependence on mushrooms.

Hieronymus led us to a network of uninhabited passageways lined with desiccated corpses. I could not tell
if this was an actual catacomb, such as are used in Rome
for entombing the lower classes, or whether it was actually some kind of refueling station for pyramids. We

crept along the tunnel until it widened and turned into an enormous chamber. It was piled high with junk of every description—indeed, most of it beggared description. There were devices with flashing lights, levers, and switches, including a battered model of the spatiotemporal bewilderizer which the Green Pig had originally used to enter our continuum. On a table stood rows of bottles, most of them empty, bearing labels in Greek or Latin such as:

HERCVLANÆVM
ΜΥΚΗΝΑΙ
ΒΥΖΑΝΤΙΟΝ
ΘΗΒΑΙ
ΚΑΝΣΑΠΟΛΙΣ

and the names of various other cities of the Roman Empire.

A few of the bottles seemed to contain a kind of sediment at the bottom, but it was Lupus who, scrutinizing them closely, first noticed what they were.

"Per magnum spiritum!" he cried. "If that isn't the town of Caesarea-on-Miserabilis, I'll eat my war bonnet!"

I bent down and peered. Sure enough, though the curvature of the glass blurred the image, I could see, if I really squinted, the capital city of the Lacotia. There was the forum; there, if I was not mistaken, was the palace once occupied by Titus Papinianus when he was the procurator of that province.

And were those tiny dots people? I shuddered.

"We've got to find the device, fast," I said. "Before the rest of the bottles get filled—and then, I suppose, we'll have to return the cities to their rightful places. More bloody heroism!"

"The device! The device!" Lupus said anxiously. "Where is it?"

"What does it look like?" Euphonius asked. It was the only reasonable question I had heard him ask, and I must confess that I felt quite the fool for not having thought of it before.

"How should I know?" I said. "Like any other sort of shrinking ray, I suppose." My classical education had not covered shrinking rays.

"Is it that thing?" Lupus asked, and pointed at the one device I recognized.

"No," I said, "that's a uranograph—used for examining the entrails of sacrificial animals on the hoof. It also kills androids," I added, though I realized that since none of the present company had been with me on the building of the trans–Terra Novan railroad, my explanation would mean very little to them. "Let's take it with us," I said. "It may come in useful—if we encounter any androids. Or sacrificial animals, for that matter."

I handed the device to Lupus to hold.

We looked all around us, not speaking for some moments as it slowly dawned on us that there were hundreds of machines in the room and that any one of them could be it.

"Well," I said at last, "there's nothing for it but we'll have to try pushing all the buttons until we get something to shrink."

At that moment we heard footsteps outside the chamber. There was no time to lose. I pushed a button on one of the nearest devices—and instantly bumped my head against the ceiling!

I looked down. "Well, that's obviously some kind of levitating device," I said. "Now let me down!" As Lupus twiddled a knob on the device, I landed unceremoniously on my arse. "Better take that one, too—here, Euphonius, you use it." Lupus tossed it to the bard.

We found several devices that did not seem to do anything at all. Then there was one that made one's hair stand on end. There was another machine with a round, flat rotating disk on which reposed a bent wooden arm with a sort of a toothpick sticking down onto the disk; as it spun around and around, a faint buzzing music issued from the disk. There was a huge pile of the disks, each within a sleeve of preternaturally smooth papyrus.

There seemed to be no purpose to it until we discovered that the disks, when thrown, arced smoothly in the air and could doubtless give some unsuspecting person quite a gash in the head.

At that moment an Anasazius came charging into the room, shouting at us. *"Huka hey!"* Lupus shouted, and ran at him with the uranograph. Unamused, the Anasazius stepped aside to reveal about a dozen more of his number, armed with war clubs, bows and arrows, and scalping knives, all bearing down on us!

"We come in peace!" I said. "You're all in the thrall of an evil Time Criminal, and I can rescue you from his power!"

They did not say anything—of course, I would not have been able to understand them, anyway—but just kept advancing. They did not look entirely pleased that we had invaded the domain of their god—or whatever it was that Equus Insanus was claiming to be.

"Quick!" I said, grabbing an armful of the disks. "Lupus, run as fast as you can toward us—everyone huddle together. Euphonius—levitate us!" The others gathered around, except Lupus, who was surrounded.

"It is a good day to die!" he shouted at me in his squeaky little voice.

I threw a pile of disks to Hieronymus; he and I and Euphonius linked arms as the bard pointed the device at ourselves—and we found ourselves soaring over the enemy! With my free hand, I threw a disk as hard as I could. It sailed over to the Anasazius who was in the process of holding Lupus and bonked him on the head. He looked up in surprise, and Lupus sprinted toward us. We were flying rapidly around the room, pelting the Anasazii with disks, and Lupus could not keep up. The disks were good as shields as well as missiles, although the little hole in the middle did not seem to be that useful as a finger grip. Whoever designed these weapons must have been in a mushroom-induced trance.

"Drop us down a little lower," I said to Euphonius. He did something, and we plummeted—right onto the heads of some angry Anasazii! As they sat up, Lupus managed to grasp hold of the hem of my Anasazian blanket, and Euphonius steered us up to the ceiling again. We resumed our barrage of circular missiles, but ammunition was running low, and the blanket was unraveling, and Lupus was dangling precariously and swinging back and forth like a pendulum.

Suddenly one of the Anasazii, who appeared to be a chief, pulled out something from under his blanket. It was tubular, like a piece of piping such as one might see at the baths, but it had a handle at one end and what appeared to be a trigger.

He aimed it at us—and at the same moment, I threw one of the disks at him.

A ray of jagged blue light struck the disk, and it began to grow!

An expletive escaped the Anasazius's throat. Doubtless he had intended to use the device on us—and, like the gigapithecus, had pointed the wrong end! Indeed, even as the disk was rapidly expanding, he was shrinking, and the disk, now almost as big as the room, was crashing on top of all of them!

"Land us!" I yelled, and Euphonius brought us down on top of the huge disk, which was still spinning from the momentum of my throw. I could see that the disk was engraved with thousands of concentric grooves, and when we landed inside one of the grooves, an eerie music came forth as the disk rotated!

"Sublime!" Euphonius cried. "Surely it is the music of the spheres! For these disks—resembling as they do the perfect circles that form the basis of the structure of the universe—have clearly been designed to emit music that reflects the supreme joy of the primum mobile."

But blended with that jangling was the sound of crunching Anasazii bones, and blood was spurting up from the hole in the center of the disk. It was time to grab the device and depart.

I saw that the table on which the bottled cities rested was still intact. We would have to come back for those later. I could not quite see trying to reconstitute all the cities of the known world on a single plateau in the middle of Zona Arida.

Where was the device? I saw it lying not far from the edge of the disk; quickly, on our next pass, I seized it. Lupus had the uranograph; Euphonius had the levitator; Hieronymus had a bundle of the throwing disks—or celestial music disks, depending on whose theory one followed. We attached ourselves to one another by means of belts and pieces of rawhide from our costumes; then Euphonius turned his machine on us once more, and hovering at a distance of some four cubits from the floor, we quit the chamber and made our way back through the city. Despite the fact that a group of strangers was flying through their dwelling places, the Anasazii exhibited little interest in us, and those who did kick up a fuss were quickly put out of action by a swift blow on the head from a flying music disk.

Thus it was that, sailing through the air at the breakneck speed of perhaps thirty mille passuum per horam, we managed to arrive back at the Olmechian citadel shortly before sunset. We all gathered in the courtyard of the palace, in front of the head and buttocks of the Sphinx, to restore poor old Joshua bar-Joseph to his proper size.

CHAPTER
XX

THE INCREDIBLE SHRINKING SASQUATCH

THINGS HAD HEATED UP CONSIDERABLY AT THE OL-mechian city when we got back. The Apaxae war-riors, having been revived from their mushroom trances by a liberal dousing with highly potent aqua cocacola, were now dancing up a storm. They were using an old altar on which victims had only recently been sacrificed to me to dance around, and were whooping, leaping, and waving old scalp sticks with glee. I noticed that their manner of dancing was considerably stranger than that of the Lacotii—perhaps it was merely that I was more used to the Terra Novans of the Roman Empire—and there were those among them wearing strange masks that represented mythological wolves, birds, and arma-tilli.

The Olmechian populace, too, was in a state of great excitement; I learned that the high priest had told them that all their great stone heads would shortly be restored and that I, as the incarnation of the unpronounceable, was about to bring about an event of apocalyptic, nay, eschatological importance, videlicet, the "harmonic convergence"—something to do with having all the stars, planets, moons, and deities perfectly aligned. Aaye, who had been bored in our absence, had decided to teach the natives the principles of encephalometry; many of them were going around with little bronze pyramids on their heads, attached by wires to one another, and chanting mystical formulae.

"Hurrah!" Euphonius said. "These savages have seen the light!" He started going on and on about how encephalometrists would one day take over the world by gaining control of the major industries, like tourism and the priesthood. But his voice was drowned by the general hubbub: the clashing of cymbals, the bleating of giant cornua made from conch shells, and the cries of joy and victory. I assumed that was what they were, though I had as yet learned nothing of their language.

We had entered the city in triumph, and as we strode down the central boulevard, with maidens scattering flowers and encephalometrists chanting on every side, we approached the outer courtyard of the palace.

Callipygia, who as my bride was officially a goddess, was formally enthroned and had her own circle of devotees, all babbling endlessly about the conjunctions of heavenly bodies.

When she saw me approach, she clapped her hands for all to be silent. Laden down with trophies from the city of the Anasazii, we staggered into the circle of celebrants.

"Let's go to the inner courtyard," I said, "and save old Joshua bar-Joseph before he squashes the whole crowd."

Swarms of curious people followed us. The sun was setting; the two-thirds Sphinx stood forlornly in the middle of the courtyard, with a blank space where its torso should have been, and the gigapithecus was leaning against the palace, propping himself up against the eaves. "Shrinking ray!" I said, and brandished the tubular device proudly. Everyone immediately rushed for cover. I stood, my back to the trunkless Sphinx, pointing the device at Joshua bar-Joseph.

Abraham was hovering about me, worrying. "Be careful with that thing," he said. "And when you're through with it, I'd like to take it apart to see how it works."

His cousin said, "Make sure you're pointing the right end at me. I've no intention of getting any bigger—there'd be nothing to eat. And don't point the back end at yourself, or you're liable to turn into the next teen titan!"

"What's its range?" I said. I did not want to expand some praying mantis or something; I have always had nightmares about giant insects.

"I'm not sure," he said. "Just make sure there's nothing in the direct line of fire from the rear."

Suddenly I realized that there was no one in the vicinity at all, save for the gigapithecus and myself. I placed the device over my shoulder. I pointed the shrinking end of it straight at the gigapithecus's face. The other end was directed straight at the empty space between the two segments of the Sphinx.

It was a simple enough thing to operate; it had only one button, and presumably, all one had to do was push it.

"Well, what are you waiting for?" the giant Sasquatius said impatiently. "It's no fun, you know, being the way I am. I feel unloved. People seem to feel threatened by my very presence." He spit out a human bone. "It's not as though I suffered from halitosis, you know!"

I had never been close enough to his face to tell, but judging by the way all the birds were steering clear of his mouth, I was not too sure that his breath *didn't* stink. But I was too polite to say anything—it is easy to be polite to someone that much bigger than oneself—and I merely smiled and pushed the button.

A beam of blue light shot from the open end and smacked him in the eye—and he was fibrillating all over and collapsing in on himself, all the while shouting, "By the unspeakable name—look behind you!"

I did so. The spectacle was even more astonishing

than the incredible shrinking ape. For, getting bigger and bigger until it was already almost filling the gap in the Sphinx was the missing torso! The shrinking ape—the self-reconstituting Sphinx—I was whipping back and forth, trying to watch the entire thing, and the shrinking ray was still switched on, so I kept alternately expanding and contracting the palace.

Eventually I had the presence of mind to drop the device. I saw the two Sasquatii embracing each other with joy. Then I turned to the Sphinx. I shouted with glee. For, emerging from the Sphinx's torso, white mane flapping in the wind, a coup stick raised high in his withered hand, was no less a figure than Aquila himself; behind him stood His Bumbling Bulbosity, General Titus Papinianus, surnamed Lacoticus Sasquaticus!

"Well," he said to me, "it's bloody about time!"

"But—but—" I said.

"We've been trying to attract your attention for days," the general said. "And that fool of a telegraph boy almost squashed me under his sandal."

"Enough, O Titus Papinianus!" old Aquila said. "How were they to know that, although the homing beacon locked on in time, our portion of the starship had been swung around the event horizon of the spatiotemporal anomaly with such force as to cause a runaway collapse of our molecular structures? I consider it a miracle that we have been restored to our proper size. What a coincidence that a device for creating localized warpings of the spacetime fabric happened to be available—else we would have been trapped forever in a space vehicle the size of a pea. *Hechitu welo!*"

No more danger, then. Our friends crawled out from behind altars and under stones. As I told Aquila of our adventures up to that point, he became increasingly grave, though he laughed when I talked of fending off the Anasazii with the disks—from a machine he referred to as a "victrola." He was particularly attentive when I told him that Equus Insanus had gone off on a mushroom hunt.

"That explains everything," he said, though it all

seemed pretty enigmatic to me. "But they won't have much luck, alas; by now they will have plucked most of the fungi magici in the surrounding desert, if, as you say, the Evil One has been using massive doses of the hallucinogen to control the minds of his subjects."

At that moment, we heard a whirring noise from overhead, like a swarm of locusts.

"It looks like the pyramids are returning," Aaye said, and sure enough, we could see dozens of pyramids crossing the face of the setting sun. They were swooping down toward the pyramid parking lot, flying somewhat erratically.

"Their pilots seem a little drunk, don't they?" Lupus Ferox commented.

"Almost as if they had no flight plan," Abraham bar-David said.

"Of course!" I said. "Hieronymus... all the Apaxish air traffic controllers... they're in the streets of the city, dancing like mad... which means that all the pyramids are going to—"

Crash! I didn't have time to say it before one of the pyramids—they were almost directly overhead—smashed into the side of another. Rubble rained down on us. We ran inside, dodging the debris like crazy.

"I haven't had so much fun since the time we were stranded in the Great Asteroid Belt of Sirius during the Dogfood Riots!" Aquila said, cackling.

From the great entranceway of the throne room, we watched pyramid upon pyramid colliding, bursting into flame, spinning dizzily. One pyramid was spiraling up and down like a tornado; another kept losing a few bricks a time; another flying monument, which looked remarkably like the triumphal arch that my uncle the emperor had built for himself after his Gaulish victories, was flitting back and forth. To my horror, images of Viridiporcus Rex were beginning to form in the clouds, a sure sign that the Green Pig was somehow present.

"There's a ten-pyramid pileup!" Papinian cried gleefully. "Obviously something to have at the next games— I can't wait to bring a show like this back to Rome, eh what?" I had not yet informed him that Rome was now in a bottle.

Another pyramid came careening overhead, ejecting some Anasazii warriors, who floated to safety by means of a parasollike device that emerged automatically from their tunicae.

"Parachutes!" Aquila said mysteriously. "I didn't realize they'd been invented yet." The pyramid crashed into the side of the cliff not far from the edge of the city. We all winced.

The one pyramid that appeared to know its way around was the Great Pyramid of Cheops—the very one we had seen take off from the sands of the desert. I knew that Equus Insanus was within, that perhaps our arch enemy was with him. I shuddered.

"Look," I said, "I'm glad we're all back together again and all that, but I'm afraid we're in as big a jam as we were when we all started. Not only do we still have Equus to rescue, Viridiporcus Rex to arrest, and the universe to save—what's left of it—but there's the added problem of the bottled cities. What are we supposed to do with them?"

"Maybe Rome's better off in a bottle," Aquila said. "A lot of good she's ever done for us savages! The Lacotii may bathe more often now, but they've also turned into a bunch of namby-pambies..."

"Oh, forget this universe-saving business," General Titus said. "Just a lot of youthful nonsense, you know, what? Saved it meself, once, and once is enough, young man."

"How can you fellows be so flippant," I said, "with the fates of so many on our consciences?"

"My dear fellow," Titus said with equanimity, "surely you have experienced enough of these madcap escapades to realize that when all seems hopeless—when there seems no logical means of digging oneself out of the grave in which one has accidentally interred oneself —when death is certain—Aquila will already have thought of an ingenious, if unorthodox, solution to our dilemma?"

A ziggurat fell into the courtyard and was smashed to smithereens.

"You know," I said, "I never thought of it in those terms, but it's true, isn't it?"

We all looked at Aquila at the same time. The old man was laughing hysterically. Papinian was right! It was just like the deus ex machina so beloved of Greek tragedies. Aquila had appeared—by magic, almost—and everything was going to be all right!

"If you believe *that*," the old Terra Novan said, with a merry twinkle in his eye, "you'd better believe it's a good day to die."

EUPHONIUS IN THE UNDER WORLD

CHAPTER
XXI

A TALE OF TRUFFLES

FROM OUR VANTAGE POINT AT THE SUMMIT OF THE Olmechian citadel, we were gazing out at a scene of astonishing devastation. Some pyramids had landed with their points half-buried in the sandstone; some lay in pieces, with their inhabitants struggling to crawl out, like maggots in a corpse; others appeared to have been completely pulverized, pilots, passengers, and all. Columns of smoke rose from the wrecked starships. Anasazian pilots wandered among the debris in a daze, scratching their heads and staggering into one another.

A faded image of Viridiporcus Rex hung in the air, and the sky was rent in several places; we could see glimpses of other dimensions. For example, there was an edge of a blue sun in one, and a lone flying saucer flitting back and forth in another. The effect was strange and dreamlike and even rather beautiful; I reminded myself that this was no normal sunset but the sunset of the entire universe as we knew it, and I had better drink in every last dreg of sensation while I could, for soon my consciousness would be drowned in the Lethelike river of obliteration. I am not quite sure what rhetorical figure that was, but I am going to leave it in and try to puzzle it out later.

On top of the heap of crushed pyramids, one remained intact: It was the Great Pyramid of Cheops, naturally.

We all assumed that Aquila would now take charge, since he was the only one who had any idea what was going on. Instead, he ordered a sweat bath built on the veranda and, while Lupus drummed and yodeled outside, retired within to seek a vision.

The new high priest was really starting to stink up the palace, and the skin of the old priest hung in tatters on his body. I left Euphonius and Aaye in charge of the newly converted encephalometrists; the Sasquatius was busy taking apart the devices we had acquired from the Anasazian laboratory, the Apaxae had gone off to indulge in the remants of our mushrooms, and I was thus thrown into the company of Titus Papinianus.

"Bloody glad to be in the company of a real Roman at last, young man," he said. "And one of noble birth at that," he added, looking askance at the Olmechian—or was it Toltechian?—Callipygia, decorously draped around the couch in which we sat, "though I see you've been fraternizing with the natives."

"You did so yourself, Uncle Papinian," I said, reminding him that he had taken Cervilla of the Quaquiutii to wife. She had run off with a gladiator soon afterward, I remembered and changed the subject. "Enjoying the aqua cocacola, what?" I poured him another kraterful of the heady juice.

"Newfangled drugs—you young people are all alike, what! Give me a jug of good old resinated Lesbian wine any day—I prefer to rot my brains the old fashioned way."

"You should try the fungus magicus," I said, pulling one of the two that yet remained to me out of my tunic. "After all, unless someone can figure out what to do, we're all doomed, and if there's any new thrill you seek, you might as well indulge now."

"True, O nephew," he said, laughing. I could tell that

prolonged exposure to spectacle had made him so blasé about the forthcoming destruction of the universe that he was not even remotely depressed about it. Or perhaps he was simply confident that Aquila would save the day. He looked at the mushrooms curiously. "They don't look like much," he said, sniffing at the one I offered him.

"Oh, but they are," I said.

"Well," he said, "do you want to split one?"

When I bit into my half of the mushroom, I was instantly propelled into the visionary world I had visited once before. Colors were heightened, the slightest sounds made my being vibrate like a bell, and a celestial music seemed to fill the air about my ears. I was being drawn up into the clouds, and Papinian, who in my vision was wearing a tunica of light, was fluttering about, his butterfly wings flapping noisily.

"Oh, I say," he was saying, "bit of a spectacle, what!"

I too seemed to have wings. We were hovering over an alien landscape with red sands, pitted with craters and riddled with canals, where the air was thin and poisonous.

"Must be Mars," I said, for I remembered it from my previous visits as one of the universe's most déclassé spots. But soon Mars melted away and was replaced by images of even more alien places: worlds inhabited by intelligent insects, rocks, and even clouds; worlds shaped like skulls and omelets; worlds where Euphoniuslike poets thronged the marketplaces, all singing simultaneously. And the Green Pig was in all the worlds.

In the distance I saw Hieronymus and his Apaxae, hands linked, weaving in and out of the clouds. They were wearing pyramidal hats. They, too, were part of this vision, then. It occurred to me that perhaps they were in the dream world all the time, and they saw our world as a mere vision.

A flock of pterodactyls soared overhead. I knew them for the totemic animal peculiar to Equus Insanus, and I wondered whether he was trying to reach me again.

It seemed that we flew for many years. On the worlds

beneath, civilizations rose up, flourished, became decadent, perished; wars raged, earthquakes and volcanoes
ravaged whole continents, and flying pyramids sliced
huge canyons in the earth with bursts of blue flame.

"This is better than the arena," Papinian said. "We've
the best seats in the house, and there's something to
watch whichever way you look. And what's more, the
spectacles aren't fixed the way they are with, say, feeding criminals to the lions."

His chatter did not bother me. The wind felt good in
my face. My wings moved with a ceaseless motion
beyond my control. I felt myself a veritable Daedalus as
I breasted the storms of the upper atmosphere.

In the distance, smoke rose from a butte. Air traffic
controllers! By the power of the fungi magici, I understood the patterns of the smoke without having to have
them translated: "Dodge the turbulence, ten degrees
north by northwest—you should have taken that left
turn at Albuquercum—approaching circle at center of
universe, continue on autopilot—"

Suddenly this gibberish all seemed to make perfect
sense. It is a common enough experience when you take
mind-altering substances, I suppose, but it never ceases
to amaze me how it makes the most obfuscatory passages clear as day. It occurred to me that maybe this was
the best way to try to read Homer.

The smoke signals brought us closer to a circle that
seemed to be described with ridges carved into a huge
plateau. It did not surprise me to see Lupus Ferox
standing just outside the circle, next to the skull of an
aurochs that had been painted in the magical pigments so
beloved among the Lacotii. There seemed to be some
kind of barrier that prevented us from seeing who was
within the circle. Clouds of steam rose from it, and as we
landed Lupus Ferox greeted us both.

"Salvete, O Lucius Vinicius and Titus Papinianus!"
He continued to pound madly on his drum. Still we could
not see into the circle, though now and then the smoke
of the sacred pipe came billowing from within.

"This is strange sort of a dream, isn't it?" Papinian said, looking about him with a none-too-trusting expression. "Are we supposed to go inside the circle?"

Lupus Ferox sang a song that went something like this:

This is the center of the universe;
If you fear visions, turn back.

We stepped inside and were immediately transported to a very familiar scene, one I had not hoped to encounter quite yet.

On the one hand, it looked like a Lacotian council lodge, with walls of buffalo hide, painted with representations of hunts, aurochs, and warriors. But there was a see-through quality to the lodge, and the various Terra Novans who sat within it, smoking peace pipes and dressed in all their feathered finery, were translucent, like ghosts.

Behind this vision was something that appeared more solid: the arbitration hall of Mars, where a green elephant from the future had once sat in judgment over us and threatened to sentence our entire world to extinction!

The elephant stared sternly at me. "Where is the Green Pig?" he said. "You said you would capture him for us, and the sands of time are rapidly running out!"

"But—but—" I had no time to finish, for the elephant was blurring, vanishing from view.

"Ah, there you are," Aquila said. He looked up from the center of the lodge, where he had been puffing on a long-stemmed pipe, and was enveloped in smoke. "Been waiting for you to join us."

"Where are we?" I asked.

"The center of the universe," Aquila said. "I thought Lupus told you so already."

"Not quite what I expected, what," Papinian said. "Are we dead?"

"All realities meet here," Aquila said, "and everything that is, is not. It's all very Zenlike."

"Don't try to explain," I said, realizing it was just another enigma Aquila had picked up on his travels through space and time. "We are all part of one another's dreaming, I know that."

"And we are all connected through the dance of Heisenbergian tachyons," Aquila said sagely. "You came here by way of a fungus magicus; I used the sweat bath. And there is someone else among us, someone whom, I think, you have missed greatly."

The smoke clouds parted. I saw the futuristic jury in the background quite clearly for a moment, the implacable face of the elephant judge and his adviser, an enormous green tapir who reared up on his hind legs and waggled his snout at me. Then they shimmered and melded with the patterns on the buffalo robes again, and I saw Equus Insanus.

"About time," he said. "Are you going to rescue me now?"

"Rescue you? I'm not even quite sure where you are —or who, for that matter."

Equus was fading in and out of view. Although he was striving to maintain the devil-may-care expression I was so used to, I knew something was wrong. "You don't look well," I said.

"You're telling me! It's only by the skin of my teeth that I'm here talking to you at all! I told you that the Green Pig had control of me, didn't I? Before I was rudely yanked away, in the middle of that last vision of yours."

"But—"

"Listen to me, Lucius, you confounded dolt of a half brother. According to the laws of conservation of multiplex realities, the Green Pig, who fled just before we were all shunted into this holding universe, can't penetrate the barrier that's holding us in without causing so many spatiotemporal anomalies that everything would just go up in a puff of smoke—see? So he's used a new technique for invading our universe, projecting a psychic simulacrum of himself into my brain! So when you finally come into the presence of His Viridiporcine Majesty, it will be the body of your half brother that you see,

with your poor half brother's personality trapped in a
little cage inside the brain, about the dimensions of a
knucklebone—and the Green Pig in charge of all the
rest! Only through the mushroom trance can you contact
me at all, and—"

He started to fade again, and I realized that *everything* was fading, not just him. I reached out to touch
him, crying "Equus! Equus!" but instead, I embraced the
harsh and arid air of southwestern Terra Nova and found
myself outside the sweat lodge in the courtyard of the
palace, beneath the flanks of the Sphinx.

"I say! Are you all right, old chap?" General Titus
looked at me in concern. I sat up. Aquila, sweating pro-
fusely, had just emerged from the lodge, and Lupus was
throwing a blanket over him and shaking a rattle.

The others of our company, leaning against the
Sphinx's paws, watched me worriedly. "Where is Equus
Insanus?" I asked, and pulled out my one remaining
mushroom, hoping thereby to be sped back into the visionary universe so that I could continue my chat with
him.

"Don't you dare pop that in your mouth, *michinkshi*!"
Aquila said. "The fate of the universe hangs on that
mushroom, I'm afraid."

Quickly I stopped myself from swallowing it. It was
night, a clear moonlit night; the Great Pyramid was
swathed in an eerie radiance, and our courtyard was lit
by torches. We all stood in a circle around the old Lacotian warrior, waiting for the wisdom his vision had
brought him.

"All of us," he said, "have gone on a spirit journey
together, and we have learned where the soul of my son
Equus Insanus is trapped. But how to lure away the
Green Pig and deliver him up to the Dimensional Patrol?
I have pondered long on the problem, and I have asked
questions of those grandfathers among the little green
men who know about the time when the world was
young. In the course of these questions, I learned much
about the Green Pig, and I propose to tell you of his

home world, his birth, and his first falling victim to the clutches of evil."

"Bit of a tall order, wouldn't you say?" I said. "Couldn't you just give us the highlights?"

Aquila raised an eyebrow. "This *is* the 'good parts' version," he said. "If you want the whole story, you can read the Green Pig's ten-volume autobiography, *In Memoria Semper Viridis*—available from the central galactic information retrieval system, transcribed onto 273 papyri."

"Oh, let the man speak," Titus Papinianus said. "You should know by now how these expository lumps work; just grin and bear it."

"Oh, all right, all right," we all mumbled, and Aquila began.

"You all know of truffles, do you not?" he said

"Of course," I said, for as you know I pride myself on my encyclopedic grasp of the culinary arts. "They're fungi porcini—id est, enormous mushrooms, rooted out from the ground by specially trained pigs, especially good braised with a stuffing of breaded gazelle's brains."

He held up his hand for silence and launched into the following narrative.

"As you may have noticed," he said, "most of the denizens of the future that one encounters in the Dimensional Patrol bear little resemblance to humans; one tends to meet green lobsters, green were-jaguars, green elephants, and so on, but seldom a green person. That is because, some ten million anni hence, most members of the human race will have evolved into creatures of pure energy and be inhabiting the empty spaces between the stars, feeding off cosmic radiation. The Earth, then, will be inhabited by the descendants of various animals, their mental powers genetically enhanced by the human beings, but long since abandoned by them, for energy beings have no ties whatsoever to the sublunary levels of existence."

"Fascinating," Abraham and Joshua said simultaneously; they were the only ones who seemed to be

able to follow Aquila's argument, although Aaye tried
very hard to look intelligent through it all.

"Now, at some intermediate stage in the future, before the formation of the Dimensional Patrol, when
humans were still in human form and colonizing the galaxy and what have you, there was, for a time, a truffle
fad that swept the known worlds. The desire for truffles
was so powerful that an entire planet was created, 'ter-
raformed,' as they said—will say, rather—for the pro-
duction of truffles—monstrous truffles, many as big as
the Flavian Amphitheater or even the Temple of Capitoline Jove—and pigs, genetically engineered for superior
truffle-sniffing skills, were brought to the planet from
Earth. A truffle-centered culture arose upon this world,
but when the fad ended, the planet was left to the pigs,
who eventually developed a superior intelligence.

"Viridiporcus Rex is a native of this planet of truffle-
seeking pigs—a mutant, to be sure, with intellectual
powers far beyond those of the average pig—and, in his
youth, he developed a passion for the study of ancient
civilizations. He became particularly enamored of Earth,
the mother planet of his race—for had Earth not engen-
dered the first pigs?—and became obsessed with the am-
bition of traveling to ancient times. Unfortunately, the
early model spatiotemporal bewilderizer that he created
kept sending him back to the wrong dimension, and each
time he used it, more and more spatiotemporal anomalies were created, and more and more alternate universes
kept branching off, until the different aspects of reality
became so perplexing that the Dimensional Patrol was
formed to keep track of them all, though the act of form-
ing the Dimensional Patrol was in itself enough to spawn
a whole host of new realities, which in turn—"

"Wait a minute, O Aquila," I said, for I thought I saw
what he was driving at, even though the *scientifictive*
aspects of it were beyond my grasp. "Are you telling me
that Viridiporcus Rex ... suffers from mushroom dependency?"

"You're not so dumb," he said, "for a Roman whelp.
The fact is, though his mind is overlaid with a massive,

twisted intellect, yet beneath it lies a dark animal instinct which understands but a single idea: truffles—truffles— *truffles!*"

"Then he can be lured with—these things?" I held up the little mushroom. "But it is hardly a fungus porcinus —only an itty-bitty fungus magicus."

"Ah," said Aquila, "but did you not steal an expanding ray from the abandoned laboratory in the Anasazian city?"

I began to see a glimmer of hope.

Chapter
XXII

Setting the Trap

THE NIGHT WAS ONE OF NIGHTMARES; WE SLEPT within the throne room, our rest interrupted now and then by the ministrations of dancing girls; frequently, the Viridiporcine visage would appear, glowing, in the air about our faces, and occasionally we would hear his mocking laughter in the darkness.

"Don't worry," Aquila said, "it's only the Evil One, channeling his psychic double, or doppelgänger, in our direction. It's merely an illusion."

The city, too, was in grave trouble. Peasants with torches overran the streets, pausing now and then to sacrifice themselves to the gods; the food supply was low, for we had left the crops behind in Olmechia, and the stores were running out. As we lay abed, we would frequently hear the wails of the dying and the complaints of the destitute; an odor of burning flesh permeated the air, as so often occurs on the eve of apocalyptic events. We had not landed all that securely in the pyramid parking lot, and now and then the city would shift or settle, sending couches careening across the chamber, making torches fly off their brackets, and making the sacrificial knives miss their targets, so that from the terrace outside we would frequently hear irritated victims saying, "You idiot of a high priest! That was my toe!".

It was in the small hours that Aquila explained his plan to us. It all seemed pretty hair-raising, but the old Lacotian chief emphasized that we had to do something soon, or the fabric of the universe would destroy us anyway, and the little green men would not save us then— for they would not risk the destruction of the metauniverse in which our whole universe was of less consequence than an iota.

For the rest of the night, the Terra Novans among us put on their war paint and sang their war songs, bloodcurdling music accompanied by the screams of the dying from the streets outside. Euphonius spent the time tuning his lyre, for he did not want to go to the bosom of his muse with an off-pitch string. I donned a bit of war paint myself, just a touch of yellow lightning beneath each eye and a few red splotches on the forehead, just enough to scare someone if I should sneak up on him from behind.

Dawn broke over the city, the field of crashed pyramids, and our desultory band of adventurers. It was time to put our plan into action. We boarded the Sphinx, which had cemented itself back into a single vehicle, and Aquila gave a few last-minute instructions to the Olmechii and Apaxae, who were to remain behind.

"Hieronymus," Aquila said, "while the Pig is occupied with us, you're going to storm the Anasazian citadel, rescue the bottled cities, and bring them back to the rendezvous point."

"Right," said Hieronymus, who was putting on his war paint even as they spoke. His men were gathering around him, wearing their finest encephalometric hats and covering their faces with fierce-looking streaks of paint.

"Serpens Plumatus," Aquila said to the high priest, whose second skin had now almost entirely rotted off, "you and your Olmechii will guard the rendezvous point, this courtyard—and be under General Titus's command."

The old general was striding about, overseeing the battle stations. Here a makeshift catapulta had been set up, along with piles of ammunition salvaged from the debris of the previous crash landings. Elsewhere, they were setting up other commonplace devices for defending citadels: here a cauldron of boiling oil, there a group of archers, in another place a group of gleaming, naked savages from the humid forests, each carrying a blowpipe and a handful of poisonous darts.

"March, you damned savages!" Papinian was shouting. "What an undisciplined lot! You there—stand up straight, or you'll get fifty lashes, on the double!" He was doing what he did best—whipping an army into shape. Meanwhile, the Egyptian and the Sasquatii were seeing to the construction of various war engines, wooden towers from which the boiling oil could be thrown, and so on. My heart swelled as I saw the ease with which a Roman general had been able to get these natives to work together like a well-oiled machina. And all without slaves, too!

"This citadel will surely be impregnable, Aquila," I said, "if the Anasazii should decide to attack."

"Attack, my foot," Aquila said. "I just wanted to give old Titus something to do. Or he's liable to get on all our nerves."

"I shall sing a noble rhapsody," Euphonius said, "to inspire these savages into a frenzy of patriotism." He rushed out, lyre in hand, into the throng.

"Good idea," Aquila said, as he and I and the young Lupus entered the Sphinx and the stone solidified behind us.

"Gave him the slip, didn't we?" Lupus Ferox said, sniggering.

We heard an earsplitting jangling sound, and Euphonius slithered into the chamber through the naked rock. "Ha! You failed to reckon with the chord of doom!" he said, alternately strumming the lyre and slamming it against the side of his head. "Music can melt the living rock, as witness the career of the great Orpheus—the most famed songster of all time, whose music so moved the Queen of Hades that she allowed him to bring his beloved Euridice back from the dead."

"You may recall," Aquila said, "that not only did Orpheus lose Euridice again, he also met an unpleasant end—being torn in pieces by a gang of madwomen that roamed the countryside of ancient Greece."

"Those were the days before good old Roman law and order," I said.

"If Orpheus was anything like you," Lupus said, "I'm not surprised the women ripped him up. I wonder if they scalped him."

"Enough bickering!" Aquila said. "Children—the mushroom!"

"Check," I said.

"Expanding ray?"

"Check." Lupus was holding it.

"Uranograph?"

"I've got it," I said, "though I can't figure out why you would want it."

"Levitator gun?'"

"Aye," said Euphonius, who had retrieved it from the palace before storming the Sphinx, thus proving himself of some use, after all.

"Thread?"

We all looked at one another. No one had mentioned thread. "We'd better get some," Aquila said, and I had to go back outside. I managed to find thread only by the expedient of borrowing one of Callipygia's robes, which she unraveled for me; she then insisted that this proved her indispensability, so we had to take her along, too.

"Very well, then . . . cleared for takeoff . . . all hands on deck," Aquila said. "That's astronautiloi talk for getting our arses in gear."

Whatever *that* meant!

We trooped up to the head chamber, deopaqued the viewscreens, and prepared ourselves; then I took the vessel up about two hundred cubits. Callipygia had learned how to fly the spacecraft from watching me at the helm of the city, and I let her take the Sphinx for a quick spin.

We surveyed the entire plateau. From the Anasazian citadel at one end, to the distant butte that no longer broadcast smoke signals to warn distant flying pyramids of collisions, across the shambles that had been the pyramid parking lot, to the city—somewhat the worse for wear—that rose athwart a vista of crushed monuments, we could see that our odyssey had already wrought its share of destruction on the world.

After a flight of about a half hora, we found ourselves above a flat stretch of plateau, large enough, we hoped, to encompass the task that lay ahead. Then we parked the Sphinx and, bearing the various devices, stepped onto the rocky terrain.

"Now," Aquila said, "the fungus magicus."

I put it down on the ground, wedging it in a crevasse.

Then, taking the ball of thread, I tied one end to the mushroom and the other to Callipygia's waist.

"Now, my dear," Aquila said, "go inside and keep the throttles on standby. If something should go wrong..."

"Yes, O mystic warrior," said the priestess, scampering off, the thread unraveling as she went. Soon she disappeared inside the craft, and the thread, caught within the tesseracting field, formed a link between the mushroom and the alternate reality within the Sphinx.

"All right!" Aquila said. "First, we bombard the mushroom with uranographic rays—"

"Right!" I said, and aimed the uranograph. "Er, why are we doing this?"

"That fungus magicus contains millions of spores, and when irradiated, these spores will begin to mutate, thus guaranteeing that at least one of them will react the way I want it to to the expanding device," Aquila said, and I took him at his word, turning the uranograph on and seeing it do absolutely nothing to the mushroom. Then Aquila signaled to Lupus, who, aiming the shrinking portion of the tube carefully away from us, pointed it at the fungus while Euphonius turned on the levitator.

At first the mushroom began to sizzle and sputter;

rainbow sparks came shooting from it, and an aura of purplish light seemed to emanate from it.

"What now?" I asked Aquila.

"Oh, anything could happen. For example, this fungus could suddenly achieve sentience, decide that we're repulsive aliens, and attack us."

"Wow!" Lupus said.

"Or nothing could happen at all—or—"

The mushroom was shaking violently, jumping up and down, yanking at the thread that bound it to the belly of the Sphinx—and Callipygia's costume.

"Stand back!" Aquila cried. "Unless you want to be thrust prematurely into the Land of Many Tipis!"

We all obeyed. The mushroom was positively bursting, emitting Jovian jags of lightning, as though there were another, bigger mushroom inside, struggling to burst loose from the seams of the first mushroom! Then, like a snake sloughing its skin, it happened. A bigger, meaner mushroom emerged from within the first, then another, then another, then another—until we were facing a fungus magicus taller than an adult sasquatch!

"Full power!" Aquila said and Lupus turned the expander up a few notches. We stepped back, farther and farther, as the mushroom grew and grew and grew... until finally we had backed up all the way against the flanks of the Sphinx.

The fungus magicus was now approximately the size of a small house and showed no signs of ceasing to grow. It was pressing us uncomfortably against the Sphinx, and I feared we might be squashed. It's not pleasant to have a palpitating megamushroom thrusting itself in your face, let me tell you. At length, Aquila said to Lupus, "Probably big enough, you'd better turn it off."

"I can't! It's stuck!"

And indeed, Lupus was pressed so hard against the stone that he had no room to maneuver, and if he shifted the device any further, we would all be the size of ants in no time.

"We'd best go back inside," Aquila said, and repeated the mystical formula that softened the stone so we could reenter the Sphinx. We rushed to the control chamber, where Callipygia was sitting at the console, tapping her fingers.

"About time," she said. "Where to?"

Through the eyes of the Sphinx, we could see that the mushroom was still getting bigger, and bigger, and bigger.

"If that doesn't get our friend right here," Aquila said, tapping his heart, "I don't know what will."

"Why is it still growing?" Lupus asked. "I've turned off the device."

"Obviously, my child, the effects of the radioactivity and the expansion of the molecular structure of the fungus magicus combined to create a runaway effect—a complete breakdown of the mushroom's ability to cope with the normal confines of spacetime. It has become a rogue mushroom and will continue to grow, perhaps indefinitely, until—"

"The Great Pyramid of Cheops—*tunkashila*, its coming after us!" Lupus Ferox cried.

"Evasive action!" Aquila said, and our stomachs all churned in unison as we lifted off. The mushroom, of course, dangled from the thread around Callipygia's waist, and so she was pinned to the wall, with the thread trying to pull her out of our alternate reality into the reality of the fungus.

"Won't the thing drag us down to Earth like an anchor?" I asked Aquila.

"Oh, do not worry," he said. "It will experience no increase in mass; its molecular structure will merely become more and more attenuated until it's little more than a phantom fungus." And I had to say that the thing was now nearly as big as our spacecraft, and I was hard put to tell whether the Sphinx was towing the mushroom, or the mushroom the Sphinx.

"Take the helm, Lucius Vinicius," Aquila said. I sat down, with Lupus as my copilot.

We saw the giant pyramid not far off, riding the clouds, brilliant against the midmorning sun. It didn't look quite the same as it had in Egypt, and I realized that it must be the visage of the Green Pig, in living color, which formed a bas-relief splayed all over each of the faces of the pyramid—grinning hideously. A booming voice—I knew it for the voice of Viridiporcus Rex, even though it seemed to come, thundering, from the sky itself—cried out something that sounded like "'SHRRRROOOOOMS! 'SHRRRROOOOOOOMS!"

"Ramming speed!" I cried, and the blood rushed to my head as I brought the Sphinx around to face the charging pyramid and prepared to pile snout first into the face of the leering Pig.

CHAPTER
XXIII

TRUFFLE WARS

CALLIPYGIA WAS BEING FLUNG ACROSS THE chamber as the rogue mushroom tugged at her tunic strings. "Ouch!" she squealed as she slammed into the bosom of the statue of the composite god. She clung to the god as the strand of thread pulled at her clothes, placing her in a most alluring state of deshabillé. But I had no time to enjoy her buttocks, for I was engaged in steering the Sphinx toward the grinning countenance of Viridiporcus Rex.

"Quick! Anchor down the thread!" Aquila said, and Lupus and Euphonius involved themselves with winding it around everything in the chamber: the sacrificial altar, the bas-reliefs, column stumps, even the distended phallus of a statue of Priapus in a niche in the wall.

We were flying directly over the pyramid parking lot; below we could see the piles of smoking wreckage and antlike people crawling about. The fungus was growing by leaps and bounds; it was much bigger now—as big as the Sphinx itself. "We're not going to be able to ram the pyramid!" Lupus cried. "The bleeding mushroom's in the way!"

187

It was true. The thing had swelled to such proportions that it formed a kind of cushiony buffer between our two vehicles.

"Back up," Aquila said, "and try again!"

I backed up, causing Callipygia to fly across the room, a fate that she endured with commendable sang-froid; indeed, she was evincing a stiff upper lip commensurate with that of a Roman matron. I wondered whether my mother would approve of her; it would not cost much to have her declared a Roman citizen, and having a dusky Terra Novan barbarian as a concubine, or even a wife, would not be a bad status symbol. It was worth looking into, I thought, listening to her as she babbled prettily in Nahvatish—the translating device was, as usual, unable to keep up with her—seeing her torn garments, with their convenient windows to her opulent flesh, flapping hither and thither. So absorbed was I in the contemplation of her beauty that I let go of the joy-stick, and we went soaring up so high that the sky turned black and stars became visible.

It was just as well. The mushroom by then was the size of a small hillock and would doubtless have crushed all the inhabitants of the plateau had I not brought the Sphinx into the stratosphere.

The Great Pyramid came whizzing into view again, expelling a jet of purple smoke from its base. I brought the Sphinx down low, hoping to drag the pyramid along —thinking, like a fisherman, that the pyramid might tire and be easier to restrain. Looking down from the aft windows of the control room, we saw a ragtag phalanx sidling out of the Olmechian city. "Jove help us!" I said. "Titus Papinianus is leading the assault on the Anasazian city in his own inimitable style, I see."

I pushed a button that magnified the view through the screen, and we saw a straggly row of Olmechii, bedecked in their finest plumage, struggling to march in formation, with Papinianus at their head, riding a sort of war engine that looked as though it had been put to-gether from old motorcar parts. He was in full military dress, waving an enormous gladius so heavy that it might have taxed a trained gladiator and shouting orders at the high priests, who were ignoring him. The Olmechian warriors, with their plumes, jaguar skins, and feathered spears, moved inexorably forward and from our vantage point resembled a string of gaudy beads rolling across the sandstone plain. "I guess they don't have much concept of camouflage," I said, for each of the soldiers was so brightly attired that he had to be a sitting duck—nay, a sitting peacock.

"No time to review our troops," Aquila said. "We've got mushroom troubles."

The fungus seemed to fill the whole field of our forward viewscreens, and the Great Pyramid of Cheops was sort of stuck in it and was bobbing up and down like a sausage in a soup pot. Callipygia, meanwhile, had been completely divested of her garments, save for a small strand about her waist that was still connected to the giant mushroom, and was clinging to the composite god for dear life.

"Don't worry," Aquila said. "Soon all will be well. When that overwhelming mushroom odor percolates into the olfactory senses of Viridiporcus, there will be nothing left—no intellect, no mind as we know it, nothing but the need to envelop himself in the mushroom, to possess the mushroom, to be absorbed into the all-pervading allness of the fungoid universe."

"Sounds like a commercial for encephalometry," I said, noting with some distaste that the surface of the mushroom was erupting with little miniature volcanoes that resembled nothing so much as the pimples of an adolescent who has feasted on too many rich foods. There were mushroomquakes, too, and huge snakelike creatures were writhing around on it. There were some bloblike animals, too, resembling enormous fried eggs, slithering about on the surface and occasionally eating the snakelike things.

"Do not worry about them," Aquila said. "They are merely giant microorganisms that got enlarged along with the mushroom. They may be big, but they're very dumb; they're not about to gang up on us."

The mushroom grew. Below us, I saw the massed Anasazii rushing toward Papinian's army, leaping, whooping, brandishing their flint-tipped weapons. I was not worried about them. They were no match for anything organized by a Roman—even a Roman as inept as old Bubblenose. It was pretty exciting to watch the two groups edge slowly toward each other from this height; it was an excellent view, almost as good as the two-denarii seats at the arena, and without the unedifying aroma of dead meat that often arises from the sand on a hot day.

"It's going to be a rout," I said, rubbing my hands together. Unfortunately, I let go of the controls, and the next moment we were sort of half-buried in the mushroom ourselves, with the giant microorganisms, whatever *they* were, crawling up and down our viewscreens.

"Oh, a streptococcus," Aquila said, as one wiggly thing swam past. "Give the Sphinx a sore throat."

Across the grayish terrain of the mushroom that bound our two spaceships together, I saw a portal open in the Great Pyramid, and armed men come charging out!

"Prepare to board," Aquila said.

"Board? You must be out of your mind."

"Why not?"

I looked out. There were dozens of men running toward us, all of them very, very green. They all looked much alike, wearing identical loincloths and feather headdresses and waving identical spears—as though they had all been copied from the same Anasazius. "Androids," I said. "But the uranograph can handle that."

"Callipygia," Aquila said, addressing the high priestess, who had not entirely managed to extricate herself from the statue of old Amon-Ptah-Isis-Hathor. "Mind the autopilot, will you, and stoke up the reactor now and then?"

"*Málista, málista, kyrie,*" she said, saluting, and reached for the sarcophagus we had replenished with fresh Olmechian mummy parts that morning.

I looked around for something that might serve as an assault vehicle. Everything seemed pretty much bolted down, except for the statue of the composite god, which, though made of solid bronze, could be levitated easily enough with our levitator. "All right," I said, "everyone pile onto the statue."

Euphonius sat down on the altar itself and aimed the levitator at the base of the statue; Lupus, with a war club and scalping knife, and I, with the uranograph, took up positions perched on the arms, while Aquila squatted with his legs wrapped around the god's horns. He had a huge war lance, decorated with about a dozen scalps, blond, brunette, and black, and a glistening point of Roman iron, and the flippant demeanor had vanished from his face, for, ridiculous though we might look, war was still war.

At a signal from the old man, Euphonius turned on the levitator, Aquila uttered the mystic formula for releasing us from the Sphinx, and we sallied forth. The wind whipped at us, icy and painful, and we wove through veils of cloud.

I had endured so many peculiar events in the last few months that I was not a bit surprised to find myself riding a statue, bursting through layers of cloud over the spectral surface of a distended mushroom. It seemed almost natural. Ahead were the androids; I could see that they were not about to attack us at all. They were on their hands and knees, shoveling, hacking away with hoes, and shoving chunks of mushroom into sacks. "By Mars, they're mining the mushroom!" I said.

"*Huka hey!*" Aquila cried.

By leaning in one direction or another, and with Euphonius treating the levitator as a sort of rudder, we were able more or less to control the statue. We brought it up high, arced over the heads of the androids, and then came plummeting down on top of them, and I loosed a stream of uranographic radiation into their midst.

The androids began to sizzle and explode, and it started to rain slime and little metal body parts. Unfazed, we soared up and swooped once more, hawklike, as those androids who remained continued, machines that they were, to attempt to perform their tasks, many without the benefit of heads or limbs. A lake of green slime was spreading across the surface of the mushroom. A gaggle of giant amoebae sucked up the slime to the accompaniment of unnerving slurping noises.

The androids that remained were drawing themselves into a huddle. We circled them, bombarding them with uranographic rays.

"Closer!" Lupus cried. "I want to count coup!" He leaned across with his cudgel and fetched one of them a smart blow over the head. It keeled over, spattering us with seething innards. Another android tried to board the statue and was actually dangling from the altar. Euphonius tried to dislodge it by pounding it with the levitator, but that threw our flight path out of kilter, and we were wobbling back and forth across the sky, and I was sure I was going to be airsick at any moment.

"Abandon statue!" Aquila cried. "Slaughter at will!"

We leapt down onto the spongy surface of the mushroom. Immediately, one of the long, slinky-looking microorganisms came darting out of the mist and tried to throttle me. Aquila cut it in half with his war lance, and the two halves went wriggling off in opposite directions.

"Mitosis," he said, and I scarcely had time to ponder what he might mean, for an android, leaking slime from the top of his head, with an eyeball dangling from a coiled metal spring, was shambling toward me! I turned the uranograph on him full blast, but he floated away, sent flying by a burst of Euphonius's levitator. The rays from my device went into a more distant group of androids, who all exploded instantly, showering us with more slime. We were drenched in the stuff, and I could see that Aquila was upset that it had ruined his makeup.

"These creatures have no manners," he was grumbling as he ran one through. "You spend all evening making yourself look beautiful, so if you die you will not go into the Land of Many Tipis looking like an idiot— and these androids don't even have the decency to explode away from your face. They have no honor at all. They're not even worth scalping." As he said this, he neatly lifted a scalp, long distance, with a flick of his war lance—a very deft trick and one he had clearly practiced many times.

"*Whee!*" Lupus was shouting as he ran from android to android, bashing them with his coup stick. "This is fun!"

But there seemed to be many, many more androids where these came from, and no sign of Equus Insanus yet.

CHAPTER
XXIV

A MAN CALLED EQUUS

THERE WE STOOD, FOUR MEN—IF YOU COUNT Euphonius—against an army of brainless automatae battling mightily in a manner that would have done Homer proud.

Unfortunately, Homer was not around, and the bard whom the muses had chosen to send in his place had just been visited by a fit of inspiration. Sticking the levitator between his legs, he struck up a mighty chord upon his instrument, resonant as an amphora of wine being smashed against the skull of a pregnant elephant. So impassioned was he that he was not even counting syllables anymore but singing in a kind of avant-garde free form, and occasionally plucking the lyre strings with his teeth. Since we were not doing at all badly in spite of the enemy's hundred-to-one superiority in numbers, I suppose he thought it would be all right to leave the dirty work to us and to work us into a frenzy by singing of the glorious exploits of great heroes of legend:

Warlike Mars! Great Zeus! Mighty Apollo,
In your brave exploits let these heroes wallow!

194

In your gore-drenched footsteps let them follow,
Retreat, you say? With one voice, answer "Nolo!"

Never before had I heard a more ludicrous example of
Euphonius's art. But he seemed more intense than usual,
more flamboyant, more flushed with inspiration. Every
few measures, he would cry out, "Oh, ye muses! Eu-
reka! Eu-reeeeee-ka! I have arrived at an epiphanic plateau in my creative outpourings—I'm throwing away the
final crutches of meter, rhyme, nay, even sense itself,
that final barrier in the revelation of an utter purity, a
semiotic null state."

He was weeping for joy, capering about on the tram-
polinelike surface of the mushroom—at last, even putting his head through the lyre strings and almost
garroting himself—all the while with that levitating device clenched between his legs, wagging like those huge
leather phalli that Greek actors wear in comedy.

And we were surrounded!

Chasms yawned in the fabric of the mushroom, from
which gusts of incandescent steam arose! Sparks of blue
lightning flew across the surface, tickling our feet and
making Euphonius caper about even more wildly! I
whirled and whirled like a child's top, squeezing the uranograph until I was sure there was no juice left...until
we were soaked with the quivering, gelatinous green
stuff from the androids' explosions...until the ground
was a shivering mass of green, with spokes and bolts and
machine parts dissolving in the wind...and a solitary
figure remained standing, his face bright green but re-
cognizably that of a young Lacotian.

"Equus!" I cried.

He tottered forward. His face was entirely caked with
pulped fungus. His eyes were like beads of cold green
glass. He did not seem to be in control of his own limbs; he
staggered, he groped, he lurched unseeing in our direction.

"*Hau, chinkshi,*" Aquila said, greeting his long-lost
son.

Lupus Ferox said, "I mean, I expected something a
little different."

Euphonius was off in his own universe. Perhaps the fumes of mushroom—he was taking very deep breaths in order to sing those lengthy musical phrases without having to stop for air—had begun to get to him, for he seemed rapidly to be sinking into the dream universe to which the fungus magicus provided the key. His words were becoming increasingly unmusical, nonsensical, and imbued with a kind of pseudo-metaphysical twaddle:

> *Ye pregnant portals, ope perception's doors,*
> *Release the starchild; Saturn never snores,*
> *Take me away, ye magical mystery tours,*
> *For Lucius in the sky with diamond spores*
> *Doth wipe the mop that waxeth marble floors—*

He stopped, mouth agape, awed by his own brilliance. "Oh...wow...oh...wow," he said. "Similis, quam in toto psychedelicus est."

"Ignore him," Aquila said, "for he straddles the interface between the dimensions; it's the early stages of mushroom dependency."

I paid no more heed to him. I was more concerned with Equus Insanus, who was not a pretty sight. "Equus," I said, "look at all the trouble you've caused us; come home and let's just get on with saving the universe and capturing the Pig and all this other nonsense." I went up to him and attempted to embrace him, but he brushed me off angrily. "I say, you're not still mad about—"

"Mad—that's it! Mad, mad, mad, mad, mad!" my brother cried. It was not his voice. He spit out an enormous wad of partially chewed mushroom. His eyes glowed with the kind of eerie light one associates with the denizens of the underworld; he did not look at me but seemed to see straight through me. His voice indeed bore the unmistakable resonance of Viridiporcus Rex.

"You're the Green Pig!" I screamed. "Get out of my brother's body, you evil creature!"

He laughed. This was, indeed, the demoniacal cackling of which Lupus Ferox's "three quick spurts followed by a long" was the smoke-signal translation. Now and then, while never ceasing to cackle, Equus would get down on his hands and knees and assume a position not unlike that of a pig in a poke, and he would bite off huge chunks of the mushroom at our feet and swallow them without even appearing to chew.

The cackling continued for some time, during which the levitated androids and assorted android body parts fluttered about over our heads, amoebae waddled about, blue lightning darted about our feet, the mushroom continued to erupt, and so on—lest my readers forget the spectacle that was transpiring during the entire course of my conversation with the being that inhabited the body of my half brother. At length, the voice of the Green Pig said, "I'll never leave Equus's body, for Equus no longer exists! I alone control him—my own body in cybernetic storage within the confines of a parallel universe! Those fools, the Dimensional Patrol, thought they could isolate your world in a holding universe. Little did they know that, even though I can no longer physically travel between the dimensions, I have become an adept at the art of channeling."

"Pseudoscience!" I scoffed, for I had read all about it in the scrolls of those mystical mountebanks who, not unlike Aquila's encephalometrists, offered courses in their exotic lore with the sole purpose of stealing from the rich and giving to the even richer.

"I'm afraid there *is* something in it," Aquila said, "for, as you know, in infinity all worlds are possible, and, implicit within the Seventh Law of the Conservation of Multiplex Realities—"

"Wait a minute! What happened to the fourth, fifth and sixth laws?" I asked, for in the previous adventure the Dimensional Patrol had been entirely certain of only three.

"They were taken off the books at the last metagalactic science conference," Aquila said, "but they kept the old numbering to avoid having to rewrite too many textbooks."

Equus continued to bound about on all fours, scarfing up pieces of the fungus magicus.

Aquila sighed. "I suppose I'd better do my duty now," he said, and walked up to Equus, managing to command a remarkable nobility of bearing despite the ludicrousness of our situation. "In the name of the Dimensional Patrol, Viridiporcus, I place you under arrest," he said, "on the charge of violating the laws of the conservation of multiplex realities."

Lupus Ferox turned to me. "How can you violate a law of nature?" he said.

I shrugged. "Have to ask the metagalactic science conference, I suppose."

Equus snarled. "You can't arrest me—you're not authorized! You've been disbarred and exiled! Everyone knows that." He turned to his flock of levitating android parts. "Attack!" he shrieked, and ate some more of the mushroom.

The android body parts gathered into an aerial V formation, like a flock of geese, and flew at us, but since they were just body parts, they did not succeed in doing anything except baptizing us in more slime.

Aquila whacked Equus over the head with his war lance. "This'll hurt me more than it hurts you, my son," he said sadly.

"You're cornered," I said. "Give yourself up." I was full of bitterness, for I had longed to see my friend these many years, and all I saw was his shell, inhabited by what I most loathed. "What can you do?"

Equus Insanus said nothing but continued to claw at the ground and swallow pieces of it, ignoring the giant amoebae as they crawled past.

"Leave the body," I said to Viridiporcus. "Channel yourself back to wherever you came from. I don't care about saving the universe, I just want Equus Insanus back."

"Yes," Lupus said. "Give us back our friend."

"That's where you're wrong," said Equus-Viridiporcus. "I'll never leave. I've got you fellows over a barrel—if you turn me in the way I am, you'll also be killing

Equus Insanus! You know the Dimensional Patrol's going to erase my brain, and that, of course, will include every last figment of the personality of your beloved friend—ha, ha! Talk about a hostage crisis!"

"A real dilemma," Aquila said.

"O Aquila, what shall I do?" I looked at him in consternation.

"Beats me," he said.

We all looked at little Lupus.

He looked at all of us—and at Euphonius, who was wrapped up in some private cosmos of his own—and said, "Well, it boils down to a conflict between love and duty, doesn't it? And, well, Lucius Vinicius, you're a Roman. You're the expert on all this philosophical stuff; we're just dumb old natives."

"Don't look at me," Aquila said.

"But he's your son!" I said.

"What is death?" Aquila said. "Equus Insanus rode off to the west to find and subdue Viridiporcus Rex. He had already sung his death song, and if he is extinguished as a result of the Green Pig's capture, he will have died with honor, and I am proud of him."

"But I don't want him to die at all!"

"Tough moral choice, isn't it? Your call."

If there is one real drawback to being a Roman—and I mean, we *are* better than everybody else, no false modesty now, just the whole truth of it—it is this whole Roman man's burden business. I mean, well, all these colonials were brave and noble and what have you, but when it came to actually deciding the fate of the universe, they ended up passing the denarius. Alea jacta est! *There's* a saying to live by! The point is, one had better be bloody sure that one's stiff upper is *really* stiff, and not just a put-on for the natives, or else—or else—I mean, Rome was not built in a day, and—

"Look, uh, maybe the Dimensional Patrol can figure out something," I said weakly.

It was a simple matter to tie him up and drag him back to our Sphinx. But as we entered, we saw that Callipygia was stalking about the control room (still naked) in a frenzy, tearing her hair. She threw herself into my arms, jabbering wildly, and at first I thought she was simply rapturous at my return and wanted an instant celebratory consummation of the ars amatoria. Then her translator kicked on.

"Where have you fellows been?" she shrieked. "We're rapidly losing altitude. Plenty of fuel, but something seems to be jammed. In about five minuti, we're going to squash the entire Olmechian army like bugs—and all your friends along with it!"

CHAPTER
XXV

ONCE MORE,
THE BRINK OF DOOM

"**H**EE HEE!" SQUAWKED THE GREEN PIG OUT OF the mouth of my half brother. "Ex sartagine in ignem!"

"What frying pan? What fire?" Euphonius said, looking around wildly, for in his dementia he could not tell metaphor from reality.

"Someone shut him up," I said, and Lupus obediently hit him over the head with his coup stick. He passed out against the control console, a smile on his lips.

We were falling rapidly. Equus Insanus said, "You fellows are not nearly as smart as you think. Even in my fungus-induced delirium, I am still capable of devilishly clever planning! When I saw you coming, I had the forethought to train an immensely powerful cosmic radiation generator on your Sphinx, which transformed all your mummiform fuel capsules into useless isotopes—incapable of releasing the πmeson streams required to stoke your warp drive!"

It was just the kind of nightmare that writers of *scien-*

tifictiones love to torment their readers with. Often, reading one of the lesser authors in the genre, I had come across a scene where the plot required that a certain disaster occur, but there was no explanation for that disaster other than a string of incomprehensible scientific terms—nothing you could find even in an unabridged Aristotle. "Can't you come up with anything better than that?" I asked.

The Green Pig merely launched into a peculiarly prolonged and odious cackle.

"I've got all the brakes on," Callipygia said, "but we're still plummeting—mushroom, pyramid, and all. Impact soon—in fact, they're within shouting range, if I turn up the sound."

"Let's take a look," I said.

I turned up the magnification on the Sphinx's eyes. Below, a scene of triumph: Olmechii were leaping up and down in the air, and Titus Papinianus was driving around in his makeshift chariot, towing a cart behind him in which reposed all the bottle cities we had seen in the Anasazian city. The bodies of slain warriors lay in heaps about the field.

"Ho, down there!" I shouted, trusting that the Sphinx's speaker system would relay my voice to the throngs below and that there would be a way to listen to their responses.

I saw the warriors look up. But they did not seem at all frightened; they were waving cheerfully, holding up various grisly trophies of the fray, and pointing exuberantly at the bottled cities.

We heard the crowing voice of Aaye. "We took the Anasazian city by storm—we've retrieved the bottled cities—on the way back to celebrate a triumph, now—all in a day's work for veteran universe savers like us!"

Papinian's voice came in loud and clear. "I say, chaps! We defeated those Anasazii without much of a struggle; pretty easy, actually, considering they were all high on mushrooms. Victory for you, too, I take it; good old Roman discipline strikes again. Masters of the world and all that, eh what?" He waved. "I suppose you'll be re-

questing flyby or some such flamboyant thing. Well, I'm
not one to stand in the way of spectacle; carry on!"

"Flee! Scatter!" I screamed. "Or you'll be crushed!
And half the cities of the civilized world along with you!"

Papinian frowned. "Crushed? What insolence! Who's
driving that thing? Give that driver fifty lashes!"

"You don't understand, Uncle Papinian. We're out of
control. Even though we're braking as hard as we can,
we're going to have impact in about—ah—a minute."

"Good heavens!" Papinian looked about him. There
did not seem to be much hope of shifting the Olmechii
out of the way. He called to old Serpens Plumatus—his
skin, that is, which was in filthy shape and hanging in
ribbons all over the new priest's body—and started ex-
plaining things to him. Then he shouted up, "Won't do,
I'm afraid; they don't mind being crushed to death.
Think it's a novel method of self-sacrifice—keep the sun
shining and all that, you know."

"Can't you steer at all?" I asked Callipygia. But I
knew it was useless. She was leaning into the joystick
with all her might, and I feared it might break off entirely.

"Get us out of this," I said to Equus Insanus. "Come
on, brother, if there's a shred of Equus Insanus left inside you. Perhaps we'll be pulverized ourselves."

"So? I can just depart the host body and insinuate
myself into some other physical soma. I've always
wanted to be one of the ant men of Epsilon Eridani, for
example."

Meanwhile, I could see that a certain amount of panic
was spreading in the ranks below. Abraham bar-David
was sheltering the bottle cities with his body—not a very
useful thing to be doing, to be sure—and Titus Papinianus was looking at his sword, wondering perhaps
whether it was time to do the Roman thing and do away
with himself rather than be ignominiously crushed by a
block of sandstone.

It was at that moment that Euphonius began to speak
—with every appearance of lucidity, though I knew that
he was deep in some hallucinogenic trance—punctuating

each sentence with a lyre twang. "What need we fear?"
—*twang, twang*—"Are we not encephalometrists? Do
we not believe that the proper exercise of pyramid power
can cause levitations, telekinesis, and transmutations?"
—*twang*—"and is there not an entire army of true be-
lievers down there—not just the Apaxae, but the
Olmechii, whom we have just converted?"

"Oh, shut up," I said. "We haven't got time for any
nonsense. We all know that Aquila and Papinian concocted that thing as a scam for raising money so that we
could get an expedition together to go capture the Green
Pig."

Equus Insanus took a bow.

"Wait a minute!" said Aquila. "It's true we made up
the whole thing, but the *principles* are sound. The whole
universe *is* linked by an all-pervasive force that can be
evoked by the proper exercise of—"

"Oh, you've really gone too far now."

"Well, what else is there to do? You want me to do a
rain dance? You *washichun* just don't have any faith in
the ability of nature to heal itself." Aquila marched over
to the control panel and punched a few buttons. "Ahem!
Papinian! Plan Epsilon!"

The image of Papinian's face was ever closer now, and
I could see that he was paling. "Oh, jolly good," he said
at last. "Good day to die, that is. Been nice knowing
you." He turned and barked out some brusque orders. A
bucina blared, but it was no military signal that I had
ever heard.

At the sound, all the Olmechii lined up, straightened
their pyramidal hats, and began chanting.

"A useless maneuver!" Equus Insanus screeched.

Wildly, I looked around. Euphonius too was chanting,
and to my amazement, Aquila was doing a rain dance.
After a moment, Lupus joined him, banging on the control panel with his fists and ululating in a childish treble
over the old man's wheezing.

Callipygia was watching the proceedings wide-eyed.
"It's beginning to occur to me that you people might not

be entirely sane," she said. "Nevertheless, god or man, I must say you're still a pretty remarkable person, Lucius Vinicius, and, I mean, what I'm trying to say is—since we're all going to die anyway—I love you, O Lucius Vinicius! I love you! *Pheu, pheu, aiaiai,* I love you!"

I have always known that I am irresistible. All women love me, but somehow it was peculiarly touching hearing it from the lips of this native girl. After all, in Rome, everyone has something to gain from trysting with the emperor's nephew, whereas this poor thing probably could not tell the emperor from a hole in the ground.

I had never said it to any woman before—and meant it, that is, for in the heat of passion one says anything one must in order to squeeze the last juice from the sacred grapes—but I said it now. "My dear, I really do think I'm rather fond of you, actually."

I embraced her passionately. The sacred grapes became somewhat engorged, and, as I saw the screaming face of Titus Papinianus filling the entire viewscreen, I became decidedly nonplussed that I would not have the opportunity to discharge them one last time.

At that moment—as I was later to learn, approximately half a cubit from the top of Papinian's head—the Sphinx screeched to a halt. In midair.

I heard the sound of chanting coming from below. The very air seemed to vibrate. The Sphinx, giant mushroom, and Great Pyramid seemed to be floating upon a cushion of that resonating air. "It's not possible," I said.

"Ah, but it is," Aquila said, taking a brief breather from his rain dance, "for I based the encephalometric chants on some ancient formulae left behind by the long-dead race of ancient astronautiloi. The astronautiloi had a theory that, if one could only generate the correct vibrations, one might learn all the mysteries of the universe—causality could be reversed—what was falling could be made to rise, the dead could come back to life; indeed, it is widely rumored that some members of this long-extinct race, prior to the cataclysm that destroyed their civilization, placed themselves within certain vaults *in statu suspensae animationis,* and that when some future race should randomly chance upon the same vibration, these astronautiloi may be released from their confinement."

"Lovely, Aquila, but how long can they go on chanting before the precise vibration starts going a little off-key?" I said, noting that many of the Olmechii down below seemed to be getting pretty purple in the face from the effort of keeping up their cantiones sacrae.

"We'll have to see," Aquila said. "Steering mechanism still jammed?" I checked; indeed, nothing on the console was working.

"A check to my villainy, not defeat!" Equus Insanus said. "Soon your cohorts will run out of breath; and then, O Aquila, you're all doomed!"

"By Jupiter Vacantanca!" Lupus Ferox squealed suddenly, pointing across to the other side of the mushroom through the forward viewscreens. "The Great Pyramid's disappearing!"

We gaped. It was true! It was slowly dissipating into the air, and we heard the beating of mighty wings, for where the pyramid once stood there was a second sphinx—not a sphinx of sandstone, such as the one we rode in, but a living creature, its body made of some crystalline material that cast a shimmering rainbow halo about its noble visage. It gazed upon us with an incommensurable nobility of bearing, now and then flapping its wings with a resounding *thwack* that seemed to turn our very stomachs to stone.

"Well," Aquila said softly, "life is certainly full of surprises. I never thought I'd live to see an ancient astronautilos in the flesh."

"What happened to the Great Pyramid of Cheops?" Callipygia asked. Aquila pointed; in the distance, atop a towering butte, the pyramid was neatly balanced on its point, looking for all the world as though it had been there since the dawn of creation.

"The chanting's stopped!" Lupus cried. "We're falling."

No sooner had he said this than the Sphinx in which we were riding began to dissolve into the air, and the giant mushroom began to sail off into the distance. One moment we were plummeting to the Earth inside a vast stone edifice; the next, we were landing lightly on our feet, and we beheld the great stone Sphinx on another butte, not far from the Great Pyramid, sitting on its haunches like a dog begging for a bone.

"Ah, there you are! Bloody good show," Papinian said. He was the only one who was not entirely in awe of the ancient astronautilos, who was circling overhead.

At length, the creature landed in front of us. The Olmechii all prostrated themselves instantly, with the practiced ease of those who are used to bumping into some new god every other day.

Meanwhile, those of our party—we, the latter-day Argonauts, always at the threshold of new worlds, always going where no man has gone before—stood face to face with a creature older even than the brontosauruses we had encountered on previous adventures. I could hear Joshua and Abraham arguing in low tones about whether this was one of the Cherubim, id est, a species of Judean chimaera that sits around adoring their nameless god all day.

"She's going to speak!" Lupus whispered fearfully in my ear. I agreed that the creature was probably a female, since it had all the endowments of that sex.

The astronautilos looked at each of us in turn. Papinian was puffing and primping; naturally, as the senior Roman official present, he assumed he was going to be the one spoken to. Aaye, too, was busy trying out various inscrutable expressions; since he considered himself, too, a member of an ancient race, perhaps he thought that the Sphinx would subscribe to the "birds of a feather" theory of communication. The rest of us, however, were simply nervous. After all, were not the ancient astronautiloi the repositories of unimaginable wisdom and unthinkable high technology? And did it not stand to reason that whatever words came from its lips would change our lives forever?

I was absolutely startled when the creature looked right at me and uttered, in tones amazingly dulcet for a being of such magnitude, the following question: "Cur pullus viam transit?"

Chapter
XXVI

To Get to the Other Side

"**W**HY," I BEGAN, BEFORE I HAD WIT ENOUGH to control my tongue, "that's the dumbest thing I ever heard a superbeing say. Every child knows the answer to *that* one: 'To get to the other side'!" I answered her in Greek, even though she had asked me in Latin, because I instinctively wanted to show her that I knew my place, even if *she* did not!

The Sphinx looked very forlorn. "Oh!" she said. "I had rather hoped that that riddle had a more profound answer than that."

"I say," Titus Papinianus asked, brightening up, "do you know any Judean jokes?"

Equus Insanus, who was still tightly bound, said, "Wait a minute. I am a master interdimensional criminal; these people here are goody-goodies who are trying to spoil the fun and take me back to the Dimensional Patrol, where I'll get my brain erased; over there are a bunch of Olmechii and Apaxae, and off in the distance there you'll see a whole lot of dead bodies. But you don't seem to figure in this drama at all, unless you're the deus ex machina."

"Why not?" Aquila asked. "Every single one of us has been mistaken for a god by someone during the course of this adventure. It's about time *we* mistook someone for one."

The Sphinx looked rather bewildered for a moment; then a throaty, bubbly laugh came rippling from her tongue. "Very good! Ha, ha, ha!" she said.

"This is an ancient astronautilos?" Lupus Ferox said as the creature began to giggle herself into knots, and huge tears welled up and rolled down her cheeks and splashed us. As they sloshed onto the desert earth, flowers sprang up here and there.

I turned to Aquila. "After this buildup," I said, "she asks me why the chicken crossed the road?"

"By the wagging tail of Anubis!" Aaye cried. "Don't you realize who this is? This is the Sphinx—not just *any* sphinx, *the Sphinx*! The one who used to ask riddles— you know, with Oedipus Rex and that lot, back in ancient times."

"No autographs, please," the Sphinx said, scratching herself behind the ears.

"But your kind have been extinct for billions of years," Aquila said, mystified.

"Always an exception," the Sphinx said. "I'm a time traveler meself; had that pyramid retrofitted for time as well as space, you know; could never resist a good riddle, you see. I'm doing this massive thesis about the enigmatic riddles of the Earthlings of the future—your past, that is."

"But didn't you throw yourself off a cliff when Oedipus answered your riddle correctly?" I have always been a stickler for historical accuracy.

"Oh, that! My getaway vehicle was parked at the bottom of the cliff, out of sight."

"But you used to devour alive anyone who was unable to answer the riddle; isn't that, well, a bit unethical?" I asked.

"Look, young man, when you've been gallivanting about the universe as long as I have, doing this gods-from-space shtick, you'd better be ready to put your money where your mouth is. Those ancient Thebans wanted spectacle, and, by gumbo, they got it."

"Would you have devoured me if I hadn't answered your riddle?"

"Don't know, really; depends."

Emboldened, the high priest was now crawling forward. "Might I humbly inquire as to whether you will be requiring any human sacrifices?" he asked.

"Oh! Why, I'd be flattered," said the Sphinx, blushing.

"At last! A god who looks, talks and eats like a proper god!" Serpens Plumatus said, leaping up and down with joy and incidentally shedding the last shreds of his predecessor's skin. He ran out and began regaling the Olmechii, but they were all shaking their heads.

"What's happening?" I asked Callipygia.

"They're all refusing to be sacrificed!" she said. "After the empirical proof of the efficacy of encephalometry, they're all ready to abandon the old religion and go for something a little more streamlined; in fact, they're saying that the priestly rulers should be deposed completely and replaced by someone who gets slightly better results—like Titus Papinianus, for example."

"Oh, I say, what," Papinian said, "just doing my duty and all that; Roman ingenuity, eh? Builds character."

"Perhaps, O Sphinx," I said, "you could help us with our mission?"

"Enough of this dillydallying," Aquila said. "We've got to finish saving the universe—just a few loose ends to tie up—deliver the Green Pig to the Dimensional Patrol—expand the cities back to their rightful sizes and drop them off at the different portions of the globe. So, if you don't mind, madam—"

"Not so fast, O withered one!" she said, and did not sound nearly so nice anymore. "I've got a deadline on this thesis, and you're the first test subjects I've found in a million years, so—" She whipped out an enormous sheet of papyrus, probably about the size of a general's war tent, and began scribbling on it in hieroglyphics. "—you're going to have to answer a few questions first."

"Then will you help us with our dilemma?" I asked. Though we were tantalizingly close to the end of our mission, I knew that there was another terrifying hurdle left: how to rescue my brother from the grip of the Green Pig—how to destroy the Pig without destroying Equus Insanus in the process. In a way, I was glad of a brief diversion, for I feared the worst. I was ready to cling to any hope, no matter how remote, and this astronautiloscum-anthropologist seemed to offer the only ticket.

"Yes, yes, yes," she said. "Oh, these natives—promise them anything—results! Publish or perish!"

"Very well," I said. "We'll answer your riddles."

She cleared her throat, a sound like the tinkle of a talent bag of silver denarii. Then she turned to Aquila and said, "What's black and white and red all over?"

"A newspapyrus," Aquila said, "and that's no fair, because it's only funny in Anglic, a language that doesn't even exist yet. You really ought to do your homework on those timelines."

"Oh, very well, very well," she said, and turned to Titus Papinianus, who was looking decidedly nervous even though he had just been elevated to the kingship of the Olmechii. "Tell me then: How many effete Roman patricians does it take to refill an oil lamp?"

"Two," he said. "One to stand around wringing his hands, and one to call the slaves."

"I object to that!" I said. "I can change an oil lamp as well as any plebeian."

She made a notation and then turned to Abraham bar-David. "And how many encephalometrists does it take to change an oil lamp?"

"One," the Sasquatius answered, "but it has to *want* to change."

"I can't believe that we're standing around trading schoolchildren's riddles," I said, "when we've so much at stake! An end to all this!" I saw that Equus Insanus was shaking all over with a kind of lunatic palsy and occasionally frothing at the mouth, and I was deathly afraid that unless the Green Pig was soon exorcised, he would be no more. "I bet you can't even answer any riddles yourself," I screamed. "You'll probably flunk your thesis!"

"Would you rather I devoured you?"

"No, but I'll bet you can't answer even one simple riddle, despite your millennialong study of them."

"Humph! If you're going to be that way about it," she said, "fine. If I can answer it, you'll all be devoured; if not, I will help you save your silly little tenth-rate universe. Tush! Natives! Natives! Can't live with 'em, can't live without 'em."

"Very well, then." I racked my brains. Everyone stared at me; the discus was clearly in my palaestra now. I could not think of a single riddle.

The Sphinx tapped her foot. Each time she did so, it made our very bones rattle; it seemed, indeed, to be the very tympanon of doom.

I had to say something. And when I blurted it out, I knew it was going to be the end of all of us, for what sprang unbidden to my lips was, "What has four legs in the morning, two legs at noon, and three in the evening?"

Like a madman, I stared about me. Titus Papinianus was rolling his eyes; Aaye and the two Sasquatii were lifting their arms to their various Middle Eastern deities, imploring them to strike me down with a thunderbolt; even Lupus Ferox would not look into my eyes. I had blown it; I had murdered the lot of us; I had committed a boo-boo of universe-shattering proportions.

The Sphinx glared at me for a long, long time and finally asked, "Is it some kind of a trick question?"

CHAPTER
XXVII

THE RETURN OF V'DENNI-KENNI

AFTER I TOLD THE SPHINX THE ANSWER TO THE RID-
dle, though, she began hooting with laughter and
finally collapsed in a fit of raucous guffawing, spraying
the desert once more with her tears and causing the very
ground beneath our feet to sprout amazing flowers. "I
haven't heard such a good one in eons!" she shrieked.
"Wait'll I go back to ancient Thebes and try *that* one on
dumb old Oedipus! He'll never guess it. I'm finally going
to succeed in having history go my way for a change!"

Aquila looked grimly at me. "Little does she know,"
he said, "that the Dimensional Patrol is constantly on
guard against the sort of thing she's into. She won't get
very far."

"Teeheeheehee!" the Sphinx said, and then, sobering
up, continued. "I suppose I'll have to keep my end of the
bargain—ancient astronautiloi burden and what have
you."

I explained to her the exact problem, and she became
rather grave. "There's only one way you can save him, if
I'm not mistaken," she said, "and it involves great peril
to yourself."

214

"I'm not afraid," I said, exercising what little stiffness yet remained in my upper lip.

"The real Equus Insanus—his original personality, that is—exists as patterns of neural impulses stored in the brain of that composite creature." She pointed at Equus with one paw as he strained against the ropes that bound him. "The Green Pig has probably reduced his personality into a single disposable module, much like a plug-in chip, and his possession of Equus's brain is probably not dissimilar to the invasion of a computer virus into an operating system."

"Oh, please! No more scientific marvels!"

"No, wait. If you could somehow invade Equus's brain and disable the Green Pig module—"

Aquila laughed. "Of course! The shrinking ray! We could inject ourselves directly into the brain and—"

I stared in bewilderment at the ancient warrior and the ancient astronautilos. "What? You mean, miniaturize ourselves and physically enter Equus's brain to find and destroy some device we cannot even imagine? Isn't that the stuff of *scientifictiones*? Didn't I read something about that in the scrolls of one of those 'Golden Age' hacks?"

The Sphinx said, "Of course, it is a little hard for a layman, especially an inferior being such as yourself, to grasp. You'd just be wandering about in an endless morass of flesh and gray matter and corpuscles. You'd not be able to tell blood from pus—not to mention the fact that you'd be battling endless armies of bacteria and leukocytes hell-bent on destroying you. But if, somehow, the world inside Equus Insanus could be made to fit your normal perceptual cosmos—if it could be remade in the image of your external world by some means that used familiar metaphorical symbology—then it would be fairly easy."

"I think I know what you're getting at," Aquila said. "A Terra Novan youth who seeks a vision is not unlike Jason seeking the Golden Fleece. Everything is an aspect of everything else, and therefore, with the right mind-altering substance, anything can be made to look like anything else—for example, the inside of the human brain could be made to appear like downtown Rome in the off-season—and so—"

"More mushrooms?" Abraham bar-David asked.

"Whatever did happen to the giant mushroom, anyway?" I asked.

At that moment, there was an eclipse of the sun.

I had not noticed it grow suddenly dark until I started to hear the cries of *"Ai-eee!"* from the Olmechii. Then I saw a small black patch in the side of the sun, steadily growing, and I felt a sudden chill; in the distance, quoiotuli, wolflike animals indigenous to these parts, howled.

I also heard a sound I had not heard in some hours: the ecstatic cry of an Olmechius who has just declared himself ready to die for the god and whose heart is being ripped out of his chest. I looked around. Sure enough, the high priest was in the middle of dispatching some wretched native.

"But I thought you fellows had given up human sacrifice!" I said.

"See what our impiety has brought us!" Serpens Plumatus cried angrily, and pointed at the sun, which was only about half there. It turned bitter cold and windy. Serpens barked out an impassioned speech in Nahvatish, and people began ripping off their pyramidal encephalometric hats and trampling them into the sand.

"Sic transit," Aquila said, shrugging.

"They were never real encephalometrists, anyway," Titus added. "Never paid for their counseling sessions."

Shivering, I looked up at the sky. Why is it that an eclipse of the sun never occurs when you want it to? I had read dozens of stories about the brilliant Roman intellectual captured by ignorant, savage Terra Novans, Numidians, or Scythians, tied to a stake, about to be eaten by natives—who managed to escape by cleverly happening to know that an eclipse of the sun was imminent; it's an old trick and one that every adventurer keeps up his sleeve for just such an eventuality. That was why I had memorized a list of the lunar and solar eclipses predicted for the next ten years, which had been drawn up for me by Abraham bar-David on consultation with a Babylonian astronomer he knew. That was why I knew for a fact that while we were slated for a partial eclipse on the Kalends of Julius, no way in infernum was there supposed to be an eclipse of the sun today. "It can't be a real eclipse—it's got to be—"

Suddenly I realized what it was. "By the armpits of Æsculepius! It's the mushroom!"

"The mushroom?" Several of the Olmechii, who had lain down and were preparing to be sacrificed, pushed off their sacrificers and started scrabbling in the sand for the cast-off pyramid hats.

"Never too late," Aquila said smugly.

The stars were coming out. The mushroom was still growing; though I could not judge its distance, it seemed to me that it was probably about the size of Rome by now.

Or bigger.

There were other strange goings-on. Twisty thunderbolts dancing across the sky. The aurora borealis. A ghostly image of a chariot drawn by reindeer flashing across the sky, driven by the Emperor Nero in a nightcap and imperial robes. Wailing faces. A faint whiff of brimstone.

"It's finally here," Equus Insanus said, in between bouts of demoniacal cackling, "the end of the universe—and there's nothing you fellows can do about it!"

The mushroom filled the sky.

Then it blew up.

We saw brilliant bursts of sunlight. Quoiotuline howlings turned to gurglings. The clouds were roiling. Gossamer sheets of mushroom-stuff, finer than veils of Chinish silk, fell upon us out of the sky. Sand gusted. A flock of pterodactyls broke through a layer of cloud and soared over our heads. The Olmechii were cheering loudly, some opining that they had been saved by the heroic self-sacrifice of a few stouthearted conservatives, the rest maintaining the triumph of encephalometric science over the superstitious past. Indeed, some came to blows, bashing each other on the head with the not unhefty bronze pyramid helmets. (*Phew!* Managed to get in a litotes at long last.)

While attempting to think of a clever metaphor, zeugma, or even histeron proteron that would encompass the entirety of the spectacle I was witness to, I noticed that the sky itself seemed to be tearing itself in twain, that an enormous curving marble staircase appeared to be descending from the clouds, and that a number of little green men were ambling down toward us!

I recognized one of them at once: V'Denni-Kenni, the green-faced were-jaguar, the lordly commander of the Dimensional Patrol. Behind him, on a litter borne by a dozen little green spiny anteaters, was a figure I had hoped never to see again in the flesh: the green elephant who had sat in judgment over me, nay, over the entire planet Earth.

These lordly creatures came wafting down from the sky as, behind them, the scenery continued its eschatalogical convulsions.

"Enough of this!" V'Denni-Kenni cried, holding up his hand and revealing, at last, who the true deus ex machina in the story was. I saw Equus Insanus straining hard against his bonds, and even the Sphinx looked a little nervous as V'Denni-Kenni turned to her. "And what are you doing out of your epoch, little girl?" he said. "The corridors of time are not for any child to wander at will. You know that."

"Uh . . . um . . ." the Sphinx said.

"Show me your hall pass!"

Sheepishly, the Sphinx pulled out a document from under her armpit. This one was about the size of the awning that covers the Flavian Amphitheater during certain spectacles; it was covered all over with hieroglyphics.

"That's expired," V'Denni-Kenni said wearily, "and you're not even a registered student anymore, are you?"

"Look, let's make a deal. I'll ask you a riddle, and if you can't guess it, you'll promise not to report me to the Sphingean High Principate?"

V'Denni-Kenni simply brushed her aside—not an easy thing to do, considering that she probably weighed as much as the Temple of Capitoline Jove—and turned to us. "I see you have captured the Green Pig," he said. "Thought he'd hide out in an alien soma, did he? Well, we've good news for you, too—and not a moment too soon. Your universe is going to self-destruct in approximately seventeen blinks of an eye, but I have received authorization to apply a new spatiotemporal reversal process to it, in exchange for the Time Criminal, and I see that you've kept up your end of the bargain." He clapped his hands, and his underlings, two green lobsters, marched forward to claim their prize.

Equus Insanus looked imploringly at me.

Titus Papinianus said, "Well, it's a shame to lose my adoptive nephew Equus Insanus, but I suppose the needs of the many and all that..."

Aquila said, "He is my son, but he has given of his pain, *hecel lena oyate kin nipi kte lo*—that the people may live. His will have been a good death. *Heya-heya-ha!* I honor him. *Hechitu welo!*"

"Daddy?" Equus Insanus said, in a voice that bore no trace whatsoever of the Green Pig's. Aquila turned away.

"It's a trick," Aaye said, "some kind of ventriloquism. In Egypt we do things like this all the time, so that the common people will think that words of wisdom come from the mouths of statues of the gods."

"Lucius! Lucius!" Equus Insanus cried. "Do you turn your back on me? False to the sacred honor of our blood brotherhood? Is this the Lucius Vinicius who defended me in school from the flagellating schoolmaster Androcles, who pissed on the emperor out of the eye of the statue of Jove? Can this be he who—"

Euphonius looked up from his lyric stupor. "Hey, not a bad 'pleading speech' after the Ciceronian school of rhetoric," he said.

"O Lucius! Friend! Roman! Countryman! My tears flow like the tears of Niobe, grieving for her fifty daughters; like Hecuba for her lost city; like Atlanta, losing the footrace to Meleager."

Poor Equus. In moments of stress, he could never speak Greek very idiomatically, and he would always end up using one of the set speeches from the rhetoric textbooks, complete with irrelevant, obscure classical allusions. I knew that the Green Pig could never have faked that—I knew that my friend was in there somewhere, and, by Jupiter Optimus Maximus, I was bloody well going to get him out.

"Hold!" I cried as V'Denni-Kenni prepared to drag him away. "You can't have him yet!"

"What is it now, young man?" the were-jaguar said. "We haven't much time."

"Seventeen blinks of an eye, wasn't it?"

"Sixteen by now."

"Right." I gulped. "Jolly good. Where's the shrinking ray, and how do I go about navigating through Equus's body, and what does this disposable personality module look like?"

CHAPTER
XXVIII

ASTOUNDING VOYAGE

"**L**OOK," V'DENNI-KENNI SAID IN EARNEST, "last-minute heroics can be very tiresome. If you want, I can put in a request for a brain dump, and we can have your friend returned to you—not, of course, in the flesh, but we could have his personality installed in something useful, a paperweight, perhaps, or a favorite fibula; there's no reason for you to fuss now."

"You don't seem to understand, do you? At the end of the sixteen blinks, you can have your Green Pig; I'll be stuck in there too, of course, but I won't have it said of me that I didn't even try to rescue my best friend!"

Honor can really be a pain sometimes. But I am a Roman and I am not going to go around acting like a cowardly savage. Equus Insanus had honor, too, of a sort, for honor was not a quality lacking in the Lacotii. The cackling of the Pig crescendoed as the Sphinx flapped her wings and an obelisk appeared before us.

"Get inside," she said. "It only *looks* like an obelisk; in reality, it's a subaqueous vehicle which, when shrunk, can be used to negotiate the bloodstream." She then gave me a small amphora containing a potion, which, she

221

said, was the distilled essence of the fungus magicus. "When the going gets tough," she said, "swig a bit of this, and it will alter your perceptual cosmos; the unfamiliar will seem familiar—you know, veins and arteries will look like rivers, that sort of thing. Time will become subjective as you shrink, so the adventure might appear longer than a few blinks of an eye; but then, why is a raven like a writing desk?"

A portal opened in the obelisk, and I entered to find a control room not unlike that of the Sphinx or the flying citadel of the Olmechii. There were, of course, the usual sarcophagi containing fuel, the statues of various deities, and murals depicting ancient Egyptian dinner parties.

I sat down and waited to be shrunk. Presently, having deopaqued the viewscreens—I was now most familiar with the workings of these devices and had no trouble operating one at all—I noticed that everything was starting to get bigger. One minute I was looking at the face of Aquila, stern yet touched with a profound concern; the next, his eyeball filled the entire screen; the next, a mere pupil of an eye, behind which I could see a wall of glittering, iridescent flesh that I knew to be the back of the eyeball.

Then the vision was whisked out of view. I fell backward. A seat belt descended from the ceiling and fastened me to a nearby sarcophagus. The obelisk was jerked up in the air, and I almost disgorged the contents of my stomach upon the floor of inlaid marble. No sooner was I used to the sensations than the entire vessel was turned upside down, and I was launched forward with such force that I feared my head would explode.

Kaleidoscopic streaks of color through the viewscreens—then, suddenly, everything was uniformly red —literally the wine-dark sea. I had no idea where I was going, but I assumed that the sphinx had set me on the right path. I unfastened my seat belt and strode over to the console; presumably there would be some device that would let me know what was going on. Indeed there was: a square glass painting of a human body in which a tiny, pulsating red dot was shown slowly progressing up one of the arteries. It was with some distaste that I realized I had been injected into a blood vessel in Equus Insanus's buttocks. As I grew used to the sea of red in the viewscreen, I began to distinguish red disks floating about, the occasional amoebalike creature slithering back and forth, and, now and then, a bacterium. I remembered them from the giant mushroom, for, whereas then they had grown to almost the size of a man, now I had been reduced to their level.

Suddenly, I heard a tapping sound coming from one of the sarcophagi. The lid creaked open.

"Lupus! Whatever are you doing here?"

He got out and shook himself. "Whew! This thing certainly shakes you around, doesn't it?" he said. "I'm glad I didn't vomit."

"But this could be dangerous!" I said. "Whatever possessed you to—"

"Good day to die and all that, Master Vinicius," he said, sticking out his chin and looking every inch the young brave.

"You naughty boy," I said. "I've half a mind to tan your hide."

"Oh, you Romans and your floggings!"

I had no time to chide the lad, however, because a ferocious jangling assailed my ears. My heart sank. I knew that Euphonius the bard had managed to stow away aboard this obelisk. "Come out at once!" I said angrily.

Another sarcophagus lid slid off. And there he was, the silly little man, lyre and all, grinning. Unlike Lupus, he had been unable to hold his stomach, and he was covered in odoriferous gunk. I must say, though, that it suited him.

"How could I fail to come with you?" he said. "A journey into the very soul of a man, into the heart of darkness—it's a poet's dream. I feel like Orpheus descending into the underworld to redeem his beloved Euridice. Perhaps I shall sing so sweetly for the rulers of infernum that they will release Equus Insanus to us . . .

perhaps, O my friends, it will be my song that melts the cold, cursed, callous, compassionless, contorted, cunning, calumniating, cowardly, contumacious, nay, cacogenic—" deep breath, "—heart of Viridiporcus Rex."

And that, O reader, is an example of alliteration. Since I have not been able to use that one during the entire story thus far, I include, verbatim, a sample from the mouth of Euphonius, just so I can say I have covered in this little compendium every rhetorical device I have been referring to as I write.

"All right. You're here now, but I must insist that you only observe. This is *my* battle. Equus is my friend, and I alone must save him. Lupus, would you be kind enough to gag our friend?"

Lupus leapt at the bard and gagged him with his headband, then tied his hands behind him with a strip of rawhide from his leggings.

Presently, as the Sphinx had predicted, the scenery became too much for me. Pipes that dripped dark rheum pushed out from fibrillating fleshy walls. Round red objects pulsed. A smell not unlike that of stale vomit seemed to seep in from outside. My head was aching from the strangeness of it all, and I could see that the other two looked a little nauseated themselves, so I passed around the amphora of mushroom juice.

As the distilled fungus magicus took effect, we became aware of changes in our surroundings. The obelisk was turning into a kind of trireme, and one could hear the steady drumbeat of the hortator; we could smell the scent of the sea wind, and a blue sky shone over our heads. I gasped, for I had not seen a sky this clear since we had been shunted into the holding universe, and I longed for the world to be returned to rights.

There were islands here and there, jutting from the waves; now and then one would start to resemble a kidney or a gallbladder, but mostly the illusion seemed to hold.

Then, for a long time, there were no islands.

At last, after what seemed to be many days—for the sun rose and set, and only now and then did I become aware that the rising and setting was in fact the beating of Equus Insanus's heart—we sighted land in the distance.

A huge statue—much like the Statua Libertatis that guards the harbor of Eburacum Novum in Iracuavia—rose from the water; on close examination, it bore a remarkable resemblance to the Green Pig, and as we sailed past it leered at us and spoke in a booming, metallic voice. "You'll never make it! You'll never save your friend!"

Despair touched me; the mushroom-induced illusions slipped for a moment, and the sky turned into a quivering mass of brain tissue. But presently we sailed into a harbor not unlike that of Alexandria, with bustling merchants—all with the face of the Green Pig—hawking their wares, a slave market, a prostitutes' quarter (even all these had remarkably viridiporcine visages), and, in the distance, a vast amphitheater. We docked the obelisk and marched into the crowd.

People were flocking into the theater, and I found myself following them, with Lupus and the still-gagged Euphonius not far behind, pushed along by the clamoring mob. They jostled, they jabbered incessantly, their eyes lusting for blood.

"I wonder what sort of spectacle it's going to be," I said. But we soon saw, suspended from Corinthian columns next to the theater, banners painted with my image and that of the Green Pig, with inscriptions that read: VIRIDIPORCUS REX VERSUS LUCIUS VINICIUS!

We entered the arena. It was just like the Flavian Amphitheater—or Colosseum, as some vulgarly call it—except that the tiers seemed to go on and on toward infinity; a canvas awning, painted with apocalyptic scenes of the universe's destruction, covered it, and the place was lit by a hundred thousand torches. Through holes in the awning, we could see the wrinkled, glistening-moist texture of Equus Insanus's brain.

Instinctively, I started walking toward the Imperial Box—there is always a secret passageway leading to it that also runs all the way to the Palatium.

A guard stood in the way: a centurion in too-shiny armor, with a war bonnet that reached down to the ground. "That way!" he said, pointing with a deadly looking pilum. "This passageway is reserved for His Viridiporcine Majesty!"

I looked at the path he indicated: a long twisty narrow opening that seemed to vanish into the depths. I shuddered.

Meanwhile, Euphonius had somehow managed to dislodge his gag. "I knew it! A symbolic descent into Hades, from which the beauty of my art will redeem us!"

"Gag him again!" I told Lupus as we entered the dark corridor, dank, smelly, and covered with obscene graffiti.

"Don't you dare, you uncultured savage! Don't you know who I am?"

"I should think I'd know by now, you effete pseudo-intellectual!"

The two of them struggled behind me as I continued walking. I was trying to concentrate on the purpose of this odyssey, to think of nothing but my captured friend. Surely, if I drank enough of this mushroom juice, I would soon be communicating with him.

Soon I began to hear his voice. "Lucius—help me—"

We emerged on the sand of the arena. I looked up. Tier upon tier of Green Pigs gazed down at us, thousands upon thousands. I knew that it was the effect of the fungus magicus, distorting my friend's brain cells into an image of something familiar. In the Imperial Box sat Viridiporcus himself, in a purple robe, with a gold wreath about his head. A female Green Pig—she wore loose-fitting garments of Chinish silk, and her teats could be seen peeping out here and there—sat beside him. She had two humans on leashes at her feet, humans that looked remarkably like Equus Insanus. They were sniveling and snarling.

"Hee, hee!" the Green Pig said. "Never thought you'd end up on *that* side of the seats, did you now, my boy?"

"Give me back my brother!" I cried out, realizing only

then that I really did not have any plan whatsoever for effecting his rescue.

"Very well," he said, and with a languid wave of his hand he commanded a troupe of instrumentalists to sound a fanfare. Bucinae and trombae blared, a tympanon pounded, and we heard the raucous tones of a water organ. As the music grew louder, we saw something being lowered from the awning. The crowd began to cheer and scream for blood. I knew the sound well. I had often been a part of it myself. Then came a growling from the lion gates.

The Green Pig laughed. I looked at the gates. There were creatures there, not quite lions; there was something slimy about them. "They're actually specially trained killer microbes," the Pig said, "but doubtless, because you've gone and taken hallucinogenic drugs, you see them as something else."

The thing from the awning came lower and lower. With a start I recognized Equus Insanus, tied hand and foot, dangling from the end of a rusty windlass. The crowd was feverish, and they were not rooting for me.

I looked at my two companions. "Look, I'm frightfully sorry I got you into this," I said.

"Hey, it's casual," Lupus said.

"I don't think it's casual at all!" came the muffled voice of Euphonius, for Lupus had not been able to get the gag all the way on. "We're all about to get killed, and you're not even going to let me get in a final ode!"

The Green Pig's eyes shone with that fiery glow that is the provenance of all evil villains. He raised his hand and, as a split second collective hush fell over the throng, cried, "Release the killer microbes!"

CHAPTER
XXIX

THE LOST CHORD

"UNTIE EUPHONIUS," I SAID TO LUPUS FEROX, "for I won't have it said that I didn't give him a chance at life just because I wanted my own last moments to be free of his hideous singing." As Lupus did so, Euphonius leapt up and down for joy. He was about to strum his lyre when he noticed that all its strings were broken. Perhaps it was mean-spirited of me to feel relieved, but there it was; if there was to be a battle to the death, I preferred to be able to choose my own background music.

A Green Pig in black, with a skull mask, with snakes about his arms, pounded on the Gates of Death, and the lions were released into the arena. It was not a pretty sight, for these lions were not entirely like lions; they were also something like gelatinous blobs—and something like sharks—and something like corkscrews—and they roared, growled, and snarled as they bounded toward us out of their cages.

"These microbes haven't been fed in days," Viridiporcus Rex said. "Equus Insanus will have the pleasure of watching you die before he is himself consumed."

Some weapons were tossed onto the sand. "It would not do," the Green Pig said, "to let you die ignominiously, without due spectacle; therefore, I am allowing you these few devices." I looked about and saw some of the musical disks, a couple of devices I could not identify, and some good old Roman weapons: a gladius, a retiarus's net, a pilum, and a couple of daggers. They were scattered all over the arena, though, and we would have to run for it—through a mass of maddened microbes.

"Quick! Let me sing a special song designed to melt their very hearts!" Euphonius said. He looked imploringly at the orchestra stalls and began shouting up to the instrumentalists. "I beg of you! Throw down a lyre—a kithara—even an out-of-tune one."

"Shut up!" I said. The creatures were running all about us, their jaws snapping, their teeth glistening with drool. I must confess that I was not unfrightened by my impending doom.

One of them leapt at me! I ducked, and it flew right over my head, narrowly missing the feet of the dangling Equus Insanus. For the first time in my life, I was glad that I had been sent to the local gymnasium for training in some of those, well, more effeminate Greek sports, like wrestling, running, and throwing the discus. I somersaulted over the nearest few creatures, grabbed a pilum, and ran one through. It did not have any blood, just a frothy, gelatinous material that bubbled as it ran over the sand. I looked around to see that one of them had Euphonius by the leg, and he was hopping about, screeching hideously; Lupus Ferox was actually managing rather well, for his smallness stood him in good stead, and he had managed to seize hold of the net, with which he was holding off several of the cerberuslike creatures.

The audience reaction was rather unnerving, though; they completely lacked the Roman sense of fair play, and they never rooted for us at all. Every time a killer microbe was dispatched, they would boo and hiss, and without the feeling that one is pleasing a mob, it is difficult to experience any particular joy at killing a bunch of animals. Lupus, I noticed, paused before running any of them through, to beg their pardon; this was a Lacotian custom, all very well if you are trying to bag a couple of deer for dinner but something of a waste of time when one is surrounded by mindless monsters.

Equus was now touching the sand, which was covered with quivering carcasses. He was jerking back and forth in an effort to avoid the microbes, which were jumping up and down, going for those parts that are most precious in a man.

"Nay! I shall endure no more!" Euphonius screamed. "I shall do that which I was born to do, for I feel the muse hovering about my head, bidding me ope the pregnant portals of my soul; nor will she be denied, for it is impiety to fail to vouchsafe the gods their just due!" The audience howled with laughter, but he paid them no heed; hotly pursued by beasts, he managed to vault up to the orchestra stall and, kicking the fattest of the viridiporcine musicians off his instrument, began to play!

> *Sing, O ye Muses! Sing, ye resplendent Immortals,*
> *And open our eyes, yea, fling wide Perception's*
>   *Proud Portals,*
> *Into the hearts of the enemy strike Direst Terror*
> *That of his ways the Green Pig may at last see the*
>   *Error!*
> *May he be slain, like the Hydra, the Sphinx, and*
>   *the Kraken,*
> *And may Lucius Vinicius, thy Servant, bring home*
>   *the Bacon!*

So striking was the melody Euphonius sang, so full of bizarre grace notes and stratospheric melismas, that I began to wonder whether he had somehow actually become inspired by the god. But then it occurred to me that each of those poignant high notes seemed to coincide with the exceptional propinquity of a killer microbe, and I was forced to conclude that these were not brilliant musical passages but yelps of terror—but that's contemporary music for you. Indeed, perhaps I should have loosed this monster on the mob sooner, for the crowd appeared quite confused.

"What else can we do?" I shouted to Lupus. He and I were back to back, fending off monsters and trying to protect Equus Insanus.

"What a hideous din!" Equus said. "It sounds like a pterodactyl puking." I was amazed that he still had the presence of mind to come up with a colorful simile, but his calmness lent me courage. Then came a booming voice from somewhere overhead, like the voice of a god:

"Attention, micronauts! You have two blinks of an eye left to disrupt the Green Pig's control and return from within the brain cavity of Equus Insanus—or you will all perish within it!"

It was V'Denni-Kenni. The Dimensional Patrol was looking out for us in its inimitable fashion.

"We must wreak havoc!" I said.

"How?" Equus Insanus asked as a creature climbed onto his face.

"I know! I'll set off a smoke bomb!" Lupus Ferox said.

"Smoke," I said. "How could you possibly—"

"Yes! I told you I always carry the tools of my trade for emergencies," he said, looking a little resentful that I would doubt him. But before I could reassure him, he was already doing his business, whirling about, seeming to exude great plumes of smoke from his bare hands.

The microbes retreated into a huddle about twenty passi away. They did not look terribly pleased. "More smoke!" I said, endeavoring to cut Equus down with a sword I had just found lying in the vicinity. Lupus obligingly threw smoke bombs at the stands, and pretty soon the nearby stalls of green pigs were all coughing madly.

"We've got to find a way out," I said. "It's probably too late to go out the way we came and—"

"Through the nose!" said Equus. "Get out through the nose!"

"Nose? What nose? This is an amphitheater, not a—"
For the effects of the fungus magicus were still powerful.

"The nose is the only part of a man that links the brain directly with the outside world," he said. "Now, if you descend beneath this amphitheater, you will find a maze that resembles the catacombs of Rome but is, in reality, the nasal passageway."

"I can't leave you here, not without the Green Pig."

"After him, then!" And the three of us—Euphonius was still singing furiously away—rushed the Imperial Box. The guards were too busy coughing to fight us off, and the Green Pig and his consort were left to fend for themselves.

We chased them around and around the golden couches on which they had been reclining. The little chained Equus Insanuses that the female Viridiporca had had sitting at her feet barked and yelped and got underfoot, and presently the Green Pig tripped and went flying over the balcony!

He did not land in the sand full of writhing microbes, for a pair of wings suddenly sprouted on each of his sandals, and he began darting about like a fat Hermes, his robe of imperial purple fluttering in the smoke-laden air. The sound of coughing resonated through the theater's excellent acoustics. Lupus ran after him, flinging smoke bombs in his face. He sputtered but zoomed up toward the awning, the wings flapping faster than a hummingbird's. I seized the retiarus's net, which Lupus had dropped, and ran after the pig myself, but he kept whizzing in and out of reach, cackling all the while.

It was at that moment that Euphonius struck a chord upon his lyre so militantly obnoxious that the Green Pig seemed to lose his composure. He stumbled in midflight, and the wings on one of his sandals seemed to go out of phase, so that he was flying in circles.

"What a splendid chord!" Euphonius cried, and began strumming it over and over. "A chord previously unknown to music, a chord that unlocks the fundamental mysteries of the universe!"

What a chord it was! I looked about me. Cracks had appeared in the columns of the amphitheater. The awning was rent in a dozen places, and through it one could see the naked surface of Equus Insanus's brain. Green pigs were screaming, holding their ears, running about through the tiers, jumping onto the sand and landing in the mass of fibrillating microbes. With a loud crack, the very underpinnings of the circus appeared to collapse, and a great wind rose up just as I managed to snag the Green Pig with my net.

Equus Insanus said, "I'm going to sneeze!"

"So what?" I said.

"No, you don't understand. *I'm* going to sneeze—I'm back in control—me, my body—not this tiny simulacrum of my personality—but my verum corpus is going to *sneeze*—farewell, O my friends—I will see you back in the real world."

A final time, Euphonius's chord cut through the screaming.

I yanked the Green Pig down out of the air just as the great wind took hold of me and Euphonius and Lupus. Explosions, screams, and the sound of falling rubble rent the air. "What is this?" I asked. "The last days of Pompeii?"

"I hope we're not dying," Lupus said. "I was just starting to have fun!"

The illusion of the circus was coming apart. Huge spheres of snot were flying all about us, and then we were soaring, borne aloft by the mighty wind of sneezing. The wind carried us through countless catacombs, where I could see thousands of corpses of Equus Insanus laid to rest, but now all were rising up, stretching, shambling about, and I realized that this was the fungus magicus showing me Equus Insanus regaining possession of his body. And then—

We came bursting into the open air, with the obelisk at our heels, and we could see, shimmering in the distance, the monstrous giants that were our friends, and then they were shrinking, shrinking, as we fell into the path of the expanding ray...

I looked about me. We were no longer in the land of the Anasazii; indeed, we appeared to be in the vomitorium of my uncle's palace. In the distance, echoing down marble halls, came the sounds of a mediocre orgy.

Equus Insanus was standing by my side, almost exploding with laughter, as was Lupus Ferox; and when I looked at where he was pointing, I saw what the matter was.

Euphonius had landed squarely in the vomit vat. "Can't find my bloody lyre!" he was crying as he bobbed up and down. "I've got to find that chord again before I forget it—I've got to find that bloody chord—ah, the miserable suffering of the true artist—else never shall I find rest again!"

CHAPTER
XXX

BACK TO THE ORGY

I WAS TOO BEFUDDLED TO WANT TO PULL EUPHONIUS out quite yet, but luckily, one of the vomitorium slaves had already thrown him a length of rope, and he was dragging himself out. The chamber was crowded, for not only were Aquila, Titus Papinianus, Aaye, Callipygia, the two Sasquatii, Lupus, and Equus Insanus present, but also V'Denni-Kenni and several of his attendants, and the green elephant of judgment, who sat upon an ornate chair. Through the window, one could see stately olive trees and the Corinthian columns of a portico, and beyond them the fires of the city, so I knew we were in Rome. But, superimposed on this familiar scene, there were also the tiers of judges and spectators such as I remembered seeing on Mars, and I knew that all was not quite over.

Nevertheless, I was not feeling in a particularly good humor; I had just been through too much. "All right, all right," I said. "Did we save the universe, or didn't we?"

Equus said, "What do you think? Do I sound like a Green Pig to you?"

I therefore realized that somehow everything was

going to be all right, and I embraced my brother with great fondness. So delighted was I to see him that I gushed with positively plebeian emotions. However, he did not seem to mind; for that I was grateful.

"I'll have to tell you all about life under the Green Pig sometime," he said, hinting of dark mysteries. "But let's not spoil the fun of my first day back in the flesh, shall we?"

It remained, however, for the Dimensional Patrol to have its say, and have its say it did.

"The Green Pig—or at least, his personality module —has been captured at last," V'Denni-Kenni said, holding up a tiny diskos no bigger than my thumb. "As you can see, while you were within Equus's brain, battling the Viridiporcine forces in a manner which we can but dimly comprehend, we have been busy! All the bottled cities have been returned to their rightful locations, and, using, as we promised, the hidden ramifications of the Fourth Law of the Conservation of Multiplex Realities, we have restored the universe to you. The fabric of the cosmos, however, cannot be resewn entirely seamlessly. It's a bit like mending a ripped toga, you see; we had to snip a bit out, and stitch it back together—so that's why you have been returned to an earlier moment in your history—the night of the Saturnalia when this adventure began."

Then the green elephant spoke, and we all inclined our heads at his grave voice, full of millennial wisdom and authority. "O Aquila, we have misjudged you. Might you be interested in a new place on the Dimensional Patrol? We could really use someone like you."

"I think not, O elephant," Aquila replied. "My place is with these people; crazy as they are, I love them."

"I thought as much," the judge said. "Nevertheless, we are going to make all of you honorary members of the Dimensional Patrol Reserve. Here." He handed each of us a jade were-jaguar on a chain. "These are symbols of your membership in the society of those who travel between the universes. You can use them to contact us. Whenever there is a disturbance in the fabric of spacetime—if ever the Green Pig should rear his head again, though I really doubt it, considering what we're going to do to this personality module—perhaps then you will hear the call to arms, perhaps you will be ready to battle once more in the cause of truth, of justice—of spatio-temporal integrity!"

"Your were-jaguars will glow bright red," V'Denni-Kenni said, "and then it will be up to you to decide whether you wish to join us in our next great exploit."

"No more of this for me," Euphonius said, having managed to crawl out of the vat with his lyre. "I'm devoting the rest of my life to seeking out that lost chord." I hoped he would never find it, and if he did, that he would refrain from plucking it in the Circus Maximus with a full house.

"And I'm going to make up for lost time," Equus said, "with my friends. I'm so glad to see them—I'll never complain about eating larks' tongues again!" How good of him to be so sporting, I thought. Tomorrow we will go on a gourmet binge; we will eat our guts out—peacocks' feet stew! Poached hummingbirds' brains stuffed into gazelle tripe! Ha, ha, that'll teach him!

"And we're going to emigrate to Judea," the two Sasquatii said. "We've heard that the *kwisatz haderach* is coming soon, and we thought we'd offer our services to him. Maybe he'll even overthrow the Romans!" Fat chance, I thought.

"And I'm going back to studying ancient mysticism," Aaye said. "After all we've learned about sphinxes and pyramids, I could probably turn the entire world of archaeology upside down. The lecture circuit! I could probably charge half a talent a lecture."

"And *I'm* going to become an encephalometric adept," Callipygia said. "I've already signed up for the beginners' course." That was a rather aerocephalic thing to say, I thought, but she was entitled to think for herself—if you call that thinking. "And tomorrow, I'm going to go shopping in the Forum." By Jove, I should never have told her about all the things you could buy in

Rome. I could imagine whose house the bills would be coming to.

Titus Papinianus said, "I'll just write another volume of my memoirs." I groaned. The world could well survive without another *Papiniad*.

And Aquila said, "I shall do nothing; after all, I'm old, and it's time I was supported by my sons." Equus Insanus beamed sheepishly.

Lupus Ferox said, "I'm going to have Lucius Vinicius buy my freedom—I think I can probably persuade him to do that—and return to Lacotia."

And that, I supposed, left me.

To my astonishment, I found myself saying, "Where's your sense of adventure, my friends? Frankly, I wouldn't mind being in the Dimensional Reserve. It'd be a jolly sight more entertaining than spending my life going to third-rate orgies like the one down the hall."

Which is where—the various members of the Dimensional Patrol having departed and the entire world having been restored to a pre-Viridiporcine state—we all ended up.

All of us trooped into the orgy room. Since we had not arrived in the regular manner, none of us had been searched, and it was with some surprise that my uncle awoke from his drunken stupor to find our group standing there among the snoring guests.

"I don't remember inviting some of you," he said.

"Just some of my friends," I said, hoping he would not ask too many questions.

"Your Divinity—it's me, Aquila," the old warrior said. Of course, the emperor would not mind seeing him; his exile was yet to occur, and, knowing how mutable the past and future could be, I realized we could make tomorrow's events quite different from the way they were last time. "Happy Saturnalia!"

"Oh, I say, what! Happy Saturnalia, old thing!" said Marcus Ulpius Trajanus, Caes. Imp. Aug., etcetera etcetera, and he put his face back in his plate.

Dancing girls, jugglers, and wrestlers were beginning

to bestir themselves. Several of the girls eyed Callipygia with a smidgen of jealousy, thinking perhaps that she was some new variety of Terra Novan call girl; indeed, her Olmechian mode of dress did render her somewhat conspicuous, for the feathers she wore, in crimson, shocking pink, turquoise, and forest green, pointed almost all the way up to the ceiling.

The XXVIIth course was just being served. It was a really boring thing, a compote of giant chicken giblets and sweet potatii, garnished with shaved hummingbird egg omelet slices and topped with a kind of coriander relish and the heads of unborn dormice. But I was so delighted to see something approaching real food, after all our hideous experiences with longi porci, that I soon revealed myself to be a trencherman of the first water.

The wrestling match was proceeding apace, and I found myself more absorbed by the finer points than I had been since I was a little boy. Everything seemed new and fresh. Was it perhaps the knowledge that the entire universe was there, outside this palace and this city, and not a mere simulacrum? The thought that we had liberated all these people, more people than we could ever count, from certain destruction?

Suddenly I realized that I did not really want to be in the Dimensional Reserve, or anything else, for that matter. Indeed, as I watched the fair Callipygia moving, with an easy and natural grace among the not unsleazy flute girls who had been not unhired for the orgy, I realized that perhaps she would be a not unfitting partner for my not unfuture. (I did it! I used four litotes in one sentence! Wait till I tell old Diogenes, the rhetoric teacher!)

I went up to her and asked her to marry me.

She raised an eyebrow. "But surely, Lucius," she said, "you know that, now that I have devoted my life to encephalometry, there can be no place in it for outside interests."

"What! You told me you loved me!" I said, wounded to the quick, for her declaration had managed to elicit a sincere response from me, and I was afraid she had completely forgotten that moment.

"Well, of course I did, and still do, but my life has been consecrated to religion, and I can only be the bride of a god; now that you're no longer a god, I shall be forced to satisfy my marital urges elsewhere."

"What a pile of merda," I said.

"Try the quoiotulus brains, Lucius, old chap!" the emperor said.

"Entertainment Number XXXVIII!" came the booming voice of the majordomo. "Elephants trampling counterfeiters to death!"

"Ah, the spectacle, the savagery, the decadence!" Joshua bar-Joseph said to his cousin, staring at everything with that childlike wonder that so many foreigners evince upon coming to our Eternal City for the first time.

I saw Callipygia running into the arms of Aquila, and I wondered whether he had convinced her that he was a god. Of course—why else would she be taking encephalometry courses? I felt absolutely furious for about a minute, but then I shrugged it off. Who could begrudge the ancient warrior his pleasures? I felt my upper lip stiffen satisfactorily and went looking for other game.

Presently I found it, in a woman who was lying alone on a couch, scribbling on some kind of wax tablet. She had ravishing, wide eyes, like those of a cat; indeed, all her movements seemed to have something feline about them, and a few ringlets of blond hair peered from one of those Egyptian headdresses that some of the rich women of Rome like to affect.

"My dear," I said, in my most lady-killing voice, "what unjust fate has decreed that a woman of such beauty should sit alone whilst others far less fair are occupied?"

A hideous racket assailed my ears. Euphonius had begun to sing. I had to move quickly or the merda would soon hit the flabellum.

The woman looked at me, fluttering her kohl-darkened eyelashes. When she spoke, it was in a soft, sensuous voice, her Greek mutated by the accents of

Alexandria. "How many Judean mothers," she asked, "does it take to refill an oil lamp?"

"You!"

Suddenly she realized who she was talking to. "I'm in disguise!" she said. "Don't give me away. This dissertation's all that's left to me."

Suddenly I noticed that my jade were-jaguar was glowing. I hit it a couple of times, hoping it would stop, but it kept blinking on and off, red-green, red-green.

The Sphinx, now a beautiful woman, her eyes holding the promise of ancient secrets, beckoned to me. I was sure that if I did not reveal her identity to the Dimensional Patrol, I could win a night of rapture from her— maybe more.

"None," I said, responding to her question, and then added, in the voice of an old Judean matron, "'So I'll sit in the dark!'"

She laughed. I would have known that laugh anywhere.

The were-jaguar continued to blink. Was the universe at stake again? Was it the Sphinx they were after, or had some unrelated crisis turned up? I did not care. My friend was returned to me; tomorrow Equus Insanus and I would go sacrifice a pair of doves at the Temple of Capitoline Jove to give thanks for being reunited.

I was a young, rich, and lusty Roman; the Pax Romana ruled; the world was at peace. Any red-blooded Roman patrician will choose decadence over altruism any time. I had done enough good already, and since it would not do to dishonor my family's reputation, I resolved to spend the rest of the evening in the pursuit of wanton pleasures.

I took off the were-jaguar and handed it to the Sphinx. "Take this pendant," I said with smooth and practiced insincerity, "as a token of my devotion to you..."

It did not stop blinking. But I did not plan to go seeking adventure for a while. Let adventure come to me, I thought. For I had my friends and my fortune, and the morrow's mishaps had been erased as though by magic.

And the thousands of Olmechii who had sacrificed themselves that the world might be renewed—why, the world *was* renewed, by Jove, and those poor natives given another chance, though they would never know how Fortuna had smiled upon them.

I put the amulet about the Sphinx's neck and waited for the next riddle.

About the Author

Somtow Papinian Sucharitkul (S. P. Somtow) was born in Bangkok in 1952 and grew up in Europe. He was educated at Eton and Cambridge. His first career was as a composer, and his musical works have been performed, televised, and broadcast in more than a dozen countries on four continents. He was artistic director of the Asian Composers EXPO 78 in Bangkok and was chosen Thai representative to the International Music Council of UNESCO. In the late 1970s he took up writing speculative fiction and won the 1981 John W. Campbell Award for best new writer, as well as the Locus Award for his first novel, *Starship & Haiku*. His short fiction has twice been nominated for the Hugo Award.

Somtow now lives in Los Angeles. He is working on more satirical novels, a serious ambitious horror novel and has recently written the script for a forthcoming motion picture. *Aquila and the Sphinx* is the third volume in *The Aquiliad*.